Sugar and Vice

Also by
Eve Calder

AND THEN THERE WERE CRUMBS

Sugar and Vice

Eve Calder

St. Martin's Paperbacks

This is a work of fiction. All of the characters, organizations, and events portrayed in this novel are either products of the author's imagination or are used fictitiously.

First published in the United States by St. Martin's Paperbacks, an imprint of St. Martin's Publishing Group.

SUGAR AND VICE

Copyright © 2020 by Eve Calder.

Excerpt from *A Tale of Two Cookies* copyright © 2020 by Eve Calder.

All rights reserved.

For information, address St. Martin's Publishing Group, 120 Broadway, New York, NY 10271.

www.stmartins.com

ISBN: 978-1-250-31301-0

Our books may be purchased in bulk for promotional, educational, or business use. Please contact your local bookseller or the Macmillan Corporate and Premium Sales Department at 1-800-221-7945, ext. 5442, or by email at MacmillanSpecialMarkets@macmillan.com.

Printed in the United States of America

St. Martin's Paperbacks edition / May 2020

10 9 8 7 6 5 4 3 2 1

To my mom, who makes it all look easy.

Chapter 1

As schooner-sized white clouds sailed high across the turquoise South Florida sky, Kate McGuire tugged at her green gardening gloves. Despite what the label proclaimed, one size definitely did not fit all.

"So what happens if I ditch the gloves?" she asked, pausing, as her friend rhythmically scooped wet sand.

"Nothing super horrible," replied Maxi Más-Buchanan, sinking her shovel into the soft ground with a *thunk*. "Just keep 'em away from Mr. Oliver. Thanks to him, my last three pairs are buried all over Coral Cay. One at a time. The least that puppy could do is bury them in pairs. That way, if anyone ever finds them, they can maybe use them."

Kate had to admit, the two of them had accomplished a lot in one afternoon. Two of the three raised beds were prepped and ready to go. One more and they could call it a day.

Oliver, in his wisdom, already had. Passed out under a shady tree, she could hear his soft snuffling sounds above the birdcalls on the breeze.

Maxi looked over her shoulder and grinned. "Some work ethic," the florist said. "Our best digger has up and quit. On the bright side, you get a promotion."

"Aye aye, captain," Kate said, giving a mock salute. "So what's going into this one?"

"For a couple of months, I'm gonna keep adding in compost and good stuff and build up the soil. Then, when it gets a little cooler, I can start planting. Oh, it's gonna be tasty. I'm putting in those juicy, old-fashioned tomatoes and little baby lettuces. And we're gonna surround the whole thing with hot peppers. *Muy picante.* 'Cause they keep the bugs away. That one over there," she said pointing at a completed bed, "will be herbs. Basil, dill, oregano, and chives to start. And peppermint—oooh, it'll smell so good. And that other one's gonna be filled with edible flowers. Not too shabby, huh? If these do well, I'll sell what I grow. Like a side business. Maxi's Kitchen Garden. All organic. I've talked to a couple of your chef buddies at the resorts, and they're super excited."

"I can see why," Kate said, tucking a stray lock of caramel-colored hair under her navy ball cap. "An organic, small-batch garden? Nobody's doing anything like that anywhere near Coral Cay. You'll clean up."

"But first, we dig up the yard and get super dirty. Poor Oliver's going to need another bath," she said, brushing a smudge of wet sand off her cheek. "Me too, for that matter."

"How about we take a cue from Oliver and stop for a rest?" Kate suggested. "I've got a pitcher of lemonade in the fridge at the Cookie House."

"Right now, I'd settle for cold water out of the sink. Or the hose."

Fifteen minutes later, with frosty glasses in their hands, Kate and Maxi relaxed in lawn chairs, surveying their handiwork.

As they chatted, Oliver scrambled back to the area they'd excavated for the last raised bed.

"OK, so we've removed two-and-a-half feet of sandy topsoil. Now what?" Kate asked, eyeing the neat rectangular trench on the left side of the yard.

"Just like last time. We'll fill it up with my super-secret planting soil mix. Then we drag out the frame for the raised bed, tack it down, and fill that up to the top with more planting mix. Then we're done."

Oliver circled the pit several times, then he hopped in and scratched the soil with his front paws, yelping. He put his head down, digging furiously. All they could see was sand flying past his fuzzy oatmeal-colored rump.

"What's he doing?" Kate asked.

"Probably digging up one of the gloves he buried. Or one of his other treasures. Oliver's got stuff buried all over town," Maxi said with a rueful smile.

They watched as the poodle-mix pup paddled furiously with his front paws for several minutes. Then he sat back on his haunches and howled.

Maxi sat forward, alarmed. "He's never done that before," she said, setting her glass on the ground.

"Maybe the little guy hurt himself," Kate said, as they both hurried over to the half-grown pup.

As they neared, Oliver began digging again, his oversized paws frantically clawing the sand.

"Oliver? Come here, baby," Kate called softly. "Come up here."

When he jumped out of the pit and trotted over, Kate stroked his soft curly coat and scratched him lovingly behind one ear. "Now, let me see those paws of yours," she said, gently examining each one in turn. "Nope, you're fine. Everything looks good," she called over her shoulder to Maxi.

"I don't think so," Maxi said softly.

"What do you mean?" Kate said, turning to see her friend's face pale. Maxi silently pointed down to the hole where Oliver had just been digging.

And that's when Kate spotted it. In the sandy soil. Scraps of an ancient leather boot. Long and brackish brown. In tatters. Kate could barely make out what had probably been a wide cuff at the top. And a big silver buckle, blackened with age, at the bottom. It reminded Kate of something out of *Treasure Island*. Or the Discovery Channel. Exposed at the top of the boot, yellowed with time, was a barely visible swath of bone.

"What? Who?" Kate gasped.

Maxi took a giant step back and crossed herself. "*Dios mio*," she whispered. "It's him. It's really him. It has to be."

"Who? Who is it?"

"Gentleman George Bly. The pirate king. I thought it was just a story," she said in a hushed voice, shaking her head. "Something to tell *mi niños* at bedtime. But it's real."

Kate stood and took a step closer to her friend. Oliver followed suit. The three of them stared down into the pit.

"I admit that boot looks old," Kate said. "But what makes you think it's him?"

"It's all part of the legend," Maxi said quietly. "Gentleman George, he pretty much founded Coral Cay. He and his men. They're the reason we have our Pirate Festival every year. Well, them and to celebrate the end of tourist season. His crew used to raid the Spanish treasure ships sailing to and from Florida and the Caribbean. This island was their home base. He was smart, and he was sneaky. He bested the Spanish king every single time and swiped their loot. But he had a code. A sense of honor. And he was only stealing what had already been stolen in the first place. But one time—the last time—they were attacked by a galleon. A big war ship. He was wounded, his ship was nearly sunk. But Gentleman George? He still had a few tricks up his sleeve. And he got his ship and crew to safety. Back to Coral Cay."

"What happened after that?" Kate asked, never taking her eyes off the boot buckle.

"No one really knows," Maxi said. "Local legend has it once he and his men reached the harbor, they burned the ship to cover their tracks. And shortly after that, he died. Supposedly, his men laid him out in his very best clothes and even shined up the silver buckles on his boots. And, as a gesture of respect and gratitude, they buried him in a secret spot on the island with his share of the treasure—a fortune in gold and jewels. And the site has never been found."

"And you think . . ." Kate started.

"I think our friend Oliver has discovered the last resting place of Gentleman George Bly, pirate king of Coral Cay."

Chapter 2

A few hours later, the backyard of Flowers Maximus was alive with people. A half dozen students and grad students paraded back and forth toting shovels, trowels, tarps, and plastic toolboxes like ants carrying off crumbs from a picnic.

At the center of the operation was Dr. Marian Blosky, a history professor from Gold Coast University. One extended game of "telephone" resulted in the professor and her team of students swarming the yard en masse.

Still numb from the shock of the discovery, Maxi had called Ben Abrams at the Coral Cay police department. He, in turn, phoned the medical examiner, who called Dr. Blosky.

Clad in a tan T-shirt and buff-colored hiking shorts topped off with an olive-green fishing hat over frizzy blond-gray hair, Marian Blosky would have looked perfectly at home on a bass boat or a hiking trail. But in the backyard of Flowers Maximus, she was clearly in charge.

"I can't tell you how thrilled we are with the discovery, Mrs. Más-Buchanan," Dr. Blosky said, tapping her clipboard absentmindedly with her pen. "If this truly turns out to be Sir George Bly—or even one of his men—this find could help us fill in a blank page in the history of this state. Perhaps even the nation. Pirates and piracy played a much larger role in our story than most people realize. So how did you know he was here? Local legends? An old diary? Markings in the landscape?"

"We were putting in a garden, and poof—there he was," Maxi said. "And Oliver found him."

"Which one of the lads is Oliver?" the professor asked, scanning the corner of the yard where various neighbors and shopkeepers had gathered to watch the action from the sidelines.

Kate hadn't told anyone about the find. And other than a quick call to Ben, neither had Maxi. But somehow word had gotten out, and townspeople just started showing up. By the time Dr. Blosky arrived with her team, they'd already had a crowd.

"The fuzzy one," Maxi said, pointing. By the edge of the trench, which had been haphazardly covered with a blue tarp, Oliver was stretched out, sphinx-like. Relaxed, but alert. On guard.

"So you mean you really had no idea anything was there this whole time?"

"Nope."

The professor shook her head. "When amateurs make a find like this? Well, most claim it was an accident. Or beginner's luck. Some of them even try to tell us that they picked up their artifacts at a rummage sale. Likely story! Later, we usually find out they're amateur treasure hunters. Scavengers, really. Working off some kind of tip. Local legends. Old maps. Oral stories passed down through the family. Something. And they just don't want to give up the location of the site. But this? An untouched discovery in situ? Astonishing. And truly wonderful."

"Maxi was installing raised garden beds for the flower shop," Kate said, pointing to the two completed plots on the other side of the yard. "She's growing herbs and heirloom vegetables for some of the local restaurants."

"We finished shoveling out the third one and were super tired, so we took a break," Maxi picked up. "That's when Oliver woke up, ran over to the trench, and just went nutty. Digging like mad."

"He was totally freaked," Kate added.

"And there he was," Maxi finished, shrugging. "Gentleman George."

"What happens next?" Kate asked, quietly, nodding toward the hole in the yard. "To him, I mean."

"Well, first we have to verify that it is him," Blosky said matter-of-factly. "We have an anthropologist who focuses on osteology and bioarchaeology coming for that. And he should be here"—the professor consulted a battered silver Timex on her wrist—"anytime now. He'll give us a rough estimate of how long the skeleton has been in the ground, as well as filling in a few basic characteristics that can help us determine if it might be Sir George or one of his crew."

"What do you mean?" Maxi asked.

"Well, Sir George died more than four hundred years ago. And he was a tall man, roughly six-foot-four. We also know he was fifty or so when he died. And he'd recently been injured in battle, though we don't really know the nature of his injuries. But if all of those indicators are present, then we know this stands a chance of being him. If the age of the burial is correct but the other features aren't there, then we could be dealing with a member of the crew. Either way, we'll take him to the university and run a few more tests."

"And that will tell you if it's Gentleman George?" Maxi asked.

"It will certainly help," Professor Blosky said enthusiastically. "Sir George Bly grew up in the country, outside of London. He was the second son of the Duke of Marleigh, if you can believe it. So we can check if the isotopes in his teeth match an aristocratic childhood in that part of the world. We'll also look for skeletal development and conditions consistent with a life spent largely at sea. Certain repetitive injuries, that sort of thing. And early in his naval career, Sir George was shot in the shoulder. French musket. So we'll look for evidence of that. Of course, this might not be him at all. It could very well be one of his crew. And a few of them hailed from the upper classes, as well. From what little we know—rumor, really—many of them stayed in this area. Married local women, raised families. That's my bit—the oral history. To me, that's what makes this find so fascinating. We'll finally have a few hard facts to start piecing together their story. Separating fact from fiction."

"The folks in Coral Cay will love that," Maxi said. "Sir George is practically a hometown hero."

"I didn't want to say anything before, but I heard Sam and Barb and Amos already strategizing on how Coral Cay can use the discovery to boost interest in this year's Pirate Festival," Kate said with a smile.

"Was that before or after *mi padrino* covered Sir George with the very elegant blue tarp?" Maxi asked.

"During," Kate admitted, recalling Sam Hepplewhite carefully draping a plastic sheet over the find.

"Um, just out of curiosity, what happens to the treasure?" Maxi asked.

"Treasure?" Blosky looked surprised.

"Apparently, local legend holds that Gentleman George was buried with his share of the ship's treasure," Kate explained.

"Oh, well, I don't know if that's true," the professor

Chapter 3

"So what are you going to do with your pirate treasure?" Kate asked Maxi, after Dr. Blosky went into the florist shop to make a few phone calls.

"Ah, that is the question," Maxi said, grinning. "First, college funds for mi niños. Let me tell you, school is *expensive.*"

"Maybe that's why Gentleman George went to sea. Running away from his student loans."

"Then I wouldn't blame him one bit," Maxi replied. "Super smart guy."

"I wonder why he really did go to sea?" Kate pondered. "I mean, you figure back home he was wealthy and accomplished. Why give it all up to sail the Atlantic?"

"Why didn't you stay in New York and marry Mr. Rich Guy? You'd have had a mansion and all the jewels your fingers could hold. Instead, you moved here and now you own half a bakery."

"Good point. But something must have happened. I wonder what?"

"You think he had lady trouble? The one woman he wanted was the one he couldn't have. Promised to someone else. Their love was taboo."

"Telenovela?"

"Oh yeah. *Mi mami*'s latest. *Pasión Prohibida*. Forbidden Passion."

"Have you told Peter yet?"

"I gave him a quick heads-up after I called Ben. But we're not telling the little ones anything until we know for sure. With the festival coming up, they've already got pirate fever."

"So much for a quiet Sunday afternoon," Kate said. "I'm either going to have to stay up tonight or get up extra early to get the bakery stocked for tomorrow."

"I could come over and help you catch up. After all this, it's not like I'm going to sleep anyway."

"Right now, I'm leaning toward taking a very long shower and curling up with a book this evening," Kate said. "Besides, something tells me you and Peter are going to have a lot to talk about tonight."

"The only thing I care about right now is who's making dinner," Maxi said. "And that's a problem Gentleman George and his treasure can't solve. Unless the pub started accepting gold doubloons."

"I wonder if I could make cookies that look like doubloons?" Kate said dreamily. "For the festival."

"See? I told you, pirate fever is super contagious. And once you catch it, there's no cure," Maxi said, suddenly glancing toward the street. "*Ay*, if this is our skeleton doctor, he is *muy caliente*."

Reflexively, Kate turned. "Oh, blast! That's not the anthropologist—that's Evan! What the heck is my ex-fiancé doing here?"

"Uh-oh, you want to go into the flower shop? I'll tell

him you had a very important phone call. Then I'll accidentally smack him with a shovel."

Kate smiled. "No. Might as well get this over with. Whatever this is. How bad do I look?"

"Way too good for him. But there's a little mud on your right cheek. That's it, you got it," she whispered, as Kate quickly rubbed her face. "Just remember, he's scum. Hot scum. But scum."

"Kate? Hey. Wow, you look great!" Evan said, as she turned to face him. Decked out in trim jeans and a navy blue golf shirt, he looked better than she remembered. Stronger. More chiseled. The shirt and a newly acquired tan accentuated his blue eyes.

"What are you doing here, Evan?" Kate asked flatly.

"Some teenager at the bakery said you'd be over here," he said, looking her up and down. "I wanted to say 'hi.' You look good. Really good."

"I meant what are you doing in Coral Cay?" Kate said.

"You know me," he said with an easy grin that revealed two perfect dimples. "Figured I'd get a little sun. See the sights. Do some fishing."

"You don't fish," Kate replied.

"There's more than one kind of fishing," he said, pushing aside a curly lock of nearly black hair, as his eyes twinkled. "Besides, this place seemed to mean something to you. I wanted to see it for myself. You visiting for a while?"

Kate shook her head. "I live here," she said evenly, trying to focus on a spot past his right earlobe. How could she have forgotten those eyes? And the thick dark lashes. Suddenly, she was unsteady all over again. Unsure.

"I'm Maxi Más-Buchanan," the florist said quickly,

sticking out her hand, as Kate silently thanked her for creating a distraction. "This is my flower shop."

"I'm Evan—Evan Thorpe," he said, smiling. "I'm sorry, I didn't mean to barge in. Is this a party?"

"Nope, it's a discovery," Maxi countered.

"A what?" he asked, clearly puzzled.

"We found a super old skeleton in the garden," Maxi said brightly, as though it happened every day. "We think it could be Gentleman George Bly, one of the early founders of Coral Cay."

"Wow, that's got to be pretty huge," Evan said. "Congratulations!"

He looked over at Kate, who was staring off into the distance, stone-faced, seemingly a million miles away.

"Look," he said softly to her. "I really didn't mean to intrude. I just wanted to see you. The way things ended . . ." he trailed off. "I wanted to apologize."

"You did." Kate said quietly.

"I mean really apologize. To your face. I owe you that. Much more than that. Any chance maybe I could take you to dinner?"

"I'm busy. Although Jessica has plenty of free time. I know because she spends a lot of time texting me photos."

"OK, I deserved that. Lunch? Some place very nice and very public. Nothing shady, I promise. Just a friendly meal. Maybe somewhere on the water?"

"No need, Evan," Kate replied. "I said everything I needed to say that night. Now it's time for you to go."

His face fell, his broad shoulders slumped. He looked down and appeared to be studying the grass beneath their feet. If Kate didn't know him better, she'd have thought he was truly dejected. Maybe he was?

"I'm going to be here, in Coral Cay, for a few days," he said finally. "I wasn't kidding about wanting to see this place. And why. Don't decide now. Just—I don't know.

Think about it. A quick bite somewhere. Old time's sake."
With that, he looked up and smiled. And it was like the
sun had burned through the clouds. "Please, Katie?" he
entreated. "Just think about it."

"Maxi, it was very nice to meet you," he said, offering his hand to the florist and clasping hers warmly.
"And good luck with your, uh, skeleton."

And with that Kate's former fiancé turned and strode
purposefully back across the yard toward the street.

"Damn," Maxi said.

"Yup," Kate said ruefully. "That's Evan Thorpe. Now
do you understand why I had to put thirteen hundred miles
between us?"

Chapter 4

Kate fell silent, absentmindedly chewing on her lower lip.

"Are you OK?" Maxi asked.

"I'm . . . yes . . . fine," she said haltingly. "It's just that . . . that was about the last thing I expected. I finally thought I'd gotten over him. Mostly. Then, bam! Here he is again. My sister Jeanine would be thrilled. She's still hoping I'm going to 'come to my senses and marry him,'" Kate said, using air quotes. "Do you know she actually called our reception venue after I'd cancelled and told them the wedding was going ahead as scheduled? That the cancellation had been some kind of prank."

"Your sister has nothing to do with this," Maxi said. "And you don't have to see him ever again. Just put it out of your mind and pretend he's still back in New York."

"Easier said than done," Kate said mournfully.

"Hey, I wonder if that's our bone guy," Maxi said, looking out at the street where a middle-aged man in khakis, a Dolphins cap, and a worn, sun-bleached denim shirt was rapidly approaching. He carried a battered leather knap-sack casually over one shoulder.

Kate and Maxi walked over to greet him.

"Are you the anthropologist?" Kate asked tentatively.

"Yes, I'm Joe Pollack," he said, by way of introduction. "Do you know where I can find Marian Blosky?"

"Dr. Pollack, I'm Maxi Más-Buchanan. This is my flower shop, and we're the ones who found Gentleman George. Dr. Blosky is inside. She needed to make a couple of calls on the landline. On this part of the island, cell phones don't work so good."

"Would you like a glass of tea or some lemonade?" Kate asked.

"We're losing the light. If it's alright with you, I'd like to start assessing the find. I'm guessing that's it under the tarp?"

"We wanted to protect it until you got here," Kate explained.

"Definitely," he said, scanning the horizon. "OK, I know most of Marian's kids this year. We'll get started. You're welcome to stay and watch, if you want. Is this your first time on a dig?"

"If you don't count putting in a garden," Maxi replied. "When we started out this morning, this is the last thing we were expecting."

"Yeah, Marian said this one sounded like an oops. Hopefully, we'll know a little more in the next couple of hours. One thing. Depending on the positioning, we may have to leave him here overnight. If we do, we'll need to post a security guard. Are you OK with that?"

"Yes," Maxi said. "Not that you'll need it with half of Coral Cay gathered around the pit."

"You might be surprised," Pollack said, shrugging.

Fifteen minutes later, the crew had gently peeled back

the blue plastic shroud, and Dr. Pollack was bent over the exposed area like a surgeon examining a patient.

As Kate and Maxi watched from the front of the crowd just a few steps away, he removed what looked like a large brush from his backpack and twirled it just above the exposed bone.

"Don't see what's taking so long," baker Sam Hepplewhite said loudly from the back of the crowd. "'Course it's Gentleman George. Who else is it gonna be?"

"Could be one of the crew," Amos Tully countered. "Or a Spanish sailor they took hostage."

"Didn't take hostages," Sam replied. "Sea battles were fought from a distance."

"George Bly's band settled this island," Barb Showalter interjected. "It could easily be a wife or a family member. Even a later descendent."

"That too," Amos agreed, nodding.

"In any event, this is going to add a whole new dimension to our Pirate Festival," Barb continued. "Actual history. We could invite in some of the leading experts in American history from the period—"

"T'ain't any American history from the period," Sam said. "This proves we're older than Plymouth. Older than Jamestown, too."

As more bone came into view, Dr. Pollack pulled a magnifying glass and what looked like a small broom from his pack. After a few minutes of brushing, he grimaced, removed his glasses and stood.

"OK, everyone, that's a wrap!" he yelled, clapping his hands. "Pack up and move out! We're done here!"

Kate and Maxi looked at each other, puzzled, and hurried toward the trench as he returned the last of his tools to the backpack.

"Do we have to arrange for security, or do you do that?"

Maxi asked quickly, as the anthropologist hoisted the bag onto his right shoulder.

"You need to call the police," he said tersely. "This isn't Gentleman George. I don't know who it is, but the remains have been in the ground less than ten years. This isn't an archaeological site. It's a crime scene."

Chapter 5

"So you have no idea of who that might be out there?" Detective Ben Abrams asked gently. Perched at one end of the little sofa inside the flower shop, he had taken Maxi and Kate through the afternoon's activities, right up to the point where Oliver had unearthed his find.

"Of course she doesn't," said Sam, who stood protectively behind the sofa where Maxi sat with Oliver at her feet. "What kind of fool question is that?"

Wide-eyed, Maxi shook her head.

"It's not an accusation," Ben said quietly. "Just gathering the facts we have."

"Any chance it could have already been there when we bought the shop?" Peter Buchanan interjected, pressing a mug of warm tea into his wife's trembling hands.

"*Gracias*," she said softly, looking up into his eyes.

Ben shook his head. "Could be. But the team doesn't think so. You guys have been here, what, nine years? Between you and me, though, anything they come up with at this point is pure conjecture. We don't even know for sure if it's male or female. We can safely say it's been in the ground less than a decade, so that rules out Gentleman George. Other than that? We're gonna need more time."

"Why were they dressed as a pirate?" Kate asked.

"We don't know that they were," Ben answered. "Whoever it was was wearing boots with silver buckles. Could have been a pirate costume. Could have been a fashion statement. Like I said, we'll know more in a couple of days."

"I know this is a tough situation," Ben continued. "And the last thing I want to do is make it worse. But I'd really like to have a team out here tomorrow to scope out the rest of the yard, just to make sure we've covered all the bases."

"When you say 'scope out' . . ." Peter started.

"GPR—ground penetrating radar. They won't have to dig up or disturb anything. Just a couple of guys walking back and forth with what looks a lot like a big push lawn mower."

"*Si*, of course," Maxi said, sipping the tea.

"Good," Ben said. "I'll set it up. Should take about half a day. And you can be here or not, whatever you want."

"I have orders and deliveries this week," Maxi protested. "I have to be here."

Peter glanced at Kate, a question in his eyes.

"I'll be here too," Kate said, patting her friend's shoulder and straining to sound cheerful. "You can forward the phones to the bakery when you want a break. Besides, tomorrow's Monday. And you take Mondays off sometimes, right?"

Maxi nodded.

Ben closed the small notebook and slipped it and the gold pen back into his inside blazer pocket. "OK, that about covers it for now. I'll give you a call as soon as we have any new information. And if you happen to think of anything, no matter how small, no matter how insignificant it seems, give me a buzz."

"What happens now?" Kate asked. The question left her mouth before she could stop it.

"Now we focus on getting an ID and finding out what happened. Could be natural, and someone just didn't want to pay for a funeral. Or it could have been more nefarious."

"Are we in danger?" Maxi asked, setting her mug on the coffee table.

"We're gonna get to the bottom of this," Ben said. "And we should know more over the next couple of days. If it makes you feel better, we can increase patrols past the shop in the meantime."

"That would make me feel better," Peter said. "And maybe we can get some help for the store, in the meantime. A high school kid. Just so you're not here alone."

Maxi shook her head, as she reached down to stroke Oliver's soft flank. "No. I can manage the shop. If it's safe, it's OK for me to be here alone. And if it's not, I'm not bringing anyone else into this. Besides, we have Oliver. And the bakery's right next door."

"We'll keep an eye out for each other," Kate agreed.

Sam nodded.

"Of course," Maxi said, patting the pup's downy head, as he gazed up into her eyes. "And we know our Mr. Oliver is very good at sniffing out trouble."

Chapter 6

Kate rolled over. The bedside clock read 2:07 a.m. Less than five hours of sleep. But in a few short hours, the residents of Coral Cay would be clamoring for breads, rolls, and cookies. And those don't bake themselves.

Luckily, her "commute" was just one flight of stairs down to the bakery.

Kate stretched and yawned, wondering if Maxi and Peter had gotten any sleep. Last night, she couldn't tell what bothered her friend more: that someone had used the backyard of Flowers Maximus to conceal a crime or that some people might believe the florist herself was somehow involved.

After Ben left, Maxi had shut down. Exhaustion and shock, Kate figured. As Peter bundled his wife into his car, he confessed that he was going to try and talk her into taking today off.

Normally, Kate would rate his chances at precisely zero. But after last night?

The last time she'd seen Maxi that upset was when

Kyle Hardy put Sam in handcuffs and arrested him for murder.

But that had turned out alright.

Ben Abrams was a good detective. And she and Maxi had nosed around and discovered evidence that helped clear Sam.

So maybe they could do the same thing again?

Kate rolled that idea around in her head as she got ready for the day.

Not for the first time, she missed Oliver. But the pup had realized that something was up last night. And knew where he was needed.

Kate recalled him sitting patiently by the back door of Peter's sedan. When the attorney had finally opened it, Oliver jumped into the car. The last thing Kate saw as they drove off was his furry, oatmeal-colored face smiling at her through the back window.

Could she and Maxi lend a hand this time? It was one thing to dig for information when the victim's identity was public knowledge. Especially when he was also publicly loathed.

But how do you uncover the details of a crime when you don't even know who was involved? Or when it happened? Or where?

Something told her Maxi's mind had been working overtime on those same questions last night. Maybe they could compare notes. If she came to work today.

Clad in trim dark jeans and a white T-shirt, Kate walked gingerly down the stairs into the bakery kitchen and plugged in the coffee maker.

As Sam's stylish, black nineties pot burbled and gurgled, Kate grabbed a raspberry yogurt from the fridge and tried to organize her thoughts.

First up for this morning—breads. Andy and Bridget would need a fresh supply for their pub, Oy and Begorra.

"Picture the best Jewish deli combined with an authentic Irish pub," was how Maxi first described the place to her. And all it took was one delicious meal and Kate understood. Andy Levy and Bridget O'Hanlon were both great cooks, but together they were magic. A popular hangout for locals and tourists alike, the pub was also one of the bakery's best customers.

Amos Tully wanted a dozen loaves of sliced bread for his grocery store. Along with a few dozen cookies. Kate suspected he was eating most of the oatmeal raisin ones himself. She made a note to include a few extra boxes of those.

Harper Duval was holding a wine and cheese tasting at his shop, In Vino Veritas later this week. He needed a half dozen loaves of Sam's famous sourdough.

"Nothing makes a good cheese taste better—and it will bring out the best in the reds I'm serving, too," the wine shop owner had admitted.

Since Sam had scheduled today off, it would be up to Kate to fill the orders and restock some seriously empty bakery cases, too. And after yesterday, she was grateful for the distraction. She scrubbed her hands, slipped on a fresh navy and white striped apron, and floured the stainless steel counter.

As dawn broke, the aroma of baking bread filled the shop.

Kate refilled her coffee cup, strolled to the front window, and peeked out the blue gingham curtains. Pink clouds danced on the horizon, accompanied by birdsong

Buoyed, she headed back into the kitchen to plan the day's first batch of cookies—oatmeal. This morning was an experiment. Some plain, some with raisins, and some with chocolate chips. She was curious which ones the customers would like best.

Situated in a pale pink Victorian with white ginger-bread trim, the Cookie House had been a local landmark for more than a decade. But they had only just added cookies back to the menu—after a three-year hiatus. An event that coincided with Kate McGuire becoming a junior partner in the bakery just a few scant weeks ago.

She was still fine-tuning the selection of offerings, as she discovered more about their customers' preferences. It didn't hurt that, after eight years as a trained pastry chef (and a Girl Scout before that), Kate could suss out anyone's favorite cookie pretty much at a glance.

While Sam dubbed it "that cookie nonsense," he was pretty pleased with the cash register receipts lately. And the idea of having a little extra money in the till and a little extra free time was a big part of the reason Kate now owned forty-nine percent of the Cookie House.

As she mixed, kneaded, and coaxed the dough, her mind returned to Maxi's conundrum.

Her friend ran the thriving shop next door and juggled it with a growing family. No small feat, it meant that some days the florist came in early. Some evenings she worked late. And sometimes she did both—with or without a break in the middle of the day. Even on days the shop was closed—Sundays and some Mondays—the active mom-of-three would stop by to tend plants, check on flowers, take deliveries, and chat with neighbors. Often with her kids in tow.

The skeleton they'd found had been buried fairly deep. About four feet, Kate estimated. Digging that hole would take time. Time alone and undisturbed in someone else's yard.

So how would someone know that Maxi—who popped in and out of her shop all the time—wouldn't be there?

Kate poured two cups of chocolate chips into the first batch of dough and held the large stainless bowl snug to her waist as she mixed them in with a wooden spoon. A lot of bakers used an electric mixer, but that risked breaking up the chips and breaking down the oatmeal. Besides, mix enough cookie dough by hand and who needs a gym?

As the soothing smells of vanilla, oatmeal, and brown sugar wafted up from the bowl, something nagged at the back of Kate's brain. The trench.

Kate had been in Coral Cay only a few months, but she was already learning the island's little quirks. Like the trade winds that kept them cool while the rest of the state was sweltering. Or the lack of cell phone service in the downtown area. And the fact that, in a lot of places, the water table was just five or six feet below the surface.

And a four-foot hole was just about the right depth for someone who understood that. Someone who knew the terrain.

What if the killer was from Coral Cay? What if the killer was one of them?

Chapter 7

As Kate flipped the shop sign to OPEN, she heard a key in the bakery's back door.

"I thought it was your day off?" she said, as Sam walked in and made straight for the coffeepot.

"Time enough for that later," he said. "Got sourdough to proof. If Harper Duval's fool enough to hold a wine tasting in the middle of the week and wants bread, who am I to argue with him?"

"I'm already proofing the dough. And I haven't seen any sign of Maxi. Anyway, Peter was going to try and talk her into staying home today."

"Couldn't do it," he said, shaking his head. "Just called me. That lawyer could talk the birds out of the trees. But that gal is stubborn."

Kate struggled not to smile at the irony of the baker calling anyone else "stubborn."

"Maxi's on her way in?"

"Be here any minute."

"OK, well, we'll keep an eye on her," Kate said.

Hepplewhite nodded. "Those cheese Danish?"

Kate smiled. "A test batch. I used apricot jam as a glaze."

"Might have to try one," he said, pouring coffee into a clean white mug. "That your young man yesterday?" he asked, plucking a pastry from the cooling rack without looking up.

"Evan. And he's not mine. I released him back into the wild months ago," she added lightly. "Hopefully, he'll be clearing out soon."

Sam nodded, a small smile on his face.

When the phone rang, she grabbed it. "The Cookie House, this is Kate.

"It's me," Maxi said. "I'm next door at the shop. And have I got some news for you."

Chapter 8

When Kate walked into the flower shop, Maxi was on the settee with a coffee service on the table in front of her. Exactly the same spot she had occupied the previous night. But her mood was upbeat, even bubbly.

Kate put the bakery box containing four cheese Danish on the table, just as Oliver galloped over to her. As she turned, the half-grown puppy put his paws on her knees, looking up into her face.

"You know I've missed you," she said, scratching behind his ear. "Don't you?"

"He missed you, too," Maxi said, grinning. "He only ate three eggs for breakfast. With bacon. Hey, these look really good."

"New recipe. They even earned Sam's stamp of approval. But I thought you were taking today off," Kate chided, as she settled on the sofa.

"An ugly rumor started by *mi amor*," the florist replied. "Well-meaning, but totally wrong. Besides, I figure if I'm here, we can keep an eye on things. And those guys are coming today. The ones with the radar lawn mower."

"I forgot about that," Kate said, spooning coconut cream from a dish into her coffee cup. "So what's your news?"

"The good part is I came up with a couple of ideas," the florist said. "But the news part you're not gonna like."

"Go for it anyway," Kate said, steeling herself. After last night, how bad could it be?

"I had two new orders waiting when I got in this morning. Big, expensive flower orders."

"That's wonderful. Weren't you worried that business might fall off after the . . . uh . . . you know?" Kate said, pointing discreetly at the backyard.

"That's not the bad part," Maxi said. "These flower orders—they're for you."

"Both of them?"

Maxi nodded.

"Evan," Kate said softly.

"He's one of them. The other is Harper Duval."

"Harp? No. Why? Wait, could this just be a 'thank-you' for doing a rush order on the bread?"

Maxi shook her head as she ladled more coconut cream into her own cup. "Nope. That's why I wanted to give you a heads-up. Red roses from both. And, in the language of flowers . . ."

"In the language of flowers, that's a statement even I understand."

"So I'll refuse the orders," Maxi concluded. "Both of them."

Kate swallowed. "No. Evan would just call someone else. And Harp is a neighbor and business owner. This is a small town. You don't want to alienate him."

"Evan's put in a standing order," Maxi explained. "A big arrangement to start. Then a single red rose every day for a week."

"And Harp?"

"Two dozen long-stemmed roses and a card asking you to have dinner with him."

"He's married! I mean, I know Caroline's talking about leaving him, but . . ."

"You're also much too young for him, but that doesn't seem to bother him either," Maxi countered. "He's got that disease middle-aged guys get. The one that makes them buy sports cars and join gyms and get spray tans. Except Harp has money, so he already has the car and a real tan and his own home gym. *Corizon*, I don't think he's that serious. Just a little lost right now. Apparently, Caroline's already left him and jetted off to Europe—straight out of rehab. And filed for divorce. At least, that's the latest rumor blowing around town."

"I like Harp, but not that way."

"Good," the florist said. "Just tell him that. He's a big boy. He'll understand. And if he doesn't, we threaten to plant him out back like the other one."

Kate laughed. "Oh sure, that'll be great for business."

"Your boy Evan? Super different. He's got it bad. And I don't just mean because he's spending so much money on my very beautiful flowers."

Kate shook her head. "He's just not used to hearing the word 'no.' It's over. So over. I admit, seeing him yesterday rattled me. I wasn't expecting it. But I love it here. I love my life. And I'm not going back to New York. Or a guy who cheated on me."

"Good. 'Cause I need someone to help me find out what happened to Alvin."

"Alvin?"

"Mi amor refers to our skeleton as Exhibit A. But Mr. Bones was a person. So I'm calling him Alvin."

"I've been thinking about that one, too. Although I have to admit I didn't get around to naming him."

"It also means we can talk about him, and no one will know who we mean," Maxi said.

"Like a code?" Kate said. "That's brilliant."

"But better than the pig Latin mi niños tried to use. Such gibberish. They were so bad I was *thiiiss* close to giving them lessons," she said, holding her fingers two inches apart. "I did learn something interesting about Alvin this morning. Before he left, Peter got a phone call. From Ben. It looks like Alvin was a man. Between twenty-five and forty-five, Ben said. And he'd been out there for less than a year. Probably not even six months. They're gonna do some tests to see if they can narrow it down more."

"Wow, big change from thinking he's four hundred years old," Kate said. "I'm no expert. But I have been to a few museums. And from what we saw, I'd have sworn the burial was ancient. Especially that boot."

"Ben thinks the bad guy might have done something to speed up the process. He's working on finding out about that, too."

Maxi fell silent.

"I want to know who did this," she said finally. "I know I should just leave it to the police. But whoever it was . . ." She shook her head.

"They made you part of it," Kate said softly. "You and the flower shop."

Maxi nodded.

"I think our first clue to finding out who put Alvin out there is determining *when* they put him out there," Kate said, relieved to have a puzzle to occupy her mind.

"When we were in the backyard, it took the two of us quite a while to dig each of those trenches."

"Ay, not easy work, even with mostly sand," the florist said ruefully.

"And Alvin was at least a foot or a foot-and-a-half beneath that last one. So someone would need to be out there a good long time. Even with two people digging. And nobody saw anything? I mean, you're here at all hours, and so is Sam."

"I know," Maxi agreed. "That bothered me, too. Some nights, I'm leaving at ten or eleven. And I know mi padrino is coming in to start baking at two or three."

"That's a pretty thin needle to thread." Kate looked over at Oliver, who was sitting next to the sofa, listening to their conversation. She broke off a piece of crust from her Danish and offered it to him.

The poodle mix lifted it neatly from her palm, then sat back on his haunches. She could have sworn he smiled.

"I was wondering if maybe we were away," Maxi said. "Peter and I, we take a weekend sometimes and go somewhere nice. Just us. Other times, we pack up everybody and drive over to Miami to see family."

"If you were out of town, that would explain how someone knew you wouldn't show up at the shop. That would give them plenty of time. And privacy."

"But when it's just the two of us, we never tell anybody. That's the point. Peter doesn't even let the bunch from his office know until we get back. I mean, for emergencies, they have his cell number. But they don't know where he is. Of course, *mi mami* knows where we are, because she watches the kids. But trust me, if she did it, we wouldn't have found Alvin ever."

Kate smiled, slipping Oliver another morsel. "But this is a small town."

Maxi nodded.

"So word gets around. Any of the times you got back, did you notice anything out of place in the yard?"

"You mean like a giant Alvin-shaped dip in the grass?" Maxi shook her glossy black hair. "Nope."

"Was there ever a time in the past year when you were both out of town—you and Sam? Or away from the shops at the same time? A weekend gathering? A festival?"

"Not that I remember. And I know it wasn't mi padrino."

"No, I saw the look on Sam's face. He was shocked that wasn't Gentleman George."

"Ay, Barb and Amos were pretty disappointed, too. So much for their dreams of a bigger, better Pirate Festival. Oh my gosh! Uncle Ernesto!"

"Uncle Ernesto? You don't think he's Alvin?"

"No, no, no," Maxi said quickly. "Mi mami's brother Ernesto. He runs a construction company in Miami. He was hurt in an accident. With one of those big cranes. Back in February. We didn't think he was going to make it. But Ernesto's tough. And lucky. When it first happened? It was bad. And mi mami was a mess. I didn't want her driving across the Everglades by herself, so I was gonna take her. But Peter cashed in some of his overtime and we all went. We were gone for, oh, it must have been about a week. And mi mami stayed there a few more weeks to help out. Now Ernesto's back at work, and there's no stopping the guy. He's something else."

"But if someone knew you were out of town," Kate started, reaching into the box for a second Danish.

"Everybody knew. I made arrangements with one of the floral networks to handle orders while I was gone. I talked with the events coordinators over at the resorts. Just to let them know. I even wanted to put a sign on the door, but Ben said that was a bad idea."

Kate nodded. "That doesn't tell us much. It could be someone who knows you or just someone who heard about it second or third hand through the resort. Or the local grapevine."

"Uh-uh, one thing was different this time. Besides how long we were gone. And I didn't think of it 'til just now. While we were in Miami, mi padrino was away from the bakery, too. Just for a couple of days."

"Sam Hepplewhite took a day off?"

"Like a whole super-long weekend. Valentine's Day. He does it every year. Since he lost Ginger. He leaves before the holiday and usually comes back on Sunday, to catch up on the baking so he can open the shop Monday morning. I don't know what day he came back this year, though, 'cause we weren't here."

"Where does he go?"

Maxi shrugged. "No one knows. Not even Peter and me."

"But anyone who knew about that *and* heard you were in Miami . . ."

"They would know they could have the whole back-yard—my backyard—all to themselves. For as long as they wanted."

"I hate to say it," Kate said, setting down her cup and leaning back into the little sofa. "But that narrows it down to someone who lives in Coral Cay. Someone we know and trust."

Chapter 9

"So what's this about a cookie-of-the-day contest?" Barb Showalter's voice boomed, as she planted her feet wide in front of the bakery case, hands on hips. Clad in a blue Hawaiian shirt and tan walking shorts, she eyed up several kinds of cookies.

Kate concentrated on the bookstore owner for a split second. Then she reached into the case, plucked out a peanut butter cookie still warm from the oven and handed it across the counter.

"An excuse to try out some different kinds of cookies and see what everyone likes," Kate explained. "You write the name of the cookie you'd like us to make and put it in the jar," she said, pointing to a yellow cookie jar on the counter.

"Enter as many times as you want, and as many kinds of cookies as you want. Every day, I'll pull out one entry and bake up a big batch. Whoever suggested it gets a dozen free. We'll keep track of how many we sell, too. Then, at the end of the month, whichever contest cookie sells the most, that person wins a fifty-dollar gift certificate to the Cookie House. And if their cookie suggestion is a big hit, we'll keep making them."

"That is ingenious," Barb said, munching happily.

"And dangerous," Kate said, smiling. "I've peeked at some of the suggestions. So far, there's a lot of chocolate in that jar. And, of course, I have to do some tasting. I mean, it's my job."

"You poor thing," Barb said. "So are these contest cookies things I'd like to try or old family recipes or what?"

"It can be anything. A name. A recipe. Or just something you've always wanted to sample. Or make yourself."

"I may steal a version of that contest for the book store. Hmmm. Let me have a dozen of the oatmeal and a dozen of the oatmeal with chocolate chips. We're having children's story time this afternoon. Oh, and a half dozen of the peanut butter." Barb grinned. "Those are for me."

Kate carefully assembled three bakery boxes—two large and one small. She filled them, throwing in some extra oatmeal cookies for the kids attending story hour, and sealed each box with a small piece of cellophane tape. She handed them across the counter, as the bookstore owner passed her a credit card.

"I have a confession to make," Barb said. "A favor, really. The other day, the thing with Sir George Bly? Or, what we thought was Sir George Bly?"

Kate nodded.

"I've been thinking. His story is a big part of Coral Cay. Directly or indirectly, he's the reason a lot of people visit this island."

"The Pirate Festival?" Kate asked.

Barb shook her head. "Not just that. Historians. Anthropologists. Sociologists. Even the amateur treasure hunters. That story brings in a steady stream of people. And not just during tourist season or for the festival."

Kate slipped the credit card though a machine next to the cash register and returned it.

"That burial got me thinking," Barb continued, slipping the card into her pocket. "What happened to Sir George—what really happened to him—it's still a mystery. And I have to admit, when our bunch from the book club pulled together to figure out what happened to Stewart Lord? We were pretty good. Surprisingly good. And I realize that you and Maxi did all the heavy lifting on that one. But it wouldn't have to be like that this time."

"This time?" Kate asked, puzzled.

"I love history," Barb said. "Always have. When I came here, I couldn't get enough of the local stuff. Native peoples. Conquistadors. Homesteaders. Outlaws. South Florida lore and legends. Who settled this place, how they ended up here, and why. The funny thing is, the reasons people come here haven't changed in four hundred years."

"As someone who relocated to Coral Cay for a fresh start, I can believe it," Kate said, sensing Barb was sharing something personal for the first time since they'd met.

Barb grinned. "You and me both. For some reason, though, George Bly's story has always fascinated me. Even more than some of the others. Maybe it's the old swashbuckling adventure yarn. Too much Robert Louis Stevenson as a child. Or maybe it's because no one knows what happened to him. Yesterday, I thought we were going to be able to at least write an ending to his story."

"You were disappointed it wasn't him out there," Kate said.

"Heartbroken. I know that sounds silly. I admit, some of that was because of the financial boost it would give this island. And our festival. But I also thought I was going to be one of the first people to discover what really happened to him. To find out if the legends were true."

"A four-hundred-year-old cold case," Kate summarized.

"Exactly. What we know—the actual history—stops with the records of the last Spanish galleon that attacked his ship. And you have to take that with a grain of salt. But the rest of it? Pure myth. Conjecture. Nothing concrete."

"You want to change that?" Kate asked, curious.

"I want the Coral Cay Irregulars to change that," Barb emphasized. "We meet again on Sunday. Or we're supposed to, if Harp is still hosting us. I have to check with him on that. All that nonsense with Caroline. He might not be up to it. But if we do meet, I'm going to propose that we take up the mystery of Gentleman George. And I wanted to see if you and Maxi would support me."

Kate had to admit, the pirate's story—true or not—was riveting. From a practical standpoint, it would also give her and Maxi a cover for what they were already investigating: Alvin.

Barb Showalter had also been a generous friend to Sam—despite the bookstore owner's claims to the contrary—during the weeks the baker had been in jail. Before the police figured out who really killed Stewart Lord.

"I think that's a great idea," Kate said finally. "Count me in. And I can't speak for Maxi. But I think she'd love it."

Barb beamed. "I know we had a false start the other day. But I believe we can do this. Four-hundred-year-old cold case or not, if we all put our heads together, I think we can finally solve the mystery of what really happened to Sir George Bly."

Chapter 10

As it approached noon, a lull between waves of customers gave Kate time to reload the cookie trays in the bakery case. The classic oatmeal cookies were a big hit. And the chocolate chip variety was outselling raisin three-to-one.

Kate was already planning a few more test batches—one with butterscotch chips, another with shredded coconut.

The front door banged open and Maxi struggled in lugging a large ceramic vase of red roses.

"OK, that is seriously huge," Kate said, stacking warm chocolate chip cookies into neat rows in the case. "You look like a flower arrangement with legs."

"From one of your many suitors with his compliments," Maxi said grinning, as she hoisted it up on one end of the bakery counter.

"So not funny. Which one is this?"

"The ex. I'm putting off the Harp flowers as long as possible."

"Because once I receive them, I have to say 'thank you' and let him down easy?"

"Because I keep hoping the young coot will come to his senses."

"Young coot?" Kate asked.

"He's not old enough to be an old coot," Maxi said, turning the vase slightly and readjusting several of the blooms. "But he's no spring chicken, either. You sure you don't want me to refuse to fill that one? We can invoke the mercy rule. Like at Miguel's soccer games."

"What's that?" Kate asked, handing her friend a cookie wrapped in a paper napkin.

"Gracias! If one team gets too much of a lead on the other—so much they can't possibly win—the coaches invoke the mercy rule and end the game. The winner still wins, but nobody gets super trounced. I say we need the same thing for dating. So if some guy is chasing a woman way out of his league or much too young, she can invoke the mercy rule and everybody walks away— no hard feelings."

"OK, I kind of like that," Kate said, retrieving a cookie for herself. "But no, I'm going to have to deal with Harp. And I think I'd rather do it in person than on the phone."

"Gutsy," Maxi said, taking a dainty bite. "You want me to come?"

"No, it's going to be awkward enough. But I'm definitely taking Oliver. And I might take some cookies."

"Make defeat easier to swallow?"

"Something like that. I just don't want him to interpret it as flirting."

"Ay, this makes me so glad I'm already married," she said, polishing off the last of the treat and wiping her hands with the napkin. "That and mi amor. Who has called like six times today. He pretends he has little things to ask. But really he just wants to make sure I'm OK. I love him, but he's driving me nutty."

"Sounds about right. You just missed Sam. He took a delivery over to Amos Tully. But I wouldn't be surprised if he stops by your place on the way back."

"Only four times so far this morning," Maxi said, holding up a quartet of fingers. "Mi padrino keeps finding things that need fixing. I've never had so many new light bulbs in my life."

"They're worried about you. He and Peter both. Me too, for that matter."

"I opened my purse before to get my hairbrush," Maxi said. "You know what I found? A giant can of pepper spray."

"In the language of plants, pepper spray means love," Kate said, smiling.

"At least it's easier to carry around than those roses. I can't believe your boy Evan is doing this."

"I can't believe he came all the way down here. And I keep wondering why."

"Calling on the phone didn't work. So he's kicking it up a notch. Or maybe his shiny new toy doesn't seem so shiny and new anymore."

"I'm thinking it's that last one."

"Hey, how about we pack him and Harp both off to a deserted island? One of those places at the end of the Keys? It could be like one of those buddy movies. Or a reality survival show."

"Only if the island is Manhattan. Evan wouldn't last long without room service and a good dry cleaner."

"You see? He and Harp have a lot in common. So where do you suppose your ex is staying? A fancy penthouse suite at one of the resorts? Or maybe the one where you get the little luxury bungalows all to yourself?"

"Nope. If I had to guess, I'd say he's on the yacht. I'm just praying he didn't bring his mother along. Amanda's a trip and a half. The funny thing is, I actually miss her."

"Been in touch?"

"Last month. She'd left a few messages. So I finally called her."

"Corizon, if you can handle that call, you can handle anything. What did you say? Did you tell momma that sonny-boy is a sorry hound dog?"

"No, I told her that the relationship hadn't been working, and it was better that we realized it before the wedding instead of after."

"Damn, *chica*, that's classy. I'd have been tempted to give her all the juicy details. And a couple of the photos."

"Oh, I'm sure she already knew. Amanda can read between the lines. Besides, from what I heard, Evan's father was the same way. Movie-star looks. Piles of family money. And no off switch."

"So the boy comes by it honestly?" Maxi asked.

Kate nodded.

"Well, if you want to bring some more of those cookies, I've got another show you might wanna see. Those radar guys just showed up. In a little while, we'll find out if Alvin has a friend."

Chapter 11

Sitting on the back patio of Flowers Maximus, Kate and Maxi dispatched another half dozen warm chocolate chip cookies, along with most of a pitcher of iced lemonade.

A half hour later, Kate nipped over to the bakery for another pitcher, along with some cookies for the radar crew.

While one technician happily accepted both, his co-worker quickly chugged a glass of lemonade and headed back to the machine.

"Don't take it personally," his buddy confided. "Crash diet. His twenty-year class reunion's next week,"

"So did you guys find anything?" Maxi asked.

Despite her carefree demeanor, frequent clenched fists and tension in her smile told Kate the florist was putting on a brave front.

"Uh, we're not supposed to discuss the results with civilians," he said, looking guiltily at the cookie in his hand. "But between you and me, nothing."

"Good," Kate said.

"Any luck and that last thing'll be just a one-off," the tech added, grabbing a second cookie from the box with a mammoth paw as he headed back to work.

"It's sorta hypnotic," Maxi said, as she watched them slowly crisscross the yard pushing a giant black box supported by what looked like three fat bicycle tires. "So when do you think mi padrino will stop by next?"

"Not for a while," Kate said, nodding at the lumbering machinery. "Since you have a couple of protectors over here already. Plus, he's trying out a new recipe for the festival. Pirate bread."

"Ay, the whole island has pirate fever. What in the world is pirate bread?"

"Sam wanted to do something authentic. Something that the pirates would have actually eaten. So he did some research and found a recipe for hardtack."

"That sounds like something you buy at a hardware store."

"Then it tastes pretty much like it sounds," Kate said. "Fortunately, sailors could carry it on long sea voyages because it never went bad. Unfortunately, that's because it was never good in the first place. Basically, it starts out hard and tasteless."

"Ay, poor Sam. So what's he going to do now?"

"A peace offering to the old pirates. Instead of what they actually ate, he's developing something they would have enjoyed, if they could have. He's calling it pirate bread. It's big and flat, like hardtack. But it's made up of a lot of light, flaky layers. He's using sea salt, and he adds rosemary."

"Rosemary means remembrance," Maxi said, nodding.

"That's what Sam said. And I stole a piece earlier. Buttery and good."

"OK, I'd like to try some of that," Maxi said.

Suddenly, the machine in the yard let out a cacophony

of electronic beeps. The tech stopped and rolled it back over the same area. It happened again. After a third roll-by, he stopped.

"Dios mio!" Maxi said under her breath.

"Not again," Kate whispered.

The first tech signaled and the second one marked off a patch of the yard with pink fluorescent spray paint. The spot was about four feet from where Oliver had discovered Alvin.

One tech quickly shut down the machine, while the other grabbed two shovels from their pile of tools near the patio. When the guy passed Kate and Maxi, he shrugged.

"I can't watch," Maxi said, covering her eyes.

"It's OK," Kate said softly, patting her friend's shoulder. "Whatever happens, it's going to be alright."

"We're going to have to sell this place and move the shop," she said. "Ten years making it *perfecto*. Every bush, every flower, every tree. Who's going to want it now?"

"Right now, just breathe," Kate said, as she felt her own heart hammering.

A few minutes later, the crew hit pay dirt. Kate watched them use the sides of their shovels to clear away the soil. Then one tech knelt and leaned in for a better view. Kate saw relief on his face, as the second one broke into a wide grin.

"Any chance you got a dog?" he shouted.

"Definitely!" Kate called back.

The second tech bent over, reached down into the hole and pulled out a large chew bone, waving it triumphantly in the air.

"Look, Maxi! It's OK. It's just one of Oliver's toys."

The florist pulled her hands from her eyes and took in the scene. Her face relaxed into a smile. "Gracias," she said softly.

"Hey, I know what will take your mind off things,"

Kate said. "Barb stopped by the Cookie House this morning. She wants us to find Gentleman George."

"Unless he's crouched behind those raised garden beds or hiding beside that big tree in the front yard, I haven't got a clue," Maxi said, before draining what was left of her lemonade in one long gulp.

"No, I mean, she wants the book club to take it on as a project," Kate explained. "She's going to propose it at the meeting this Sunday. She wanted to get our support in advance."

"Canvassing for votes. Very cagey. And very Barb. *La Presidenta* doesn't want to suggest an idea and fall on her face. So she's counting the votes ahead of time."

"Apparently, she's a real history buff," Kate said. "And she loves the Gentleman George story. She's also convinced it could help tourism on the island."

"OK, that I believe. Barb is a super-smart business-woman. If she thinks it will help, it probably will."

"I was also thinking it could give us an excuse for nosing around," Kate said. "Since we're trying to find out what happened with Alvin."

"Ooo, sneaky! I like it. Still, it's gonna go on one super long to-do list. Now in my spare time, when I'm not digging bones out of my yard, or chatting about little nothings with mi amor, or clearing cans of pepper spray out of my purse, or delivering giant flowers, I've gotta keep my eyes peeled for a four-hundred-year-old pirate."

Chapter 12

It took Maxi several minutes to politely work her way to the front of the crowded bakeshop. The oversized flower arrangement she was hauling didn't help. And the steady thrum of conversation among the customers meant that almost no one heard her say "excuse me," as she tried to wind her way through the throng.

"So the good news is Alvin doesn't have any friends," she said softly, sliding the large vase of roses onto the counter as she handed off the card to Kate. "The bad news is that you-know-who didn't change his mind."

"I'll go talk to him after work," Kate said crisply, pocketing the card.

"Oh, nice roses!" Bridget O'Hanlon said. "They must be from your fiancé. Is he an actor? He's really cute."

"Ex-fiancé," Kate corrected, as she herded a dozen sourdough rolls into a white wax-paper bag. "Emphasis on '*ex*.'"

"Ex as in 'exit,'" Maxi added.

"Are you sure?" Bridget asked, watching Kate fill her

order. "'Cause I swore he said 'fiancé' when he was in the pub this afternoon."

"I'm sure that was just a slip of the tongue on his part," Kate said. "We broke up this long time."

"OK, well, whatever," the pub owner said, accepting the bag. When she reached the shop door she hesitated, turning.

"But Mitzy Allen heard Delores Philpott mention he'd hired a real estate agent to find a place in town," Bridget called over the din. "She figured that you guys were house hunting. You know, for after the wedding."

With that, she disappeared out the door.

"Oh, that's sweet," said Minette Ivers, stepping up to the counter. "Let's see, I'm going to need a loaf of wheat, sliced. And a dozen of those oatmeal cookies. Oh shoot, add in a half dozen of the ones with chocolate, too. I wish my Carl would have done that. I had to find every single one of our homes my own self. 'Course that man was working all hours," she said, grinning. "Before, during, and after our wedding."

"Wedding?" Sam said, coming through the swinging doors carrying a fresh batch of garlic naan. "Who's getting married?"

"Kate is," Phyllis Webster piped up from across the crowded shop.

"Her groom's an actor," Frannie Alfano added from the other corner. "And he's buying her a big house in Coral Cay as a wedding present."

Sam wrinkled his nose and looked at Kate.

She shook her head vigorously. "There's been a misunderstanding," she enunciated clearly. "Evan's not my groom. He's not my fiancé. He's not even my boyfriend. And I seriously doubt he's shopping for a home anywhere south of Fifth Avenue. He's dating a Manhattan real estate agent."

"Why's this place look like a florist?" Sam grumbled.

"It's a new advertising campaign," Maxi announced brightly. "We put big flowers over here. And we give away cookies to customers at the flower shop."

Sam looked dubious. "Got some challah that husband of yours likes. Might taste good with dinner." With that, he retreated back to the kitchen.

"Now ladies," Kate said, cheerily. "Let me tell you all about our brand-new cookie-of-the-day contest."

Chapter 13

As Kate walked out the front door of the bakery, she turned the sign to CLOSED.

Oliver, who'd been napping on one of the white benches on the front porch of the Cookie House, leapt from his perch and fell into step.

"The name of the game is 'keep it short,'" Kate informed him, as she slipped a gingersnap to the pup. "I brought a box of anise cookies for Harp. We drop in, let him down gently, and take off. Got it?"

Oliver quickly looked away.

"OK, it's not much of a plan, I admit, but it's the best I've got."

As they passed Wheels, something in the window caught her eye. Kate stopped and peered into the bicycle shop. The object looked like an actual artifact: a large treasure map, wrinkled and yellowed with age.

Kate looked up, and Claire St. John was standing in the doorway, smiling. "So what do you think?"

"This is amazing," Kate said. "Is it real?"

Oliver galloped toward Claire, who squatted down to greet him.

"I made it, actually," Claire explained in her clipped British accent, as she tousled the silky hair on Oliver's head and patted his flank. "To advertise the bike tours I lead during the Pirate Festival. I've dubbed it the Treasure Island Tour. That's the display. And everyone on the tour will get their own copy. But they're much smaller. More the size of a letter."

"How did you do this? It looks authentic."

Claire stood and walked over to the window, next to Kate. "Old British remedy. Tea. Of course, it works best with paper that's mostly cotton. I give each sheet a bath in a dishpan of strong tea. It dries looking ancient and wrinkled. I even apply some extra with a sponge—to create the dark splotches—and make it appear more realistic. Weathered. Then once the paper dries, I print out the maps using brown ink instead of black."

"This is amazing."

"I was actually rather chuffed," she said proudly. "With that one, I even burned the edges a little. But I can't do that with every one."

"Too time consuming?"

"Too nerve wracking," Claire said, laughing. "I was a shambles. Convinced I was going to set off the fire sirens."

"This is a work of art," Kate said, shaking her head.

"You should see my storeroom. It looks more like a darkroom. Or a printer's studio. I've got a washing line with bits of damp paper strung across the place."

"A pirate bike tour is a great idea," Kate said. "Where will you go?"

"Well, I'm trying to keep it accurate. But when it comes to our pirate friends, it's all rumor and conjecture. Gossip, if you will. I've spoken with some of the local historians. And I'm sticking to a couple of the coves that the pirates supposedly used—Gentleman George and some of the bands who came later. And we finish up with a beach picnic at the nature preserve."

"I love that," Kate said.

"You should join us," Claire said enthusiastically. "It's great fun. And, if nothing else, a lovely ride on a beautiful part of the island. For me, that's the real treasure."

As Kate and Oliver approached In Vino Veritas, she sighed audibly. "I should have brought Maxi, too," she mumbled under her breath as she presented Oliver with another small gingersnap.

He lifted it softly from her palm. Then he gazed up at her. If Kate didn't know better, she'd have sworn she saw concern in the large black eyes. But dogs couldn't worry, could they?

"C'mon, sweetie. We go in, we chat, we're out of there." She opened the heavy shop door.

"Well, if it isn't my favorite pastry chef," Harper Duval drawled. Somehow, his honied, monied New Orleans accent seemed thicker. Relaxed, tanned, and clad in a turquoise dress shirt with khakis bearing a knife-edge pleat, the owner of the wine and gourmet foods shop always seemed more like a well-heeled host than a working shopkeeper. But Kate also caught a whiff of cigarettes.

Weeks ago, Harp had confessed that he smoked when he was tense. He'd also been trying to quit. And he'd had the patch on his arm to prove it.

She wondered just how bad things had gotten between him and Caroline. Although, from what Maxi had said, his soon-to-be-ex was more interested in her freedom than his money.

"Just a little something to say 'thank you' for the flowers," Kate said, presenting the bakery box.

"Are these what I think they are?" Harp said, beaming as his fingertips momentarily brushed hers.

He opened the lid. "Ah, your famous anise almond cookies. My favorite. You know what they say. 'The way to a man's heart is through his stomach.'"

He met her eyes expectantly. Kate felt the knot in her stomach tighten. Like a noose.

Sitting, but alert beside her, Oliver gave out a soft low growl.

Kate did a double take. The pup had never done that before.

"Um, there's no easy way to say this," she started. "But I have to say 'no' to the dinner invitation. I just broke off an engagement. I'm not ready to see anyone. Even casually," she added hurriedly. "I'm not ready to even entertain the idea of dating. I'm sorry. I hope you understand."

Harp smiled. "I understand completely, dear lady. When you get to know me better, you'll learn I am a very patient swain."

Kate took a small step back, shaking her head. "When I do date again, it won't be with a neighbor I consider a dear friend," she said softly, looking at him directly. "It's too hard when that doesn't work out. And this is a very small town."

Kate reminded herself to smile and tried to keep her tone light. It felt like there were boulders in her stomach. She looked down at Oliver, who was totally focused on Harp. She couldn't read the pup's expression.

"Is it your young man? The one who's been in town the past day or so? You still have feelings for him." The last sentence was a statement, not a question.

"Evan," she said softly. It would have been so easy to blame this on him. Especially since Evan Thorpe had been happily telling the world he was still her fiancé.

But that wasn't honest. Or fair. And she needed Harp to know, even after Evan left town, that she truly wasn't interested.

"No," she continued. "That's over and done. But I was in a relationship for a long time. We were getting married. Making plans together. Now I'm on my own. And I like that. I wanted to let you know how flattered I am that you'd invite me to dinner. But the bottom line is, when it comes to that kind of thing, we're not a good match."

"Well, you and I will have to agree to disagree on that part," he teased genially, placing the bakery box carefully onto the thick, white marble counter. "Perhaps as we get to know each other better . . ."

"I know what it's like to come out of a long-term relationship suddenly," Kate blurted. "It feels like everything's upside down. And I understand that ending a marriage—a long marriage—is much more devastating than breaking an engagement."

"Ah, you've heard," Harp said quietly, as the smile slipped from his face. "My almost-ex is jetting around Europe, as we speak. The good news is she doesn't want my money. The bad news is she doesn't want me, either."

He glanced from Kate to the floor, then at some spot in the back of the shop.

Finally, he looked at her again. While his mouth curved upward in a genial smile, his eyes were flat. "But you certainly can't fault a gentleman for trying."

Chapter 14

Kate sat at Maxi's breakfast bar, basking in the warmth of the bustling home kitchen. She picked up the glass of white wine at her elbow and took a small sip.

"So how bad was it?" Maxi asked, as she prepped the pot of soft-shelled crabs with generous dashes of various seasonings.

"Don't ask," Kate said. "Brutal. Let's just say I'm thinking twice about going to the book club meeting this weekend."

"No way, corizon. The Coral Cay Irregulars need you if we're gonna figure out what happened to Gentleman George. And *I* need you if we're gonna figure out who planted Alvin in my garden. Besides, Barb deputized you."

"She didn't deputize me, she just asked for my support. And for yours, too, by the way."

"And I'm going. You want things to go back to normal, right? So you just do what you always do, go where you always go, bump into Harp around town and act like everything is hunky-dory. Then pretty soon it will be. And he'll be onto his next crush."

"I don't know. It's one thing to run into the guy downtown. But going to his home? That seems a little invasive."

"Well, it would help if you could burp after the meal. You know, super loud? I have a cousin who can belch 'La Vida Loca.'"

"How about I show up to the meeting in curlers and a ratty bathrobe?"

"If you got one of those avocado face masks, that would be good, too. Or the little paper ones? They're really nice. Look, the truth is, if you want things to go back to normal, you just gotta act normal. Besides, it's not like you're going there alone. We'll ride over together. And you got the whole book club between you and him. We'll eat a little, vote for Barb's proposal, see who remembers what was going on around town back in February, and leave."

"I know you're right."

"I know what will cheer you up," Maxi said. "Barb called me just before you arrived. That new vet clinic is opening in town next week. And she wants to throw the guy a party to welcome him to the downtown business community. She's got me doing balloons. And she's hoping you can make a pretty gingerbread doghouse."

"Did she really say that? A pretty gingerbread doghouse?"

"La Presidenta requested a big doghouse made of cookies," Maxi said, spreading her arms wide. "What kind I don't think she cares. I'm just her minion. And translator."

"Mom!" Michael shouted from the next room. "Javie ate a bug!"

"Javie, did you eat a bug?" Maxi called into the den.

"We're playing pirates, and Michael dared me," Javie said, a grin on his face as he ran into the kitchen with Oliver at his heels.

"OK, what kind of bug?"

"Ant."

"Regular ant or fire ant?"

"One of the little black ones."

"Good protein. They sell those in the health food store. OK, you go get washed up and you and Mr. Oliver can set the table outside. If you're hungry enough to eat bugs, it's time to get this show on the road. And you, Miguelito," she said, pointing her index finger to where her older son was standing in the doorway. "Stop daring your brother."

"Aw, Mom! I didn't think he'd really do it. What's for dinner?"

"Steamed ants. With grasshopper sauce. Now go wash up. You can help your father boil the corn and crabs out back. *Vamanos!*"

Kate smiled. "Do they really sell ants at the health food store?"

"Chocolate covered. But I didn't want to give the little gremlins any ideas."

"Speaking of which, I brought a little something for dessert," Kate said. "A sneak preview of the first cookie contest winner. They go on sale tomorrow."

"I feel humbled and grateful," Maxi said, holding her big wooden spoon as a microphone. "And for this honor, I would like to thank the academy. . . . So how good are these cookies, really?" she added, giving the crab pot a quick stir.

"Dark chocolate and decadent. The recipe calls them 'chocolate icebox cookies,' because you have to chill the dough before you bake them. Then, once they cool from the oven, they get a generous topping of vanilla icing. I don't know who's going to win the contest, but I'm definitely keeping these around. I think they'll be a hit for parties and special orders, too."

"You had me at 'dark chocolate,'" the florist said, smiling. "OK, if mi amor is finished shucking corn, this pot is definitely ready for him. One South Florida crab boil coming up!"

"I also brought a couple of key lime pies," Kate confessed. "As a backup."

"Ay, I'm gonna have to save a piece of that for mi mami. It's her favorite."

"Where is Esperanza tonight?" Kate asked.

"Birthday party for one of her friends. And they're having it at one of those night bowling places. Cake, burgers, and bowling balls that glow in the dark. Super festive."

In the cool of twilight, Kate, Maxi, and Peter lingered at the table as the sun sank into the western sky. A gentle breeze stirred the trees as Elena, Javie, and Michael, armed with empty jelly jars, gleefully chased fireflies around the backyard. Oliver, in the thick of the action, ran in circles around them.

"At least this way, we know they're *chasing* bugs, not eating them," Maxi mused, reaching for another icebox cookie. "And you were right about these. Plus, there's plenty of room in the white icing for decorations. Or advertising. Not that I'd ever use them for that."

"And you can tint it pink or blue for baby showers— or green for St. Paddy's Day," Kate said.

"Well, I'm no advertising whiz, but I will say they taste great," Peter said, snagging another for himself. "But hey, I liked that key lime pie, too. Tangy. Not too sweet."

"Yeah, that's a mistake even the natives make," Maxi said, approvingly. "Too much sugar."

"Thank you! I was thinking of making little individual ones for the book club meeting. Now that someone has twisted my arm into going. I figured single-serve pies would be better for a buffet."

"You know who would love those too? The resorts," Maxi said. "They're always looking for local specialties for the guests. You know, giving them a taste of the real South Florida."

Across the yard, Elena held her jar carefully as Michael gently placed two more lightning bugs into it. He pulled the wax paper taut over the top and resealed it with a rubber band.

Elena stared at the luminous creatures, fascinated. "Ooooo, pretty buggy!" she said. "*Mami! Papi!* I have pretty buggies!" she called, running over to the table.

"Yes, you do have pretty buggies," Maxi said happily.

"And what do we do at the end of the night?" Peter asked, teasingly.

"Buggies go bye-bye?"

"Yup," he said, pulling the small girl into his lap, as together they studied the flashing lights emanating from the jar.

"But buggies are pretty," she protested.

"They're like your friends," Peter explained softly. "They come over and you play. But then they have to go home. They have homes, too."

"OK," she said softly, nodding. "Play now?"

"Definitely play now," he said smiling.

With that, the little girl ran back to her brothers and Oliver, chubby legs pumping as she clutched the precious jar to her chest.

"Have you heard anything else from Ben?" Kate asked. "About you-know-who?"

Peter shook his head. "It's a tough one. Right now, they're just trying to get an ID. But they're coming up blank. Obviously, they can't use fingerprints. And dental records don't help until there's a potential identity to match it to. So they're going to get a facial reconstruction sketch to circulate. To see if anyone recognizes him. So far, he doesn't seem to match any of the missing persons reports from the region, either."

"When I first hit town, Gabe Louden told me that everyone who wanted to start over either came here or went out to the West Coast. Maybe he's not from around here."

"True that," Maxi said, raising her glass. "Although we only came over from Miami."

Peter smiled, clinking his glass against hers. "A couple of lovesick kids, we were."

"Looking to build a nest," Maxi said, nudging his shoulder with her own.

"Looking to put a little distance between us and your family," he countered, grinning.

"We were not!" Maxi said, in mock outrage. "OK, maybe a little. But we still go back for all the big celebrations."

"Bottom line, the police don't know anything yet," Peter admitted.

"What about DNA?" Maxi asked, swirling the dregs of the tea and melting ice cubes in her glass.

"They may have to do that if they can't get an ID any other way," he said. "But it's expensive. And unlike what you see on TV cop shows, it takes time. Our labs are massively backed up. And there's no guarantee it would even help. DNA only works if he was a felon or a member of the armed forces and we have his DNA in a database. Or if a blood relative used one of those family-tree kits from a company that shares the results. Otherwise, we're back to square one."

"Do they know when it happened?" Kate asked.

"If they do, Ben's not telling," Peter replied, tensing slightly. "All he'd say was that it had been out there a year or less. And most likely six months or less."

"Kate and I talked about it. We think it might have been during that time in February when we went to

Miami. You remember? To see Ernesto? And Sam was away for a few days, too. So both yards would have been empty. And both shops would have been closed."

Peter sat up and looked directly into his wife's face. "Look, whoever this is, it isn't something you want to get involved in," he said softly. "I mean Stewart Lord? That was one thing. To help clear Sam. But not again. You need to stay out of this."

"Even though someone brought it to my backyard?"

"Even though," Peter said, emphasizing the words. "Ben will work it out eventually. Let him handle it."

With that, he pushed off from the table and strode across the yard toward the children and Oliver.

Maxi tilted her head, watching him join their game, all of them stalking fireflies across the thick carpet of emerald grass. "There's something he's not telling me," Maxi said quietly, never taking her eyes off her husband. "I don't know what. But Peter is hiding something."

Chapter 15

"Are you sure you still want to do this?" Kate asked anxiously, as Maxi whipped the Jeep around a hairpin curve on the beachfront road. A storm was rolling in and Kate could smell the salt water and ozone in the air. Along with something sweet. Jasmine.

"Why wouldn't I?" Maxi said, as she swung the car onto the lane that led up to Harper Duval's beachfront mansion.

"I don't mean the book club meeting itself. Or even helping Barb with her Sir George Bly project. I mean asking around about Alvin. Peter seemed pretty determined the other night that we stay well out of this one."

"Peter knew what he was getting into when he married me," Maxi said. "Somebody plants a skeleton in my yard, I want to know who. And why."

"You said you thought Peter was hiding something."

"I don't think it. I know it. I know him."

"Could it have something to do with one of the cases

he's prosecuted?" Kate asked. "Could it be some kind of warning?"

"Nah, someone wants to give you a warning, they don't hide it under four feet of sand," Maxi said, slowing as they came up behind Bridget O'Hanlon's electric green Volt. "They leave it right out in the open. Whoever put Alvin in my backyard didn't want him to be found."

"So where would you hide a body if you wanted it to disappear permanently?"

"Swamp."

"OK, that was scary quick," Kate said. "Does your brain really work that fast, or have you thought about this one before?"

Maxi grinned.

Kate wondered if Peter knew who Alvin really was. Or suspected he knew. She remembered what Maxi recounted about her husband suddenly clearing his calendar to take the family to Miami in February. Could he have done something before he left to protect them? Was that why he got them all out of town for a while?

"Maybe he's just worried about you," Kate said finally. "If someone killed Alvin—if they weren't just covering up a natural death or dodging the cost of a burial—maybe he's afraid that nosing around could get you hurt."

"Whatever else is going on, I understand mi amor is being protective. But not knowing who's using the back-yard of my shop like that? That's gonna get me hurt more. Whoever it is, they did this once. I don't want them coming around again. Not when I'm there. Not when mi niños or mi mami are there. Not when some poor teenager is watching the store for me. I need to know. And I need to know it's not going to happen again."

Kate sighed. "All right, then count me in."

"Corizon, I never counted you out," her friend said, smiling. "Even if you did."

Chapter 16

Hiking up the long wide driveway, Kate couldn't help but admire the house. Say what you will about Harper Duval, he had excellent taste. It looked like an old Florida mansion that had been part of the landscape forever. Yet it was just a decade old—built by Harp and Caroline when they first moved to town.

Kate could see glimpses of Harp's hometown of New Orleans in the structure, too. Especially the sweeping white-columned porch surrounded by tall pin oaks. Beautiful though the place was, she would have been perfectly happy to let a few days go by before she saw Harp.

As if reading her mind, Maxi looked over at her and smiled. "Just focus on the food and fun," she said softly. "And I won't leave you alone with him. Promise."

"I'm going to hold you to that," Kate replied, as they climbed the steps, joining a gaggle of fellow book club members.

Magically, the massive oak door opened before anyone had to ring the bell. "Come in, come in and welcome," their host enthused, stepping back to usher them into the two-story marble foyer.

Today, Harp wore a blue blazer over a powder blue dress shirt with jeans. Casual money. But Kate would have bet a dozen of her best chocolate chip cookies that the tan leather loafers on his sockless feet were hand tooled and handmade.

"The buffet tables are already set up in the cellar, along with a few trays of chilled champagne," their host said. "Everyone just help yourselves."

Kate smiled broadly and concentrated on staying within the thick of the crowd as they trooped through the house and into the "cellar."

Due to the realities of South Florida geology, it wasn't underground. Instead, it was the best that copious amounts of money could buy: a cavernous room with rough-hewn stucco walls, niches stacked with dusty bottles, polished gleaming hardwood racks, and a stone floor. Windowless and temperature controlled, it was always chilly, too.

Luckily, Kate had remembered to bring a sweater.

"This should be good," Maxi said, elbowing Kate in the ribs. "The theme this time was 'brunch.'"

"You know that's right," Andy Levy said, off to Kate's left. "I brought spiked orange mini pancakes. And Bridget made this French toast she does that's all eggy and really good."

"Spiked orange?" Kate asked.

"Grand Marnier," he said with a grin. "The alcohol cooks out, but the cakes taste great. And the batter has fresh orange zest, too. We use what's left when we make orange juice. Really gives it some zip. So what did you bring?"

"Key lime tarts."

"Sweet!" Andy said. "Can't wait to snag one of those. Hey, Bridget, Kate brought key lime tarts."

"Nice!" said the bubbly twentysomething blond at his elbow. "I could use one of those right now. Maxi, what'd you bring?"

"Tropical fruit salad," the florist said happily. "This one has lots of mango, 'cause that's how mi mami and aunties make it, plus lime juice to keep it fresh, and a little shredded coconut for extra sweetness."

"I'm sold," Kate said. "And it sounds like it would go really well with those orange pancakes and some nice French toast."

"Well, you helped with the French toast," Bridget confessed. "We used some of the challah from the bakery. With a little vanilla and a little cinnamon, of course. And half-and-half instead of milk. That's the secret."

"This all smells so good it's making me hungry," Maxi said. "Hey, there's Rosie and Andre."

"Don't start the party without us," Rosie teased. "Besides, my guy here went all out. Dessert crepes with strawberries and melted chocolate."

Kate's face lit up. "That sounds wonderful."

"Eh, we shall see," Andre said modestly. "The people will like them, I hope."

"Please, every time he makes them, folks lose their minds," his wife said proudly. "I couldn't compete, so I brought a giant bowl of whipped cream for on top."

"Can't go wrong with whipped cream," Maxi chimed in. "That would go with pretty much everything here. Even the coffee."

"Especially the coffee," Kate agreed.

"Hey, I see Dr. Patel over there, and Carl and Minette just walked in," Maxi said. "But where's Barb? It's not like La Presidenta to be late."

"Last I heard, she and Amos were carpooling," Andy said. "And they're bringing some sort of surprise guest. I'm guessing they'll be here anytime."

"Well, it's a brunch, so everyone can grab a plate whenever they're ready," Harp said, presenting a tray of champagne flutes. "And what's brunch without a little bubbly, I always say."

"Ooo, that would be perfect," Rosie said, lifting two glasses from the tray and handing one off to Andre.

"*Mais oui*," Andre agreed.

"Don't mind if I do," Maxi said.

"Thanks," Kate said, quickly taking a glass. As her eyes met Harp's, he smiled broadly, before disappearing across the room.

"Well, you don't have to ask me twice," Rosie said. "I'm going to get a plate and start in."

"We're right behind you," Bridget seconded.

"Uh-oh," Maxi said under her breath.

"I think you were right," Kate said softly to Maxi. "Everything's finally going back to normal."

"Hold that thought," Maxi said, eyeing the doorway. "Barb and Amos just walked in. And your ex is with them."

Chapter 17

Kate's head whipped around. Sure enough, Evan Thorpe, wearing his most devilish smile, was standing by the cellar door chatting amiably with Barb, Amos, and Dr. Patel.

"What in blazes is he doing here?" Kate stage-whispered.

"He's like one of those vampire monsters that refuses to die," Maxi said softly. "You're gonna have to go after that one with a wooden stake and some garlic."

"If he's not careful, I am going to plant him next to Alvin," Kate admitted under her breath. "I'm going over to tell him to get lost."

"No, corizon, not smart. He can always say he's here for some other reason. Then you look like *la mujer loca*, the crazy woman. Besides, Barb and Amos brought him. He's their problem, not yours. Ignore him. Like he's dead to you. And if you want to leave early, we will."

"What's up?" Claire St. John asked, as she and Gabe

Louden materialized behind Kate, champagne flutes in hand.

"Kate's ex showed up, and he's trying to make nice with everyone and win her back."

"Maxi!"

"Well, she asked," the florist replied.

"Do you want him back?" Claire asked, concern audible in her voice.

"I want him back in Manhattan where I left him," Kate quipped.

"I hope the leaving is joyful, and I hope never to return," Gabe said.

"Amen," Kate agreed.

"Why does that sound familiar?" Maxi asked.

"Frida Kahlo," Gabe said.

"No wonder. We Latinas know how to make an exit."

"I don't know which I like better, Bridget's French toast or Andy's pancakes," Maxi said softly, as they tucked into their plates.

"I accidentally got some of Andre's melted chocolate on Andy's spiked orange hotcakes," Gabe confessed. "Best discovery ever."

"Maxi, this fruit salad is wonderful," Kate said. "Really juicy."

"It's the mangoes," her friend said. "Mi mami's got this trick for knowing just when they're ripe."

"Hey, Big Guy," Evan said, appearing suddenly behind them and affably addressing Gabe. "If you slide over, I can actually sit next to my girl."

Gabe paused mid-sentence, barely turning. "Sorry, no can do. But there's an empty chair near Amos and Barb. Since you're their guest."

"Evan, I'm not your girl," Kate protested. "Not any more."

"You're right," Evan said, adopting the expression of a wounded puppy. "Absolutely right. Did you get the roses? I know they're your favorite."

"They're a big hit at Oy and Begorra. Which is where I drop them off every day. Evan, if you want to stay in Coral Cay, I can't stop you. But please stop lying about me. Our engagement ended months ago. And I've moved on with my life."

"Could we possibly talk? Privately? Just for a minute?"

"No, Evan," Kate said, feeling like a cornered animal. "Just . . . no. Please."

"Look, I'm not afraid to tell the world," he said, huskily. "I love you, Katie. From the moment we met, I've never stopped loving you. You are the best thing that ever happened to me. The very best. And I don't want to live without you." With that, he took his plate and strolled across the room toward Amos and Barb.

"He really does seem rather contrite," Claire said.

Gabe shook his head and smiled, wiping his mouth carefully with a napkin. "No comment."

Maxi looked at Kate, who appeared to be studying the plate in her lap.

Gabe shook his head and kept eating.

"I'll say one thing," Maxi said softly to Kate. "Pirates or not, La Presidenta has a lot to answer for."

A half hour later, amidst empty casserole dishes and brunch plates, Harp stepped to the front of the room and held his glass aloft.

"All right, everyone, consider this your two-minute warning. Please feel free to refill your glasses before we begin the meeting. And for those of you driving, we have a fine selection of coffee, iced tea, and lemonade."

As Barb stepped up to the podium, Kate noticed that the bookstore owner actually looked a little nervous. And that was new. From what Kate had witnessed, people got nervous approaching Barb Showalter—not the other way around.

"OK, folks," Barb started, halting as she scanned the room. Kate saw her look to the left, where Amos and Evan were seated. Each of them gave her a little nod, and the bookstore owner smiled.

"I know we're here to discuss Josephine Tey's *The Daughter of Time*, which delves into a real historic mystery. But before we start, I'd like to float a proposal."

"So how many of these folks do you think Barb has deputized?" Maxi whispered to Kate.

"Less than half," Kate said softly. "She's actually worried. But something's up."

"What do you mean?" her friend asked.

"Evan. He's involved in this somehow."

"A few days ago, we were all very disappointed that a local find turned out not to be Sir George Bly," Barb reported.

"A local find?" Maxi whispered, incredulous.

"Give her points for tact," Kate said, watching late arrival Annie Kim nibble on one of the key lime tarts. "Some folks are still eating."

"As you all know, Bly, his rumored treasure, and the legend of our pirate founders bring a lot of people to our island. And it finally looked like we were going to be able to substantiate the claim that we're actually an older settlement than Jamestown. Nearly as old as St. Augustine. Which wouldn't be bad for business, either."

Several of the business owners laughed, and Barb visibly relaxed.

"Which got me thinking. Why wait for someone to accidentally stumble over Gentleman George? This is our town, and he's our founder. Our history. Who better to launch an expedition to find evidence of his presence on this island, and perhaps even his last resting place, than us?"

A murmur started among the crowd, as everyone started talking at once.

"I've got a bad feeling about this," Kate said quietly to Maxi.

"Yeah, your former boyfriend is grinning like that *Alice in Wonderland* cartoon cat."

Barb put her palms up. "Hang on just a sec, people. Let me get this out, and we can put it to a vote. Now, we recently proved that the folks in this club are pretty good at taking a little information and piecing together the bigger picture. You'll recall the little matter of Mr. Stewart Lord."

The developer's name touched off another spate of uncontrolled chatter.

"I think Detective Ben and mi amor had a little something to do with that one," Maxi whispered. "And I didn't see La Presidenta breaking into Lord's office with us, either."

The book club leader again raised her palms, attempting to quiet the crowd. "I say we put those same skills— and our knowledge of our own island—to work on the historical mystery of Sir George Bly. Now, I've talked with a good number of the people in this room, and I know many of you feel the same way. And, with that in mind, I've spoken with Mr. Evan Thorpe of the Thorpe Family Foundation."

At the mention of Evan, Kate felt Maxi's elbow lightly in her side. And a sick feeling in the pit of her stomach.

"And," Barb continued, her voice resuming its usual stentorian timbre, "he has very generously agreed to sponsor our project."

Amid a sprinkling of light applause, Kate and Maxi exchanged a look. Instinctively, Kate knew Evan had to be beaming—he lived for the limelight. But she wouldn't let herself meet his eyes.

"So now I'd like to put this to a formal vote of this club. How many of you would like us to launch an expedition to search out and document the story of Sir George Bly and his men on Coral Cay?"

Rosie Armand stood.

"Rosie," Barb acknowledged. "You have the floor."

"I think we need to ask a few questions before we put it to a vote," she said. "For one thing, this sponsorship. If we find remains or historical artifacts, who would they belong to? And where would they go for study or display? Because it doesn't do us any good to uncover and document our local history if the evidence supporting that discovery just disappears to a museum in New York."

"Who gets George's gold?" a woman called from the back. Kate recognized the clarion voice. Stylish, eighty-plus Sunny Eisenberg, who ran the local yoga studio.

Evan stood, a broad smile on his face. Even Kate had to admit he looked good. The tan accentuated his blue eyes. Afternoons on the yacht, Kate surmised. And the South Florida humidity had added extra curl to his dark hair.

Sporting a faded indigo golf shirt, khaki Bermuda shorts, and a casual, off-handed manner, he could have been just another one of the locals. If not for the movie-star looks and piles of family money.

"You're going to need another sweater," Kate whispered to Maxi. "Because in the next few minutes, the snow in here is going to get pretty thick."

"Hi, everybody. For those of you I haven't met yet, I'm Evan Thorpe. I work with the Thorpe Family Foundation. I've been down here on vacation. And to see my, well"—he cocked his head and gestured toward Kate with his right hand—"the one that got away."

She felt her face go hot. Across the cellar, she saw Harp wince.

"Anyway," he continued, "when Barb told me Gentleman George's story, I was riveted. It's like something out of a Hollywood movie. Except it's real. It's real, and it happened right here. I mean, in school we learn that this country was founded by puritans and farmers and famous statesmen. But an outlaw pirate hero? That's cool. And the idea that the foundation could help bring that story to light? Man, that's the whole reason we exist."

"That and the massive tax write-off," Maxi hissed in Kate's ear.

"And to answer your question," Evan said, looking directly at Rosie. "Our funding this project won't change the ownership of what's found or where it would be housed. That will be your decision. It's your history." He looked to the back of the room, where Sunny was sitting. "And your gold."

Evan paused expertly, allowing half a beat for the members of the crowd to giggle. Which they did.

When he continued, his smile was electric. "We make resources available, yes. But if and how you use them? That's up to you. And we have a very similar arrangement with an archaeological dig in Montana."

"He's right about that," Kate admitted quietly to Maxi. "And they've made some amazing discoveries."

"Please, the only piece of history that boy's interested in unearthing is his past love life," Maxi whispered directly into Kate's ear. "Do you trust him?"

"No."

"You wanna vote against this craziness?"

"If we vote in favor, it might help Alvin," Kate said.

Maxi went silent. Kate could tell her friend was torn.

As Evan sat, Barb stood up. Like some kind of synchronized tag-team dance routine, Kate thought ruefully.

"Any other questions?" Barb asked.

Hardware store owner Carl Ivers stood. "Carl?" Barb said, acknowledging the former cop.

"When you say 'project,' what exactly would we be doing? 'Cause on some parts of this island, it's mighty dangerous to dig. And no matter who we're after, there's such a thing as private property rights. And you can't just wave a magic wand and make those go away."

A couple of people around him nodded, including his wife, Minette.

"Initially, we're looking at a research project," Barb said. "The only digging we'll be doing will be through stacks at the library. We'll be tracking documents, sending emails to historians and academics, and combing through private papers for clues. We'll construct a timeline for the life of Sir George Bly, along with the source material. We'll be looking to verify and cross-check the facts we do have and add more points to that timeline. At the same time, we'll be keeping an eye out for indications of what may have happened to him. Mentions of local homesteads or landmarks. Family. Funeral practices. Local burial grounds. That kind of thing. If and when we get enough evidence, then we'd look at making some kind of physical expedition. And we'd have the Thorpe Foundation to help us secure the proper experts and equipment and permissions."

Carl looked down at Minette, who smiled as he took his seat.

Evan nodded, implying he couldn't have said it better. Kate wondered how much of this had been scripted before the meeting. Was that why the three of them had been late? And how much might Amos spill if she showed up at his market later with a dozen oatmeal raisin cookies?

Maxi looked at Kate, a question in her eyes.

"We came here to vote 'yes,'" Kate reminded her softly. "Evan being part of this doesn't change why we want to do it." She put a slightly stronger emphasis on the word "why," and Maxi nodded.

"Besides," Kate added, "the foundation would be a good resource for this. Much as I hate to admit it."

"I don't want to rush anyone or cut off any questions," Barb said. "But I also know some of you want to discuss Josephine Tey, too. Any more concerns, or are we ready to put this to a vote?"

No one moved.

"OK," Barb said, "all those in favor?"

Fourteen hands. Evan, Kate noticed, holding her arm in the air, at least had the good sense to abstain.

The lone holdouts: Sunny Eisenberg and Harper Duval.

"Fourteen to two—motion carried," Barb announced triumphantly. "Let's find Gentleman George!"

Chapter 18

Maxi steered the Jeep expertly around a wide curve on the beach road. The cool breeze through the windows smelled of the ocean. Kate put her head back and closed her eyes. A good meal combined with the warm sun streaming through the windshield left her drowsy. And content.

Evan or no, she was glad she was in Coral Cay.

"So it looks like your ex is going to be sticking around for a little while," Maxi said, as she swung the Jeep onto Main Street.

"Looks like," she replied, eyes still closed. "Although, the foundation could support the Gentleman George project just as easily from Manhattan. So we'll see how long it lasts. Evan has a very short attention span."

"You really don't think he'll stay here?" the florist asked. "Mitzy swears the boy's looking at houses. Big houses. And everywhere you go, there he is. Kinda like a shadow. If a shadow had pockets full of money."

"I think the house thing is a canard. It makes him seem like a local. Evan's really good at winning people over. And he probably means it when he says it. Like a kid playing dress up. He's trying on a role. Trying it out. But long-term commitments aren't his strong suit. Trust me on that one. I'm just relieved we set the record straight on the fiancé thing. Now all I have to do is ignore him. And his flowers."

"I know. This is one flower order I wish I didn't have. Those gooey love poems he wants on each card? I'm gonna have diabetes by the time that boy leaves town."

"That's strange," Kate said, opening her eyes as she felt the Jeep pull into the driveway of Flowers Maximus. "What's Ben's car doing here?

"And Peter's too," Maxi murmured, voice barely above a whisper.

"Maybe there's been a break in the case," Kate said, trying to sound cheery. "Or maybe Ben finally found out who Alvin really is."

Deep down, Kate felt an electric tingle of fear. "Since you have company, why don't I come in and make us all some coffee? If I don't get a little caffeine after that book club buffet, I'm going to fall asleep."

Mouth set in a line, Maxi said nothing. As she put the car into park, Kate saw that her eyes were focused solely on the front door of the flower shop. And she felt her own stomach knot up.

Maxi flew up the walkway. Kate had at least six inches in height on her friend—and longer legs—but she was struggling to keep pace.

The florist pulled at the door to her shop and threw it open.

Ben was settled on the settee. In much the same spot he'd been the day they found Alvin. Kate could smell coffee brewing. Peter, she surmised.

"Is everything alright?" Maxi asked. "Mi niños and mi mami?"

"Everyone's fine," Peter said, walking into the room carrying a tray with a glass coffeepot, a carton of creamer, and several mugs. "Ben needed to talk with us, and I suggested that the shop would be better than the house. No little ears listening. Much more private."

The detective nodded but didn't smile. Peter's tone was friendly, his expression tight. Almost guarded. Professional. Not the look of a loving husband or lighthearted friend. The attorney was in courtroom mode.

Kate sensed a very heavy shoe was about to drop.

Despite the warm weather, Ben was wearing his work clothes. A navy blazer and white dress shirt with khaki slacks and wingtips. He had a small notebook in one hand and a gold ballpoint pen in the other. An official visit. On the record.

"O-kaay," Maxi said slowly, clearly coming to the same conclusion. "Do you know who put Mr. Bones out back? Or how he died? Or who he is?"

"Let's take it one step at a time," Ben said. "I just need to ask you a couple of questions. First, we're trying to narrow down the timeline of when he was buried. Any new ideas on that?"

Kate saw Maxi look at Peter, who nodded infinitesimally.

"We were talking about it," the florist said. "And I remembered something. Back in February. Valentine's Day week. We went to Miami. My uncle Ernesto had been in a really bad accident. So we went *rápido*. And we were gone for about a week. But for some of those days, right around Valentine's Day, Sam was out of town, too."

Ben nodded. "I remember the Miami thing. And I confirmed Sam's trip with him. And you're right, the timing would explain a lot. How someone could get access to the yard without your knowing about it. Without anyone seeing anything. Now, refresh my memory: Was this shop closed? Or did you just leave someone else in charge?"

"The shop was closed and locked," Maxi responded emphatically, focusing all of her attention on the detective. "I called all my regular customers to tell them before we left. I can check my records and give you the exact dates."

Ben nodded. "Who filled your orders? While you were gone?"

"I forwarded the phones to one of the wire services. They handled all of the orders through other florists while we were away."

"Any of those florists on Coral Cay?" Ben asked.

Maxi shook her head, her chin-length glossy black hair swinging, then falling neatly back into place.

"Close by?"

"A couple of places on the mainland, not so far from here," she said. "But none on the island, thank goodness. Why?"

"You have bushes around this place. What would have been blooming at the time?" .

"A lot of stuff," Maxi said, sitting back in her chair. "Hibiscus, bougainvillea, roses, jasmine, even my lemon trees. We had a very warm spring. Warm and humid, too."

"Any roses? Long-stemmed roses?"

"No, you need a hothouse for those. And they are super hard to grow. Mine are what they call old-fashioned roses. Like my *abuela* grew. Yours too, probably. They smell so good. And they have beautiful big blooms. But they're on bushes, so no long stems. Why are you asking about flowers? I thought you were going to tell us about the bones."

"Bear with me," Ben said. "During that time period—

back in February before you left—did you have long-stemmed roses in the shop? Red ones?"

"I almost always have roses. And back then, before Ernesto's accident, I was getting ready for Valentine's Day. Of course I had roses. And I was supposed to get more before the holiday. But when I decided to close the shop, I cancelled the delivery."

"Before they arrived?" Ben asked quickly.

"Si. Yes. I called the supplier."

"What happened to them?" the detective asked, tilting his head and searching Maxi's face. "The flowers. Who got them?"

The florist shrugged. "The other flower shops in the area. There's always a shortage of red roses around Valentine's Day. So I knew it would be no problem for the supplier to send them to someone else. Besides, the other flower stores would need some extra to handle my customers. The orders that would have been mine."

"What happened to the red roses you already had? Here in the shop?"

"It's a super popular time for roses. I sold a lot of them. And I took some with us. For Ernesto. And my aunties. What was left, I just added extra to all the orders I was filling before we left. I did that with all my flowers, not just the roses. I figure, better to give someone a super big bunch than just let flowers wilt in the shop. That way, the flowers—they have a chance to make people happy. What is this about? Why so much about flowers? What do my roses have to do with Mr. Bones?"

"You've had a chance to think about this a bit since the discovery," Ben said, looking up from his small notebook to make eye contact with Maxi. "Any thoughts on who it could be?"

"No," Maxi said, knitting her brows. "You mean you still don't know, either?"

"There's nothing that happened around that time? Maybe someone who stopped by?

Maxi shook her head vigorously, as Peter sat forward in his seat.

"Ben, you've asked us both that," the attorney said. "Several times. We have no idea. And if we had known there was anything out there, we sure wouldn't have been digging up the yard, now would we?"

"Technically, you didn't," Ben said, exhaling. "The trench you dug was a foot or so shy of the burial. Oliver did the rest."

"You can't think that they . . ." Kate started.

Ben held up his palm and shook his head. "I don't, no. And the trip to Miami—especially with Sam being out of town—that goes a long way toward explaining how someone else had the time. But I still have to ask. There are some things that aren't adding up. I'd be lying if I didn't admit we have to look at everything. And everyone."

Kate searched his face and found concern in his dark eyes. Worry, even. Was he worried for Maxi and Peter's safety? Or afraid one of them might be involved?

"That's it, this conversation is over," Peter said, suddenly standing. "We're getting a lawyer. From now on, you can talk to him."

"Peter, no," Maxi protested. "This is Ben. He's our friend."

For his part, the detective didn't budge.

"You said some things weren't adding up," Kate said softly. "What exactly?"

Ben looked up at Peter and over to Maxi. "This doesn't leave this room." A command, not a question.

All three of them nodded in unison.

Ben sighed. "The skeleton was recent. But someone went to a lot of trouble to make it look like it wasn't. Including adding those *fakakta* leather boots. And some kind of pirate garb. Eighteenth century, not sixteenth, by the way. Probably French. That's courtesy of one of my lab techs and something called 'cosplay.'" He shrugged. "Don't ask. Anyway, let's just say that whatever they did to age your Mr. Bones also made him a lot harder to ID. Which was probably the point. About all we know at this stage is that he's an adult male. Likely mid-twenties to mid-forties, as I mentioned earlier. With a burial range that includes that window in February. But the techs are running tests to see if we can narrow it more. Right now, all we can say is roughly six months to a year."

Kate noticed Ben's coffee sat untouched on the table in front of him. Another sign this wasn't a social call.

"We do know he would have been about six-one or six-two. He had a few old injuries. Couple of broken bones—long healed. And he had some kind of repetitive injury to both shoulders and both sides of his clavicle. Almost like slight grooves in his shoulder blades. His job, whatever it was, could have involved carrying something heavy. Sound familiar at all? Someone who made deliveries? Someone you bumped into around town?

Maxi's face relaxed. She shook her head. Peter's expression had returned to the wary, inscrutable mask. Kate glanced at Ben and sensed more was coming.

"One odd detail," the detective continued. "There was some kind of flakey powder on his hands. He'd been clutching something. It took the lab a while to figure out exactly what that was. But, give 'em credit, they finally did."

Maxi and Peter looked at each other. Maxi was confused, curious—while Peter's face was still unreadable. His legal training? Kate wondered. Or did the attorney know something he wasn't sharing?

"You wanna hear what's really weird?" Ben asked, looking Maxi straight in the eye.

Chapter 19

As the summer heat melted into the cool of evening, Kate sat at the big table in the Cookie House kitchen, cookbooks open in front of her, jotting down ingredients and calculations for her next test batch.

Suddenly, she felt something bump the side of her leg. Repeatedly.

She looked down. Oliver sat there, his purple Frisbee in his mouth. He looked up into her face.

The puppy had been napping in the front of the store for the past hour, while she baked. Now he was awake. And ready to play.

"I've been all over this island today, and I haven't been here for you, have I?"

The pup's black eyes twinkled.

"OK, message received. Those doubloon cookies won't be out of the oven for another twenty minutes. What say we toss that disc around the backyard? We've earned it. But if you see any pirates, we just leave them alone, OK?

I don't know about you, but I've had enough excitement for a while."

As they walked outside, Kate couldn't help glancing at the yard next door. Maxi and Peter went home right after Ben left. Officially, he'd been there to gather evidence and interview Maxi and Peter. Unofficially, he'd alerted them that they were on the suspect list. Even if he himself didn't believe they'd done anything wrong.

Oliver dropped the disc at her feet. She picked it up and sailed it across the yard. He chased it at top speed. Just when she thought it was past him, he leapt up and snatched it out of the air.

He trotted back and proudly laid the disc at her feet.

"How did you do that?" she said, scratching the silky hair behind one ear. "Does anyone else know you can do that? Did someone teach you?"

Kate remembered Maxi telling her how Oliver had shown up in Coral Cay out of the blue six months ago. He was just a puppy. About three months old, they'd estimated. He loved everyone. And everyone wanted him. He'd accept their hospitality, stay a few days, then move on to someone else.

"Like he was staying in a fancy hotel," Maxi had recounted.

It was a practice Oliver continued until Kate came to the island just a few short months ago. Now he'd definitely chosen a home.

Which isn't to say the half-grown pup never left her side. He still had free run of Coral Cay. Especially the downtown, where everyone knew him—and kept an eye out for him.

One of the things Kate noticed when she first visited downtown were the water bowls—all different kinds of water bowls—in front of the shops. Only much later did she learn that more than a few of those same shop owners kept dog treats under their counters. Even the ones who didn't have dogs.

So, had one of Oliver's many hosts taught him to catch a Frisbee? Or was the pup just a natural?

She picked up the disc, curled it against her shoulder and let it fly. And he dashed after it.

Time after time, he'd take to the air. And most of the time, he caught his prey.

"That purple Frisbee doesn't stand a chance," Kate murmured, shaking her head, as she watched him pluck it from the air.

Twenty minutes later, Kate scrubbed up at the kitchen sink as Oliver snoozed under the table. The pup had lapped his fill from the oversized stainless-steel bowl, then passed out under the table. She could hear soft snuffling sounds as his wooly back moved gently up and down. Asleep, the half-grown poodle mix resembled a lamb. A very large lamb.

Kate heard a loud knock on the front door, followed by the tinkle of the shop bell. "Anyone here?"

Claire.

"In the kitchen, Claire. Come on back."

"It smells lovely in here. But I wasn't certain if you were open."

"Technically, no," Kate said, grinning. "Sam's at the beach today. I'm just getting caught up for tomorrow. And you're just in time. I'm testing a recipe for the Pirate Festival, and I could use a guinea pig."

Kate looked up to see Oliver bounding over to Claire, tail wagging furiously. He planted himself at her feet like an eager suitor. Claire scratched his ear and offered him a treat from her pocket. He looked up, spellbound.

"Too bad you weren't here five minutes ago," Kate said, watching Oliver bask in Claire's attention. "Apparently, that dog can fly."

"I never doubted it," she said, slipping him a second

treat. "I can't believe how big he's getting. He looks perfect. And it's so strange you should mention pirates. That's why I'm here."

"OK, that definitely got my attention," Kate said. "Help yourself to coffee. I'm going to get these cookies on a plate. They're still warm. We can even give one to Oliver. There's no chocolate in them—just a bit of cinnamon."

"If they taste anything like they smell, you'll have people queuing up around the block."

"So how are things at the bike shop?"

"Lovely. Although, it was nice to have a few hours off today. But I think the Coral Cay Irregulars are going to have their hands full with Gentleman George."

Kate placed a platter of cookies on the table, topped off her own coffee, and added a little cream.

"My word, these are doubloons," Claire said, picking up a cookie and holding it up to examine it.

"Exactly. I'm glad they're at least recognizable."

"This is brilliant! How did you do it?"

"A round cookie cutter for the shape. Then I hit the top with a stamp before I bake them. I'm working on a second variety in chocolate, too. If it works, I thought we could sell them during the festival. But the most important part is the taste. So be honest. I need to know what you really think."

Claire popped the small cookie into her mouth and smiled.

Kate slipped a doubloon to Oliver, who took the offering gently from her palm. Seconds later, it was gone.

"Kate, these are wonderful. They melt in your mouth. I taste cinnamon. And butter. And something else. Rum?"

"Rum extract—and tons of butter," she confessed, as Claire delicately lifted three more cookies from the platter. "I'm still noodling around with the recipe."

"Well, I like them exactly as they are. And I'd like

to buy a dozen for Gabe, if I can. He'll definitely fancy them. That man's a secret biscuit fiend. So when will you start selling them in the shop?"

"I'll give you a bag for Gabe. That man rescued me when my car broke down on Main Street. As for stocking them, I'm still doing test batches. And I want to develop the chocolate ones, so we can offer two kinds for the Pirate Festival."

"Well, I won't say no to chocolate. But I wouldn't change a thing on these."

Kate smiled. "That makes me feel better—thanks. So what did you want to tell me about pirates?"

"I actually have a few books that reference the Bly family. I thought maybe the book club would like to share them. You know, swap them around and compare notes. Some are rather obscure. And from what I recall, they mention the family or the family home, rather than Sir George directly. I haven't looked at them in ages, but I thought they might help. You know, with the research."

"I never would have taken you for a pirate groupie," Kate teased.

"Tudor history, actually," Claire said, reaching for another cookie. "Got into it at uni. It was a nice break from my studies. And I've been to Marleigh Hall. Stayed there for a few days, in fact. The place is enormous. And fascinating. They could open a museum with the art alone."

"Sir George's house is still standing? That's incredible. Is it open to the public?"

"No, that's the cool part. It's one of the few stately homes that isn't. And I mean never. Not even summer weekends. And it never has been. It's still owned by the family, and they still live there."

"I bet they'd have some information on Sir George— he was their ancestor, after all," Kate said, snagging two cookies and slipping one to Oliver.

"That's the odd bit," Claire enunciated carefully between bites. "They don't, really. There's one portrait of him hanging in a side room. A room that's rarely used, by the way. I asked about it because it was actually from the Tudor period. Dashing fellow, by the look of it. But the family member I spoke with said they actually knew very little about him. Only that he'd served the Crown and had died abroad. And that he was a great-uncle or something. That was it."

"Wow, that's not much to go on. I wonder if 'abroad' means Coral Cay?"

"It very well could. And I believe 'serving the Crown' was a rather popular contemporaneous euphemism for piracy. In the beginning at least, pirates were acting at the behest of Queen Elizabeth by raiding treasure ships from Spain. The queen even issued them permits—letters of marque," Claire finished.

"Wow, I had no idea," Kate admitted. "Piracy was legal?"

"Not just legal," Claire said. "It was considered patriotic. Every doubloon taken off a Spanish ship was gold King Philip couldn't use to invade England. And that's why Queen Elizabeth knighted our George."

"Do you want to tell Barb about the books and let her divvy them up?" Kate asked. "Since she's the book club president?"

Claire hesitated, then reached for another cookie. "I did think of that," she admitted. "But project or no, this is supposed to be fun. I didn't want Barb parceling them out like assigned school reading. I love her, but the lady can be a bit of a steamroller. And she's so excited about Sir George. Plus, she's busy with your . . . I mean, the guy from the foundation."

Kate smiled. "Ex-fiancé. And it's OK to say it. Long over, and we've both moved on."

"I just thought, well," she paused, hoisting a woven multicolored satchel onto the table and carefully removing what appeared to be a mountain of books. "I brought them with me. I thought everyone could just select whatever they fancy."

Kate's face lit up. "It's a library."

Claire beamed. "I almost hate to part with them, even temporarily. But it's for a good cause. This one looks at court life and the nobility during Tudor times. And there are several mentions of George's brother, Henry Bly. This one deals with Tudor-era homes and estates, so there are a few references to Marleigh Hall. This one has to do with foreign policy from 1485 to 1603—so there are some bits about pirates and piracy in there. Oh, and this one's rather unusual," she said, placing what looked like a hand-bound manuscript off to the side.

Kate picked it up and carefully turned some of the pages. Held together with butterfly clips and bound with a black leatherette cover, it was definitely homemade.

"That was a thank-you present from Sophie, the friend who invited me to Marleigh Hall. I was helping with a charity do," Claire shrugged. "Sophie's a distant Bly cousin. It's a reproduction of a book of family correspondence. Some of it quite old. And there are some names you'll recognize in there. Royals, prime ministers, members of Parliament. Apparently, the house hosted a number of hush-hush summits during World War II."

"Anything from Sir George?" Kate asked, as she carefully turned the photocopied pages.

"Not that lucky, I'm afraid. A few things from one of his cousins. And some snippets from his brother as an old man. But nothing from George himself."

"Not so odd, I guess. It's a miracle any of the letters survived into the modern age," Kate said, scanning the pages. "I'd love to read this one, if that's OK. And this one on pirates and piracy."

"Smashing. Throw in a dozen of those doubloons and we have a deal," Claire said. "But there's something else. The main reason I didn't bring all this to Barb? Sophie told me that, until recently, George's painting had been packed away in an old outbuilding. That's likely why it was in such good shape."

"You said they had a lot of art. Maybe they didn't have room for it all?" Kate asked, carefully closing the book.

Claire shook her head. "I know Barb loves her pirate stories. Especially the ones that relate to Coral Cay. But I'm afraid that what we discover about George Bly could very well break her heart. Sophie didn't know any of the details. That's all been lost to history. But apparently there was some sort of scandal surrounding Sir George. So much so that when Henry Bly became the Duke of Marleigh, he removed George's portrait from the wall and never uttered his name again."

Chapter 20

Suddenly, Kate was cold. She opened her eyes.

Oliver was sitting at attention beside the bed, the corner of her aqua coverlet in his mouth. The rest of the spread was pooled at the foot of the bed and on the floor.

"What is it, Ollie? Do you need to go out?" She sat up and looked at the bedside clock: 1:15. They'd been out just an hour ago.

Oliver dropped the coverlet, scampered to the bedroom door, and let out three staccato barks.

"OK, you don't have to ask me twice," Kate said lightly, fishing her white terrycloth robe from the tangle of bed-covers and wrapping it around herself. "Let's go."

When they arrived downstairs at the bakery's back door, Oliver stopped and planted himself in front of the door—blocking her path.

Kate gently patted his silky shoulder. "C'mon, little guy. You need to go out, right?"

Stock-still, the dog refused to budge. He looked quickly

up at her, then at the door and barked again. A trio of short barks.

Kate stepped to the side, pushed open the curtains and looked out the window into the backyard.

It was dark and deserted. She couldn't see a thing. Not even a squirrel or a raccoon. She started to reach for the switch to the porch light. Then she heard something.

A soft scraping sound. Repetitive. Rhythmic. Familiar.

A shovel going into sand.

Kate angled herself to get a better view of the backyard. Nothing. No one.

Suddenly, she saw a flash of light. It came from the direction of the flower shop. She looked again. It was gone. Kate pressed her face flat against the window and strained to see.

Oliver was silent at her feet.

She could barely glimpse a glimmer of light, between the slats of the fence that separated the two yards. A short, strong beam. A flashlight. Coming from next door.

In the quiet she could hear something else. Men's voices. At least two. And that soft, rhythmic scraping.

Someone was digging up the yard.

Chapter 21

Thirty minutes later, the bakery's kitchen smelled of coffee, cheddar biscuits, and warm butter. Kate smoothed her jeans, grabbed a tea towel, and opened the small oven door.

"Corizon, you don't have to do that," Maxi said, from her perch at the kitchen table. "It's not like this is a party."

Clad in a red T-shirt and jeans, the florist wore not a trace of makeup. But even at two in the morning, her swingy chin-length bob was perfect.

Peter looked a little the worse for wear. Sleepy-eyed and sporting a five-o'clock shadow with his Miami Hurricanes jersey and jeans, he was on his second cup of coffee, Kate noticed.

"I need something to do with my hands," Kate explained, sliding the second tray onto the counter. "Call it high-carb stress relief. So what did the police tell you?"

"Not much," Peter replied. "Just that they were checking out reports of a prowler at the flower shop."

"Same thing they said to me," Sam said, refilling his cup.

"How did you know they were there?" Maxi asked.

"I didn't," Kate admitted. "Oliver woke me up. Kept alerting to outside, but blocked me every time I tried to open the door."

Maxi reached out and ruffled the pup's oatmeal-colored coat. "That's because our Mr. Oliver is one smart dog."

"Yup," Sam said, raising his cup as he looked over to where the dog was sitting at attention next to the table. "Definitely a keeper."

"Do you think it's really them?" Maxi asked. "The ones who buried the skeleton?"

Peter shook his head, patting his wife's hand. "No idea. But I'm sure Ben will tell us something as soon as he can."

"OK, folks, biscuits are up. Sam Hepplewhite's famous recipe."

"Smells good," the baker said, reaching for the platter.

"If nothing else, the coffee's strong enough to wake us up—and keep us up," Kate said.

Peter took a biscuit and put it on Maxi's saucer, then took a second for himself.

Whatever else had happened that evening, at least the Más-Buchanans seemed solid, Kate thought.

The back door opened and Ben stepped through it. Middle of the night or not, he was perfectly pressed and put together in a blue blazer, white golf shirt, and gray suit pants—complete with a Panama hat. As usual, his wingtips were shined and spotless.

"Right this way, gentlemen," he said, calling to someone behind him as he held open the door.

Two men with their hands cuffed behind their backs lurched into the room.

"Anybody know these two?" Ben asked, scanning the faces of everyone at the table.

In unison, all of them shook their heads.

"Isn't this against our rights or something?" whined

one of the men, bobbing a head of stringy brown hair. His grungy sleeveless white undershirt and baggy jeans were both stained with what looked like mud and grass.

"Zip it," Ben said. "You have the right to remain silent. You might want to use it."

"Hey, we didn't do anything wrong," said the other one, who wore a greasy blue trucker cap, a black T-shirt, and black pajama bottoms. "This is bogus, man! Everybody knows pirate treasure is public property. We're allowed to dig it up. And we can keep whatever we find. That's the law, man. It says so on the Internet."

"OK, in the first place, that is not the law. If you want to dig for anything on private property, which that yard is, you need permission from the owner. Which you did not have. So that makes it trespassing. Since you hopped the fence, I'm going to add breaking and entering. You also got me and all these nice people out of bed in the middle of the night, so I'm going to charge you both with disturbing the peace. You dug holes in the yard, that's vandalism. Oh yeah, and because that yard is also the scene of a recent crime, I'm adding obstruction and interfering with an ongoing police investigation. And that's just for starters. Are we clear?"

Staring at the floor, both men nodded.

"What were you two after?" Ben asked.

"The gold, man," Trucker Cap said. "Pirate gold. It's worth a fortune."

His buddy nodded eagerly.

"There's no gold on that land," Ben said evenly. "There was no pirate on that land. There was an illegal burial discovered there last week. That's it."

"No, man, that's just what they want you to think," Trucker Cap said. "But the truth is all over the blogs. They found Gentleman George. And everybody knows he was buried with piles of gold and jewels and stuff. The eggheads just want it for some museum. But if you get there first, it's yours."

"Yeah, it don't belong to nobody," Grungy T-shirt added. "'Cause it was from, like, back in the old days. Before anybody owned anything around here. Before it was a country, even. So if you dig it up, you get to keep it. That's what all the sites say."

Trucker Cap nodded vigorously.

Ben looked around the room, studying each face present. Finally, he opened the back door. "OK, Kyle, get these chuckleheads out of here. Take 'em down to the station and book 'em. I'll be down later."

Kyle Hardy appeared and herded the two men out the door.

"What was that?" Maxi asked, astonished.

"That, I'm afraid, is the first wave of what could be a bit of a problem for a while," Ben said. "Treasure hunters. And we're not talking puzzle and crypto experts. We're talking any ham-and-egger with a Wi-Fi connection, money trouble, and a shovel."

"What did he mean about the Internet?" Peter asked, concerned.

"I'm afraid that part is true, too. The Gentleman George story is out there. Along with all the misinformation about who really owns the treasure. And rumors about the find on your property last week. Bloggers and social media trolls are basically putting all of that into a blender and whipping people into a frenzy."

"Why?" Maxi asked.

"Who knows? Those two tonight are basically harmless," Ben said, swatting his hand toward the door. "Heck, they were half in the bag when we collared them. Problem is, they might not be the last."

Sam looked at Maxi and Peter. Kate could see the worry in his eyes.

"We should close the shop for a while," Peter said softly. "You could take the kids to Miami. Summer vacation. I can drive over on the weekends. Just until this blows over."

"I'm not running away from our home," Maxi said. "Just because two *bobos* show up at night? That's *loco*."

"What if the police make an announcement?" Kate asked. "That the skeleton was just a skeleton. Not Gentleman George. You could even appeal for new information to find out who it really is."

Ben nodded. "We can do that, and we still might. Look, from the beginning, as far as the news outlets, we treated this whole thing as a simple unreported burial. Which is why we're not being overrun with news crews searching for Gentleman George. Or Jimmy Hoffa. But I don't know that an official announcement will prevent more of this. You heard those two tonight. They're still convinced we're just trying to keep them away from the treasure."

"What's the smart move, Ben?" Sam asked. "What would you do?"

Ben scratched his head. "Well, I hate to admit it, but I'm with Ms. Más-Buchanan on this one."

The florist grinned triumphantly.

"But with a couple of caveats," he said, holding up an index finger. "We definitely need to step up patrols on the block. And I'd look at getting a couple of security cameras in the backyard. Even temporarily. Heck, have Carl route the feeds to the station and our folks can keep an eye on it. And if anybody shows up, you do exactly what you did tonight—call us."

Sam, Kate, and Maxi nodded. But Peter was clearly not happy.

"Come on, mi amor," Maxi said, putting her hand gently on her husband's. "We both have to get up early."

"You're right," he conceded. "If we head home now, we can at least get a couple hours' sleep."

"How about some cheddar biscuits for the road?" Kate offered Ben.

"Definitely won't say no to that," the detective replied.

"I'll throw in a few extra for the folks at the station," she promised, pulling a flat cardboard form from under the counter and deftly assembling it into a bakery box.

"Thanks, Ben," Peter said, offering the detective his hand. "I really appreciate your coming out here tonight."

"You guys need anything, you just call," the detective said, shaking his hand warmly. "Even if I'm not on duty, the dispatcher has instructions to get me on the horn. In the meantime, we'll be keeping a close eye on the entire block, just in case. If we're lucky, these two clowns are a one-off."

"Look at the bright side," Maxi said, stretching and suppressing a yawn. "With any luck, I may never have to dig my own garden beds again."

Chapter 22

Kate punched the two pillows and tucked them neatly behind her back.

"I know I should be sleeping," she confessed to Oliver, who was curled up at the foot of the bed. "But after everything that just happened, I can't."

The pup raised his head and studied her earnestly as she spoke.

"I'm thinking this might be a good time to do a little reading on the Bly family. Why don't you doze, and I'll just leaf through a couple of Claire's books?"

Seemingly satisfied, Oliver nestled his head against the coverlet and closed his eyes. Soon his regular breathing alternated with a soft whistling sound.

As Kate flipped through the hand-bound book, she marveled at the sheer scope of the volume. The family had letters going back to the sixteenth century. After her move from Manhattan to Coral Cay, she was doing good to find any of last year's Christmas cards.

The first few pages of the book were an introduction

to the Blys. There were family trees showing various branches. And recent pictures of Marleigh Hall, as well as several that appeared to be taken in the 1920s or '30s. Claire was right. The place was enormous.

There were also photographs of various family portraits. Including one of the current duke.

He was rather good-looking. Kate wondered if he resembled his great-uncle the pirate.

Turning pages, she saw that some of the letters were grouped as conversations, with the responses included. Others were simply stand-alones, clustered by date and family branches. The book was thick. And just glancing through, Kate could tell Claire was right about something else: she did recognize many of the names.

It seems the Blys had some very distinguished friends and family members over the years. Could that be why Sir George was expunged from the records?

Claire said that George Bly wasn't in this book. But his brother Henry was. Kate resolved to start there.

She turned the pages, looking for his name. Luckily, the man had a large, proud signature. Unfortunately, in an age before computers—or even typewriters—she had to work to decipher his scrawly, cramped handwriting in ink that had faded considerably over almost four hundred years. And even the magic of modern copiers could only do so much.

Kate scanned the letter, which was really more of a note. It was dated 1634 from Tuscany.

My Sweet Jayne,
I thank you verily for sending word of my beloved
father. Though it is sad news indeed, I am most
grateful in knowing that he did not suffer in his
last earthly moments. I rejoice that he enjoyed

a most long and fruitful life. Yet I do grieve that
you endured his passing alone.

 Father is with my dear brother—and truly I
feel his absence all the more sharply.

 I shall speed my journey back to Marleigh.
It has been only weeks—yea, though weeks too
long—since last I beheld your fair countenance.

 Though I have been parted from England's
green shores for lo these many years, I see it—
and you—always in my dreams.

Your loving husband,
Henry

It sounded as though Henry had been living abroad, too. So George wasn't the only one who'd left the bosom of England and the family home. Why?

It also appeared that Henry had a soft spot for George. Otherwise, why assume that his "beloved father" was spending the afterlife with his "dear brother"? And Henry's grief for George seemed genuine. If not, why mention him at all?

Perhaps the scandal—whatever it was—hadn't yet been discovered by the Bly family?

Claire recounted that, when Henry had moved into Marleigh Hall, he'd had George's portrait removed and had never spoken of him again. So what happened between the time Henry sent this note and the time he reached England?

Kate turned the pages gently and studied the family tree in the front of the book. In 1634, George's brother would have been in his seventies. And the late duke would have been a hundred or more. In an age without vaccinations— or even basic hygiene—that truly was an achievement.

She checked the birth and death dates, calculated the math in her head—then did it again. Just to be sure.

It seems that Henry Bly took after his father in more than just name. The man had been 101 or 102 when he died.

While the tree listed birth and death years for Henry Bly senior and junior, as well as junior's mother and several sisters, Kate noticed there were none for his brother George. Nor were there listings of any marriages or children.

Was that because there weren't any? Or because his family didn't know of any?

It seemed Sir George Bly wasn't simply a mystery to the residents of Coral Cay. He'd also been a bit of a mystery to his own family.

Chapter 23

Maxi carried the tray carefully through the doorway and set it on the table. While it was a warm morning, a strong breeze off the bay cooled downtown Coral Cay and carried the smell of salt water. And the promise of a storm.

Following a long walk through downtown followed by a romp around the backyard of the Cookie House chasing his favorite flying disc, Oliver was stretched out on the porch of Flowers Maximus at Kate's feet. She reached down and rubbed his back. His hair was like silk. Curly, fluffy silk.

"Two hours' sleep calls for extra caffeine," Maxi said, as she poured *café cubano* into delicate yellow china cups.

"Definitely," Kate said, flipping open the bakery box she'd brought. "Even Sam was dragging this morning. And he had yesterday off."

"I know," Maxi said smiling. "But even in the kitchen last night, did you notice he had just a *liii-itle* bit of a tan? Mi padrino looks healthy good. Ay, chocolate icebox cookies—*muy deliciosas*!

"He does," Kate agreed, reaching for the china bowl full of frothy coconut cream. "And he seems happy. Although I know he's worried about you guys."

"Not as much as Peter is. Mi amor is usually super positive. But lately? Mr. Grouchy Pants."

Stationed between them, Oliver followed the back and forth conversation with his eyes.

"Those two guys last night got me thinking," Kate said, setting down her cup. "About Alvin, I mean. I really believe that whoever put him in your yard had to be from Coral Cay."

"Why? Peter called Ben this morning. Those two bobos are from Hibiscus Springs."

"Yes, but think about it. They came here, to a place they didn't know, because that's where they thought the treasure was buried. They didn't have any choice in the location. And they got caught in record time. But what if you had the opposite problem? What if you had something you wanted to bury, and you could go anywhere?"

"You'd go somewhere you knew you wouldn't get caught," the florist added, cradling her cup. "Somewhere super private."

"Somewhere you felt comfortable," Kate added. "Somewhere you felt at home. And you'd know the spot well enough to do it when there was no one around."

"Why not bury it at your home? Why come to my place?"

"Well, maybe they wanted to avert suspicion from themselves," Kate said. "In case Alvin was ever found."

"Or throw suspicion on someone else. Like me."

"Maybe whoever it is couldn't bury it at their home. Nosy neighbors? Doesn't live alone?"

"Has a smart dog who digs up the yard?" Maxi ventured, grinning.

"Exactly," Kate said.

Oliver straightened, looking very proud of himself.

Kate retrieved a gingersnap from her pocket and offered it to him. The pup took it politely from her hand.

"So that could be a clue," Maxi said.

"Who do we know who couldn't bury Alvin in their own yard?"

"Anyone who's married, corizon. A wife won't put up with that stuff. 'Specially if she wants him taking out the trash, cleaning out the garage, and painting the spare room."

Kate smiled. "I'm not even going to ask."

"I'm telling you, something's up with Peter," Maxi said, leaning forward and putting her cup on the saucer. "Something weird."

Oliver stretched, circled a few times and curled up at Kate's feet.

"What do you mean? Peter seemed fine last night. Well, except for the sleep deprivation."

"He was talking on the phone this morning. In the bedroom closet."

"Maybe it was for a case?"

"I got curious. So I *juusst* happened to need a different bag. But the minute I opened the door, he got this funny look on his face and hung up."

"What did he say when you asked him?"

Maxi shrugged. "He said it was the office. But I saw the phone. For just a little bit. It was a 407 number. That's not his office. Something's up. That much, I can feel."

"So talk to him. Take him to lunch. Sam's at the bakery this morning, so I can keep an eye on things here."

"Nope, not yet," Maxi said, shaking her head. "For now, I let him—what is it you foodie people say?—'Stew in his own juices.' Besides, we need to find out what happened to Alvin. You really think it's someone in Coral Cay?"

"It's the only thing that makes sense. The scary thing is, if it's true, it has to be someone who knows the place pretty well."

"Everybody knew I was out of town in February. I mean, even a tourist at the resort could have overheard someone over there talking to me. It wasn't exactly a secret."

"Yes, but they wouldn't know how to find this place. Much less that it had a big backyard. I mean, when I hear the phrase 'flower shop,' I think of a little shop. Surrounded by other little shops. This is, well, amazing."

"*Es fabulosa, no*?" Maxi said, grinning.

"Si, *muy buena*!" Kate said.

"Ay, look at you. We'll make a *cubana* out of you yet."

"Seriously, only a local would know that there was a nice, undisturbed yard out back. And only a local would know how to get here. I mean, it's at the end of the block."

"And only a local would know about Sam's annual trip," Maxi said, taking another cookie.

"Exactly. And, as we foodies say, 'That's the icing on the cake.'"

"So what do we do?" Maxi asked. "It's not like we can go door to door asking, 'Hey, did you happen to lose Mr. Bones? 'Cause we found him, and we want to give him back.'"

"There's one other thing I was wondering about."

"Just one? Corizon, I got a lot of questions."

"No one's missing in Coral Cay," Kate said, looking down at Oliver, whose eyelids were getting heavy.

"You think Alvin is a tourist?"

"I don't know about a tourist. But I definitely think he's from out of town. And, wherever he comes from, either they haven't noticed he's missing—or the police haven't made the connection between that missing person report and our Alvin."

"So maybe we give them a little help," Maxi said, refilling Kate's cup and then her own. "But how?"

They sipped the inky coffee in silence, both of them turning the question—and the myriad of new complications—over in their minds.

"I don't know that I have an answer," Kate said, suddenly sitting forward. "But I think I might know who we can ask."

Chapter 24

That afternoon, Kate picked up the red slimline phone in her bedroom and dialed a familiar number.

"Stenkowski Investigations. Leave a message at the beep, and one of our agents will contact you today."

"Manny, hi, this is Kate McGuire. When you get this, just give me a call."

She left her number and prayed Manny wasn't on vacation. Or a more interesting case.

Kate had met Manny after she first moved to Coral Cay, when Evan hired the P.I. to keep tabs on her. And help her out if she needed it—but without letting her know.

Luckily for Kate, while Manny turned out to be a first-rate investigator, he wasn't exactly practiced at tailing people. So after she'd discovered him following her—and learned who was footing the bill—she'd convinced him to help her track down information on the late and unlamented Stewart Lord. On the Q.T., of course. As far as Evan Thorpe was concerned, she and Manny had never met.

Kate also had a soft spot for Manny's beagle, John Quincy, a former cadaver dog with a bad case of burnout. Manny and his ex-wife had rescued the dog, who was now a pampered family member. And the P.I. took him almost everywhere.

Suddenly, Kate heard yelling.

"I don't care who you are, I was here first! So they're mine!" A woman's voice. Angry.

"Look, lady, my kid's having a birthday party," a man hollered in response. "His tenth birthday! That doesn't happen every day. And a kid's birthday party comes first!"

"Quiet!" Sam's voice sliced through the din. "Cut the nonsense. Both of you."

Kate raced down the stairs, through the kitchen, and into the shop to find a crowd of people jammed into the small room like sardines. Directly in front of the bakery case, a man and woman were facing off.

"You people don't knock it off, no one's getting cookies," Sam said evenly. "And I mean no one."

"But there's only a dozen left," the woman whined. "And I was here first."

"Is it your birthday?" the man hissed. "'Cause it's my kid's birthday. And he wants those cookies."

"When's your child's party?" Kate asked smoothly.

"This afternoon," the man said. "Four o'clock."

Sam shook his head, sadly. "Sarah, you wanted sourdough?" he asked, moving on to the next customer in the crowd.

"Where are you staying?" Kate asked, sizing up the man's new leisurewear and the pink sunburn across his nose.

"We're at Coral Isle Resorts. We've got four kids and another four adults. Josh had some of those icebox things this morning, and he loves them."

"OK, if you have eight people, you're going to need

more than a dozen cookies. And I've got more in the oven right now. So how about you let this nice lady take these, and I'll drop off, what, four dozen at the front desk of Coral Isle by three thirty. Would that work?"

"Could we get five dozen?" the man pleaded.

"Of course," Kate said, grabbing a pad from the counter and jotting down the order. "Anything else to go with it?"

"Well, a cake would be nice. Chocolate with white icing? That's Josh's favorite."

"Happy Birthday Josh," Kate said matter-of-factly, scribbling it on the pad. "What's the birthday boy's favorite color?"

"Orange. Lady, that would be great. You're saving my life."

"Not a problem." She glanced at her notes. "Five dozen chocolate icebox cookies and a birthday cake—chocolate with white icing, orange writing, and candles. Delivered to Coral Isle Resorts by three thirty today. Will that be cash, or may I put it on your credit card?"

"Never had nothing like that when we just sold bread and rolls," Sam said gruffly, after the shop had finally emptied.

"I don't know—everyone in town raves about your sourdough," Kate said. "I'm guessing you had at least a few fistfights over the last loaf in the shop."

"Woulda rather tossed 'em both," Sam replied. "Bunch a' troublemakers."

"Look at it this way, instead of a dozen cookies, we sold six dozen, plus a cake, plus a delivery charge. And now we know those icebox cookies are a hit."

Sam shrugged. "Got a point there," he admitted, heading into the kitchen.

When the shop bell tinkled, Kate looked up. Evan.

He looked over and smiled broadly. Kate always teased him about the grin—calling it his "five hundred-watt smile." Often, it meant he wanted something. And most of the time, he got it.

Evan turned, talking to someone behind him—out on the porch. "Come on in. I want to introduce you."

"Nah, I'll just wait out here," an unseen man's voice mumbled.

"No, come on. She'll want to meet you. She's great—I promise."

Manny Stenkowski stepped through the door, a sheepish look on his face.

"Hi, Evan, what's up? And who's your friend?" Kate asked, nodding toward the private detective.

"Kate, this is Manny Stenkowski. He works in security and investigations. Look, I heard about the problem last night. At your friend's place. And I felt bad about it. I mean, the foundation is funding the search for Gentleman George—and that's ratcheted up the whole treasure hunting thing. So I've asked Manny to help us out. You know, sort of keep an eye on things. And I know what you're going to say . . ."

"Nice to meet you, Manny," she said, extending her hand across the counter. "I'm Kate McGuire. I'm one of the owners of the Cookie House. Before you go next door to meet my friend Maxi, would you guys like to come into the kitchen and have a snack?"

After she got Evan and Manny settled with coffee and a big plate of chocolate chip cookies, Kate picked up the phone. And pointedly ignored the questioning looks she was getting from Sam each time he wandered through the kitchen.

"Hi, Maxi, it's Kate. Just wanted to find out if you

could come over for a minute. Evan's here, and he's got an investigator he's hired to keep an eye out in case any more of those treasure hunters show up."

"Are you OK? You sound weird," Maxi said.

"No, I don't think you've met him. His name is Manny Stemkowski."

"Stenkowski," Manny corrected from across the kitchen.

"Excuse me, Manny Stenkowski," Kate said into the phone.

"Yowza," Maxi said.

"Exactly," Kate replied, cheerily. "So, you know, just pop in whenever you have a sec."

"Are you kidding?" the florist said. "I'd pay money to see this. I'll be right over."

After another round of "introductions," Evan outlined his plan: Manny was going to stake out the block at night, and alert the police if there were any more unwanted visitors. And, as time permitted, he would also use his skills to assist them with the search for the real Gentleman George.

"Uh, what's that?" Evan said, pointing to where Oliver perched by the bakery's back door.

"That's Oliver," Kate said. "He's the town dog, but he lives here. With me."

"I never knew you even liked dogs," Evan said. "Why didn't you say so? I'd have gotten you a dog."

For his part, Oliver sat bolt upright, chin down, saucer eyes laser-focused on Evan. If Kate didn't know better, she'd have sworn the expression on the dog's face was disapproval. Or disdain.

But that wasn't possible. Was it?

"Um, does it need to go out or something?" Evan asked.

"No, he's just been out," Kate said.

Evan looked down at his plate. Then again at the door—and quickly away. "Does it always do that? The staring thing?"

"He," Kate corrected. "And no, he doesn't."

"Kinda looks like he doesn't like you," Maxi said. "But I wouldn't worry. He probably won't bite or anything."

"Geez," Evan said, briefly looking up. "Well, anyway, I think that about covers it. And, naturally, the foundation will pay all of Manny's fees and expenses. Anyone have any questions?"

"Should be interesting," Manny said, slapping the table. "Coldest case I ever worked. The murder of a four-hundred-year-old pirate."

"If it makes it any easier, we think we know who did it," Maxi said. "The captain of the galleon was named Juan Pedro Baptiste. And he was not a nice guy."

"Might actually help to get some data on the perp," Manny said. "You got something I could read while I'm out there tonight?"

"Stop by around six," Kate said. "I'll make you up a care package with some sandwiches, a thermos, and a good book. Now, if you'll all excuse me, I've got to go see a man about a birthday cake."

Chapter 25

Kate was just turning the OPEN/CLOSED sign on the front door when she spotted Manny at the curb. This time, he had John Quincy on a black lead.

The P.I. wore the same khaki shorts he had on that afternoon. But he'd switched Hawaiian shirts. This one was springy green covered in palm fronds. And he'd traded the straw fedora for an olive-drab fishing hat. The "just another tourist" look that was his stock in trade.

The beagle made several stops, sniffing various flowers, and presumably satisfied, he ambled up the walkway.

"Your ex still here?" Manny asked, looking around.

"Long gone," Kate replied.

"Thanks for that," he said. "You know, before."

"No problem," Kate said. "I'm glad he called you. We've been a little worried about the treasure hunters."

"That's one reason I took the job. Plus John Quincy loves this place. And the idea of spending a few days at a resort didn't sound half bad, either."

"As far as Evan's concerned, we just met today," Kate

said, bending to stroke John Quincy's velvety flank. The beagle sniffed her shoes, then gazed up at her. "But there are some things you need to know. This case is a little more complicated than it looks."

"Aren't they all?"

"C'mon back to the kitchen," Kate said, standing. "I'm just finishing up your snack. And I'll tuck in a few gingersnaps for the little guy."

"That would be aces, thanks," Manny said. "Hey, where's your Oliver?"

"Next door with Maxi. He's been sticking pretty close to her lately. And that's kind of what I wanted to talk to you about. How much did Evan tell you about what's going on over there?"

"Bare bones, if you'll pardon the pun," Manny said, smiling, as he settled into his previous spot at the kitchen table. "Some kind of illegal burial from last year. But the web whackos think it's really some pirate who was buried with his loot. Which is a load of horse hockey, if you ask me."

"What do you mean?" Kate asked, washing up at the kitchen sink.

"I've dealt with a lot of criminal types. Nobody—and I mean nobody—buries money with a corpse. What good's that gonna do? Money's for the living."

"These were loyal men," Kate said. "They lived by a code. It was a show of respect for their leader."

"Un-uh," Manny said, shaking his head. "I don't know where your pirate friend is right now. But I'll bet you dollars to doughnuts he hasn't got more than a dime in his pocket. Four hundred years or not, those guys were real flesh and blood. Not some fairy tale. They fought for that money. Fought hard. No way they're just gonna toss it into some hole in the ground."

"So you believe . . ." Kate started.

"I'm sayin' your pirate friend might be out here somewhere. But his treasure is long gone. Probably spent three hundred and ninety-nine years ago on you-don't-wanna-know what."

Kate sighed. "There are a couple of things you need to know about the case—the real one, not the pirate one. I don't know what Evan told you. But the cell service is notoriously unreliable on this part of the island. So if you need to call the cops, just bang on one of the bakery doors, and you can use our landline. I live upstairs."

"Yeah, I remember the cell bit from last time," Manny nodded. "Mixed blessing."

"And the skeleton they found in Maxi's garden?" she said, folding sandwich after sandwich neatly in wax paper and stacking them in the picnic basket. "The police are telling the public it's an unreported death or an unsanctioned burial. But there could be more to it than that."

"Because her husband is an assistant state's attorney?"

"You know about that?"

"Yeah, and you're right. It does throw a new light on things. Your friend Thorpe briefed me. Even if he hadn't, I do my homework. 'Cause in this business, clients don't always tell you everything. Sometimes they don't even tell you the truth."

"Maxi says Peter's being really odd lately," Kate confessed.

"She thinks he knows more than he's letting on? Or maybe he's cheating?"

"No!"

Manny raised his hands in surrender. "Hey, I'm just asking. You say the guy's a state's attorney, he's acting squirrelly, and there's a skeleton in his yard."

"Not squirrelly, exactly. Just, I don't know, uptight. Tense. And this morning he was making a call from their closet. To a 407 number."

"Maybe he's worried about his wife?" Manny said. "I mean, one night it's fortune hunters. Another time, someone's using the place for a DIY cemetery. His office can't help. Oh yeah, and his wife refuses to leave town. Your Maxi is a lot like my Margot."

"How did you . . . ?" Kate said. "You knew all this already?"

Manny nodded. "Sure. Those treasure yahoos were the last straw. Your buddy Buchanan called Thorpe last night and demanded security. Pronto. Thorpe called me. Who do you think Buchanan was talking to in that closet?"

Chapter 26

In the kitchen of the Cookie House, Maxi perched on a barstool as Kate stood at the counter piping a wide stream of white icing onto the side of a large piece of gingerbread.

"Peter did what?" Maxi exclaimed. It was half question, half shriek.

At her feet, Oliver looked up suddenly in alarm. Maxi reached down and patted his head reassuringly.

"Look at the bright side," Kate said, carefully pressing two sections of gingerbread together to form one corner of the doghouse. "At least he won't be pushing you to pack up and go to Miami anytime soon. And it will be kind of nice to have an extra pair of eyes on the shop."

"Ay, not you, too. So how's this gonna work, anyway? Will Manny help us with Alvin?"

"Right now, Manny's just assessing the situation," Kate explained, carefully adding a third side to the structure. "He's going to stake out the block tonight from his car. And after Carl Ivers installs cameras in your yard tomorrow, he can watch the feeds from almost any-where. But he's still going to swing by regularly to make sure everything's OK. If we get more treasure hunt-ers—or if it looks like it's going to be an ongoing prob-lem—he'll hire a couple of security guards to keep an eye on the place, mostly at night. As far as anyone else is concerned, he's coordinating the search for Gentle-man George. And that part's true. But he's also agreed to reach out to his police contacts to try and find out more about Alvin. "

"Ben will love that," Maxi said, grinning.

"I know. Manny needs that sketch Ben's people are doing of Alvin. I'm supposed to get a copy so he can show it to a few of his law-enforcement contacts out of state. He's hoping someone might recognize it from a police report or a missing person's report. And he's going to try to match up descriptions of missing people from a few of the big metro-area police databases with what we know about Alvin."

"Ay, talk about a super small needle in a very big hay-stack. But at least he's helping us."

"I think that's the main reason he's here. He loves Coral Cay. That, and Evan's putting him up at one of the resorts."

"I hope it's the one with the little bungalows. I love that place. But it's super pricy."

Kate piped icing onto the fourth side of the doghouse and slipped it carefully into place. She stepped back and held her breath.

"Hey, that thing looks pretty good. If it had a roof, Mr. Oliver could grab his Frisbee and move in."

"Barb wanted big, so she's getting big," Kate said, smiling. "I'll let it firm up overnight, and tomorrow I'll put the roof on and finish decorating it. Then we're all set. So how's the new doctor getting settled in?"

"Don't know yet," Maxi said, sipping her coffee. "Barb says his clinic opens the day after tomorrow. And Mitzy says he's a real hunk."

"Mitzy also said Evan and I were settling down happily ever after in a big house in Coral Cay," Kate said ruefully. "Take anything that woman says with a grain of salt. Come to think of it, I actually met Dr. Scanlon once. When he was house hunting last month."

"OK, spill."

"There's nothing to tell. He seemed nice. He came into the shop. Well, really, Oliver brought him in."

"Mr. Oliver is drumming up business now?" Maxi asked, grinning.

Hearing his name, the pup looked up.

"Dr. Scanlon had spotted Oliver downtown and was worried he didn't appear to be with anyone. So he followed him. And they ended up here."

"Hmmm, Mr. Oliver, are you playing matchmaker now?" Maxi said, reaching down to stroke his side.

The dog's eyes twinkled.

"I'm gonna take that as a 'yes,'" Maxi said.

Kate glanced at her watch.

"Got a hot date?" her friend teased.

"We both do. The first batch of tomorrow's contest cookies are done. Carrot cake morsels."

"OK, I'll stick around for that. So how's that cookie contest thing going?"

"We had a fight break out over the last dozen icebox cookies today."

"See, I told you those things were good. I'll bet Sam just loved that."

"Sam was ready to toss everyone out and close the shop. But business has been pretty good, so . . ."

"So who came up with the icebox recipe?" Maxi asked, carefully stepping around Oliver to get to the coffee maker. "Did you ever find out?"

"Sunny. I'm going to drop her off a dozen when I take the rolls to 'stretch and starch' tomorrow morning," Kate said, using the popular moniker for the yoga instructor's six a.m. class—which was followed promptly by fresh rolls, local jams, and copious cups of steaming green tea.

"You should go for the class," Maxi said. "We both could. I don't know about you, but ever since we found Alvin, I've been a little tense."

"Actually, that's not a bad idea. Sam's opening the store tomorrow. So if I get us stocked up tonight, I could do it."

"Just remember," Maxi said, smiling over her coffee mug, "with us there, Sunny might need a little extra starch with her stretch."

Chapter 27

"And reach—ever so gently—and breathe," Sunny enthused, from the front of the class.

At eighty-plus, with a stylish champagne-blond bob and a toned body encased in a navy leotard that disguised nothing, Kate marveled that the instructor was a walking advertisement for her studio.

"Ay, what happens if my body freezes in this position?" Maxi stage-whispered to Kate.

"Then you will be permanently at one with the universe—and you won't get any tea," Sunny replied.

"That's what I was afraid of," Maxi said.

"All right now, folks, the dead man pose. And no talking. Let all those muscles relax and refresh."

Kate imagined this is what dough must feel like when she left it on the counter after a vigorous kneading. And, for all her quips, Maxi seemed to bounce through the poses without a hitch.

"And that concludes our class," Sunny announced. "Go out and meet the day—and make it joyous! And re-

member, tomorrow morning's class will be on the beach.
Weather permitting."

As the students filed into the lobby for tea, Kate rolled
up her fuchsia mat and followed.

"So how are things going with the search for Gentleman George?" Sunny asked.

"Not much progress yet," Kate said. "I think this is
probably going to be more of a long-term project. Very
long term, by the looks of it. But I didn't think you were
a Gentleman George fan."

"Oh, I like the old duffer just fine," Sunny admitted.
"I've just never seen the advantage of looking backward
when you're trying to move forward. Besides, for a lot of
these folks I suspect it's more of a marketing ploy. More
tourists, bigger crowds at the Pirate Festival. And I don't
believe we need that. A new vet in town? That we need."

"You're right," Kate said.

"Just think of what this island was like back when
Gentleman George was here," Sunny said. "Nothing
but salt marshes and sandy beaches with a dozen hid-
den coves offering safe harbor. A bay full of fish. Trees
and bushes brimming with wild fruits and berries. It was
paradise. Especially for some poor sot stuck at sea for
months at a time. It must have seemed like Eden."

Kate smiled.

"To my way of thinking, if we want to honor Gentleman George, we take good care of his home. Preserve
his real legacy. Because it's our home now. We need to
look after it—keep it up."

"That makes a lot of sense, actually," Kate said. "By
the way, do you happen to remember anything special
that was happening in town back in February?"

"Is this about that skeleton you gals found?"

Involuntarily, Kate grimaced.

"Dear, whatever you do, never take up high-stakes

poker," Sunny cackled. "Let's see. February. Well, obviously, Sam was making his annual trip. Wherever it is he goes. And Amos's nephew was in town again. Teddy. Actually stayed for a couple of weeks this time. I don't know exactly what the situation was, but I had the distinct impression the boy was moving here. Then one day, he was gone. Amos said he'd decided to go back home. He actually seemed kind of relieved," Sunny confided. "Oh, and that's about the time we were beginning to see cracks in the Duvals' marriage. Really a shame. They were such a happy couple. But at the party, it was obvious something was off."

"The party?"

"Their annual Valentine's Day bash. Of course, Caroline had taken to calling it a 'féte,'" Sunny said, shrugging. "But it raised a ton of cash for the library. Huge wingding. Chamber orchestra, costumes, dance band, fireworks. The theme was love, of course. Because of the holiday. But there wasn't a lot of love between the two of them that night. She was snipping and sniping all evening. At the time, I chalked it up to the stress of organizing the thing. Now, of course, we all know better."

"Sounds like a real blowout," Kate said. "The party, I mean."

"Oh, they used to hold it every year. And it wasn't just Coral Cay. People came from all over Florida. It was quite the event. I don't know what Harp will do next year. I can't think that he'd want to host a Valentine's Day party alone."

"No, I don't imagine he would," Kate said, feeling a pang of sympathy. "Oh, I wanted to let you know your icebox cookies were a real hit. If you're OK with it, I'd like to keep stocking them."

"I'd be delighted if you did. And Mother will be tickled pink."

"Mother?"

"My mother, dear. She hasn't made them in years. Hasn't had the time."

"Does she live in town?" Kate asked, intrigued.

"On the far side of the island. Right on the edge of the preserve. She's got a little cottage. Been in the family for ages. But she's not there now. She likes to go up north in the summer. To visit my brother, George. Between you and me, I think she just likes to avoid the heat and the tourists."

"Your brother's name is George? That's a coincidence," Kate said, smiling at the irony.

"No coincidence," Sunny replied. "It's an old family name. Word is that we're descended from Sir George Bly."

Chapter 28

Walking down Main Street after class, Kate had to admit that Sunny really knew her stuff. She hadn't felt this relaxed in days.

Just before eight in the morning, it was what Coral Cay residents called "local hour." Since tourists tended not to hit the downtown area much before ten, locals tended to shop in the cool of the morning.

She'd only been here a scant few months. But it seemed like she recognized more faces—and recalled more names—every time she walked down the street.

In Manhattan, trekking down the block meant dodging pedestrians, bikes, and traffic. Unless you knew someone, making eye contact was rude. And chancy. Here, people waved and said hello. Sometimes, they'd even stop to chat. About everything.

"Where's Oliver this morning?" Annie Kim asked, as she passed Kate and Maxi on the sidewalk.

"We left him at the flower shop, but that was two hours ago, so now there's no telling," Maxi admitted.

"If you see him, send him this way," the pharmacist said, ducking into the doorway of Kim's Drugstore. "It's heartworm pill day. They taste like liver, so he loves them."

"I'll bring him over at lunchtime, if he hasn't been here before then," Kate promised.

As they strolled down the block, Kate glanced across the street and spotted Amos Tully's market.

"By the way, what do you know about Amos's nephew?" she asked Maxi.

"Teddy? Not much. He came and stayed with Amos earlier this year. He does that from time to time. They're pretty tight. I sorta thought he might be moving to Coral Cay. But then he didn't."

"Sunny said the same thing. In fact, she said it was like he was living here one minute and vanished the next. I hate to even think this, but could he be Alvin?"

Maxi paused. "I guess he could be," the florist conceded. "Teddy's got to be about twenty-four or twenty-five."

"Right in the age bracket Ben gave us," Kate said.

"Yeah, but it was a pretty wide range. Although Teddy was here when we left for Miami, and gone when we got back, I never really thought anything of it."

"So the timing's about right, too," Kate said. "On the other hand, Amos never reported him missing."

"Teddy's always been kind of a wanderer," Maxi explained. "He never stays in one place long."

"Where's Teddy from? I mean, if he truly went home, where would that be?"

"Amos never said. You know him. He's not much with the small talk. I think the rest of the family is from up north somewhere. But I don't know about Teddy."

"Might be nice to find out," Kate suggested. "Pretty much the only thing I know about Amos is that he has a weakness for oatmeal raisin cookies."

"Well, I can't picture Amos Tully planting Teddy in my yard," Maxi said grinning. "The guy's name fits him. He's built like a Teddy bear. And you've seen Amos. Besides, no way Amos would dig down four feet. I have to beg that man to double-bag my groceries."

"Seriously, how could a person just disappear and no one notices? What if Amos thought Teddy had just cleared off for home?"

"But really something happened?" Maxi breathed. "I wouldn't want to be the one to have to tell Amos. It would break his heart."

"Let's just see if we can find out where Teddy is now," Kate said. "And confirm that he's really there. If he is, then we don't have to say anything."

"You know who knows Amos better than anyone? Mi padrino. He might know where Teddy lives."

"You think so? Because I can picture the two of them sitting on the front porch for hours watching traffic and not saying a word."

"Ay, I think that's exactly why they're friends," Maxi said, grinning.

"Speaking of which, why didn't you tell me that Sunny Eisenberg was related to Sir George Bly?"

"Sunny Eisenberg is related to Gentleman George? Who told you that?"

"Sunny. She mentioned it this morning after class."

"I didn't know that. She never told me. I don't think she ever told anybody. Must be your magic cookie powers. Were you waving one of those icebox things in front of her face when she 'fessed up? 'Cause I'd spill my guts for one of those, too."

"It's funny. Barb isn't related to him, and she can't get enough of the Gentleman George story. Sunny is an actual descendent, and her attitude is 'Live for today.'"

"Sounds just like a pirate. Plus, she knows how to punish people with those classes of hers."

"Have you ever met her mother?"

"Iris? Si, many times. She's had some get-togethers out at her place. And she gave me a few rosebush cuttings. *Muy bonita.* Some of the best roses in my yard are from her."

"You don't suppose Ben's lab got it wrong? What if it wasn't long-stemmed roses? What if it was just roses?"

"You think Sunny and Iris popped Alvin and planted him in my garden?"

"OK, it sounds ridiculous when you say it out loud. Besides, Sunny isn't the type. She's more 'Live and let live.'"

"More like 'Live and let me torture you with twisty exercises,'" Maxi countered. "But you got a point. Besides, Iris lives right next to a nature preserve. If Sunny and her mom were gonna bury a body anywhere, they'd put it there."

"Which brings us back to the original question," said Kate. "With miles of deserted beaches and a wilderness preserve on this island, why did someone bury a skeleton downtown in back of a flower shop?"

Chapter 29

When Kate walked into the bakery, it was packed with customers.

"What's today's cookie, Sam?" someone called from the back of the shop.

"Carrot cake morsels," the baker said.

"Whose entry is it?" another voice called from across the room.

"Don't know," the baker admitted. "Tasty though."

"Those sound good," Mitzy Allen said, tucking her frizzy blond hair behind her ear. "I'll take a dozen of those, and a loaf of the rye. Oh, and one of the sourdough, too."

"You want that bread sliced?" Sam said, looking up as Kate worked her way through the crowd. "You got a visitor," he added quietly. "In the back."

Kate said a silent prayer it wasn't Evan.

Luckily, Manny Stenkowski was drinking coffee at the kitchen table. And John Quincy was sacked out beneath it.

"Hey, how did it go last night?" Kate asked.

"Brutal. This town rolls up the sidewalks at nine o'clock. And I gotta tell you, absolutely nothing happened after that."

"Isn't that kind of a good thing?"

"Not if you're trying to stay awake. Good news is, cops are running regular crawl cars on the block. And your friend from the hardware store is coming to install those cameras this morning. As soon as he does, I'm going back to my room and catch some shut-eye. I'm beat."

"How did you get John Quincy past Sam?" Kate asked.

While the baker made certain exceptions for Oliver, provided the pup was discreet, he maintained a strict "no dogs" policy for all other canines.

"You mean this trained police dog? I snuck him in the back door when your partner wasn't looking."

"That works. How about some breakfast? I can scramble a couple of eggs. We've got some great challah rolls—fresh out of the oven. And I'm sure I can find some bacon for you-know-who."

"That would be swell. Sad thing is, I get a free breakfast with my room at the resort. And they put out a great spread, too. But at this rate, I'm never gonna be there to enjoy it."

"Don't worry," Kate said. "That's one thing you don't have to worry about while you're here. In Coral Cay, there may not be much of a nightlife. But you can always find a good meal."

After Manny left to supervise the installation of the security system in Maxi's yard. Kate slipped on an apron and headed out to the shop to help Sam.

When the phone rang, she grabbed the receiver off the wall. "The Cookie House, this is Kate."

"It's me," Maxi said. "The guys are here doing the security stuff in the backyard. And it reminded me of something. I think I might know why whoever it was put Alvin in my yard!"

Chapter 30

At the bakery, Kate noticed, customers came in waves. The place stayed packed throughout "local hour." As soon as there was a lull in the crowd—and before the tourists started trundling in around ten—she grabbed a box of carrot cake morsels and headed next door to Flowers Maximus.

When she walked in, Maxi was standing by the French doors in the back of her shop, watching Carl Ivers and his men install her new security cameras. Manny was off to the side of the yard. And from the body language, Kate surmised that he and Carl—both ex-cops—were mixing about as well as sugar and cold butter.

"Today's winner," Kate said, holding up the large box. "Carrot cake morsels. Think coconut macaroons with a carrot cake twist. And I brought enough to feed the crew when they're done."

"A super good idea," Maxi said over her shoulder. "Thank you."

"Maybe we should throw a couple out there now," Kate said, peering through the glass. The arm motions had gotten more animated. And their voices were getting louder. "It sounds like Carl and Manny aren't exactly getting along."

"Ay, it's not that bad. They're having a tiny disagreement on where to put the cameras. To get the most of the yard. Each of them has a slightly different idea. And, of course, each of them is the only one who can be right."

"Naturally," Kate said.

"Throw in a scheming girlfriend and an evil twin and it could be one of mi mami's telenovelas," she said, studying them from behind the glass. "Oh, and you just missed Oliver. He took off when Carl and the crew arrived. Funny thing is, he was heading right up Main Street. You don't think he's going to the drugstore?"

Kate smiled. "With that pup, anything's possible. So what did you remember?"

"That's the weird thing. And I don't know how I forgot. Remember how I told you that back in February we left for Miami quick, quick, quick?"

"Of course. It was a family emergency."

"Before all of that, Peter gave me his Valentine's Day present early. Grass for the yard."

"He gave you grass? For Valentine's Day?"

Maxi grinned. "It's a lot more romantic than it sounds. The yard behind the shop had become kind of a catchall working area. It wasn't awful. But I had this dream of what I could do with it. Make it special. Kinda like the front and side yards. Something really beautiful."

"You mean, like it is now?"

"Ay, it wasn't like that then. But I had a plan. And I was gonna do it in baby bites. A little here, and a little there. And under it all, I wanted this wonderful carpet of grass. This special stuff I heard about. But my plan was taking for*ever*. You know, with the shop and the kids and everything else. So mi amor arranged for a service to come out and put down sod. All over the backyard. My special grass that I'd wanted. It's this super cool stuff. Short and green and really tough. And it's not cheap, let me tell you."

"But how does that involve Alvin?"

"The guys who did our yard? I know them. They're the best. I recommend them to clients all the time. When we left for Miami, they had just started. They were ripping out all of the old grass. Then they were gonna leave the hoses out there for a couple of days. Give the area a good soak. Then they would come in and put down the new stuff."

"So when you left town, the yard was bare sand and dirt?" Kate said, finally seeing the full picture in her mind.

"And when we got home, all beautiful sod grass," Maxi said, nodding.

Kate sagged against the wall. "Whoever put Alvin out there—this means they had to be local. And they had to know you guys fairly well."

Maxi nodded. "Yup, I thought so, too. Because whoever it was knew their hole-digging would get covered with thick squares of nice green grass. And no one would ever know a thing."

Chapter 31

Later that morning, just after the bell on the shop door tinkled, Kate heard a familiar voice call out, "Yoo-hoo, anybody there?"

"Hi, Rosie, come on in. I'm back in the kitchen."

The antique dealer was wearing a plum-colored suit with a cream silk blouse that set off her café au lait complexion. She looked around the kitchen. "Is anyone else here?"

"Just me. Sam had to go over to Maxi's for a few minutes. Sit down and I'll get us both some coffee. What's up?"

"This stays between the two of us?" Rosie said, clearly concerned.

"Of course," Kate said. "But you've piqued my curiosity."

Rosie's face relaxed into a smile, as she seated herself at the kitchen table. "It's no big secret. Well, not most of it. Has anybody told you about Pirate Night Dinners?"

"Not a peep. What is it?"

"Well, during the festival, this place is crazy. I mean, really crazy. Especially downtown. And you can say goodbye to 'local hour.' Tourists come early, and they stay late. Which is wonderful. Especially for all of us shop owners. But it also means we're spending a lot more time at work. Even more than usual. So we came up with a little tradition of our own. Pirate Night Dinners. Every year, we pick a central location. And every night, a different shop puts on a dinner for any of the downtown business folk who want to show up."

"That sounds wonderful," Kate said, grabbing two cup-and-saucer sets from a cupboard and placing them next to Sam's coffee maker. Then she pulled out a platter and plucked a half dozen still warm shortbread cookies from a cooling rack.

"It really is," Rosie agreed. "It's a lot of fun. And some really good food. I think some of the best dishes I've had in my life have been at book club meetings and Pirate Night Dinners. And that's saying something."

"So where's the centrally located spot this year?" Kate asked, filling the cups.

"This is the tricky part," Rosie said, lowering her voice. "It was supposed to be in the backyard of Flowers Maximus."

"Oh no," Kate said, as she lifted the platter and set it in the middle of the table.

"I know," Rosie said, fingering the short strand of pearls that lay at her throat. "Maxi had her heart set on it. And frankly, so did the rest of us. Now Barb is scrambling to find another spot."

"That explains why Maxi had been working on the yard even more than usual," Kate said, as she carefully placed the coffee cups on the table.

Rosie nodded, taking a cookie. "And she would have

done a bang-up job. You know how warm she is. And her place is gorgeous. But now . . ."

"Now it's just not feasible this year," Kate finished.

"Exactly. And I know it's breaking her heart. Anyway, I was wondering if you might be open to having it here instead? And letting her host?"

"Rosie, that's a brilliant idea! Have you talked with Maxi about it?"

Rosie shook her head. "Not yet. I wanted to check with you first. I won't sugarcoat it. It's a lot of work. The location becomes sort of the unofficial hangout spot for us locals during the festival. I mean, you're only putting on a dinner, but people will show up with a bag lunch at noon just to chat and gossip and gripe. Or swing by for coffee in the afternoon. So privacy sort of goes out the window. And the dinners themselves go on for hours— because we can't all take a break at the same time. When Andre and I hosted a couple of years ago, we used the private dining room in the back of Oy and Begorra. Because there really isn't enough room in our shop. And at the end of the night we practically had to toss people out."

"Sounds like a few of the restaurants where I've worked," Kate said smiling.

Rosie looked around surreptitiously and lowered her voice to almost a whisper. "I also didn't know how Sam would feel about it. The last time he hosted was with Ginger. And that was about five years ago."

Kate nodded. "Well, I can't speak for Sam. But if it helps Maxi, I think he'd jump at the chance. Me too, for that matter. Plus, hard work or not, it sounds like fun. It'll be like being back in restaurants again."

Rosie beamed. "I'm so glad you like the idea. I feel for Maxi. It's bad enough what happened with her backyard. But now I'm hearing that some of the resorts are using other florists. You know, just until that whole situation with the remains is resolved."

"Oh my gosh, that's awful!" Kate said. "She never said a word about it."

"She wouldn't. Maxi is a trooper. And she always focuses on the positive. But I was kind of hoping this might help take her mind off of it. And maybe, if we do it right, boost her business, too."

"I know exactly what you mean, and I think it's a great idea. And as far as Sam goes, just leave that to me."

Chapter 32

"So how's the pirate bread coming?" Kate asked, as she refilled her coffee cup in the kitchen. The savory scent of rosemary perfumed the kitchen.

"Not bad," the baker said, holding out a small platter.

If Kate didn't know better, she'd have sworn the old baker was actually pleased.

"Thought we might put some samples in the shop," he said. "Go on, have a taste."

Kate took a piece from the plate and examined it. Firm with flakey layers. It smelled of pungent rosemary and warm butter. And it melted in her mouth.

"This is wonderful," she said, scooping up two more pieces. "Harp is going to want some for his next wine and cheese party. And Andy and Bridget are going to love it."

"Took a little engineering," Sam said proudly. "But I got there. Mighty tasty, if I do say so."

"Did you know that Maxi was supposed to host the

Pirate Night Dinners this year?" Kate said, as she followed him into the shop.

"Yup, a real shame," he said, shaking his head. "Woulda been really good. Don't guess she'd much care to now, though."

"Actually, I think she might," Kate said. "And if you're up for it, we could loan her the backyard of the Cookie House."

"Not a bad idea," he said, thoughtfully. "Means we'd have people around to keep an eye on her place. And she'd be over here more, too. Her husband would like that. Ben too, I imagine."

"I think she'd really love it," Kate said.

"Only one way to find out," Sam said, with a small smile. "Ask her."

Later that afternoon, while Sam worked the front counter, Kate loaded up a trio of icing bags to finish the gingerbread doghouse for Jack Scanlon's welcome party that evening at Oy and Begorra.

She'd slipped the structure onto a fresh sheet of shortbread, so that the entire house and yard would be edible—and big enough to feed an army.

Kate steadied her hand, drawing big loops on the roof to create the outline of roofing shingles. Then she filled them in, using delicate shades of pale blue for highlights.

Next she painted three sides of the house with cheery red icing, smoothing it out as she worked with an offset spatula. On the front, she did the same, carefully leaving several voids in the gingerbread.

Reclaiming the white icing, she drew on a big window, then added a large door. She filled in both with white icing, added a few highlights, and smoothed it over with the spatula.

Kate stepped back and smiled, surveying her handi-work.

Now all it needed was an Oliver-worthy yard. She returned to the batch of white icing in her mixing bowl, added a few handfuls of coconut flakes, along with a few drops of green food coloring, and carefully slipped the bowl under the stand mixer. A minute later, it was the perfect shade.

As she carefully formed little patches of icing grass, Kate thought of the news that Maxi had shared that morning. How many people would know that the flower shop was getting sod in the backyard? The people installing it, certainly. Could it have been someone on the crew or connected with the company?

And who else would have known? Kate couldn't see Peter sharing it with the folks at his office. But she could imagine Maxi telling the whole town about Peter's Valentine's Day gift.

Even if the florist only chatted with one or two friends, word would get quickly around Coral Cay. Especially if it was the right one or two people.

Gabe Louden had been spot on when he noted that downtown might not have great cell service, but the community was wired in other ways.

More important, who was Alvin? She made a mental note to ask Sam about Amos's nephew, Teddy. At this point, she didn't even know the man's last name.

And it was definitely time to pay Ben Abrams a visit and get that composite sketch for Manny. Perhaps a dozen chocolate crinkle cookies—Ben's favorite—might buy a little goodwill?

Finished with the lawn, Kate stepped back and looked at the doghouse. Almost perfect.

She went into the refrigerator and retrieved two small

plastic bags with the marzipan decorations she'd made earlier. In one, a little red fire hydrant. In the other, a small purple Frisbee.

Chapter 33

Kate shivered as she sat in the lobby of the Coral Cay police department. It wasn't just that the AC was going full blast. Her last few visits here had not been happy occasions.

She hoped this one might change her luck.

"You here to see Ben?" Officer Kyle Hardy asked brusquely, from the other side of the glass partition.

"If he has a minute," Kate said, brandishing a box of cookies. "I just wanted to chat for a sec, and give him these. And I have a box of the peanut butter ones for you. Just to say thanks for the help the other night. With the treasure hunters."

Kyle Hardy's face actually lit up. It was the first time Kate had ever seen him smile. The first time she'd met him, the twentysomething cop had all but decided she'd imagined—or staged—a break-in at the bakery. The second time they'd met, he'd arrested Sam Hepplewhite for murder. So their history was complicated.

"Now that's really nice," the officer said, looking gen-uinely pleased. "Thank you. Ben'll be free in a couple of minutes. He's just finishing up a few things."

"That works. Are you coming to the welcome party for the new vet this evening?"

"I'm working. Routine patrols. But I might try and drop by on my dinner break. You met the guy yet?"

"Last month. He was in town, and he popped into the bakery. Seems nice. And Oliver likes him."

"Good, 'cause we could really use a decent vet. My mom's schnauzer is getting up there. Seems like she's taking her in every other month or so. And the clinic is all the way over in Elmwood. Be nice to have a vet on the island for a change."

A few minutes later, Kyle reappeared behind the glass. "Ben's free now. You want to come on back?"

"Let me guess," Ben Abrams said, getting up from behind his desk to usher her into his office. "You want to give me cookies and tell me that Maxi and Peter are innocent of any wrongdoing."

"No, I just wanted to say thank you for helping us out the other night," she said. "With the prowlers. And if you have that sketch of Al—I mean, our friend from the garden, I was going to show it around. To see if anyone recognizes him."

"For what it's worth, I believe Peter and Maxi had nothing to do with this," Ben said. "I'm still concerned it might have something to do with his work, though. And I think he is too. But I will investigate every lead—no matter where it goes."

Kate nodded. "That's fair. And Carl put in the cam-eras this morning. At least that should help."

Ben flipped the lid on the bakery box and inhaled deeply. "Oh man, I love these things."

"Fresh out of the oven," Kate said proudly. She neglected to mention that she'd baked them just so she'd have an excuse to visit.

He offered her the box, and she politely took one. "You should try the chocolate icebox cookies, too. We nearly had a fight in the bakery over those."

"Yeah, I might've heard something about that," he said, reaching into his desk drawer and pulling out a single piece of paper. "OK, part of the problem with these sketches is there's a lot we don't know—like coloring and hairstyle. If the guy had a beard or a mustache. If he'd shaved his head—don't understand that one," he said, smoothing his dark hair. "But it seems to be a trend. So the artist gives us a sheet with a few options."

He slipped the page onto the desk in front of her. "These are the ones we got back for your friend."

Kate studied the faces. Or, more correctly, face. With different coloring, different hairstyles and different facial hair, each rendering looked like a completely different person. She remembered Maxi's description of Teddy. "Do you have any idea what he might have done for a living or what he weighed?"

Ben shook his head. "Not so far. But the M.E. is taking this one as a personal challenge. And I wouldn't bet against her. As far as what he did, the doc thinks it could have been some kind of manual labor. He did a lot of walking. There was some wear on his hands and feet. Plus those shallow depressions on his shoulders, where he was likely carrying something on a regular basis. Also looked like he could have had some recent injuries to his hands. Maybe been in a fight. Teeth looked OK— like he might have had braces and good care growing up. But no signs of recent work. Although it doesn't sound like he needed it. He broke an arm as a kid. That healed up fine. And it looks like his nose might have been broken once or twice in the past few years."

Kate looked at the sheet wondering if any of the thumbnails might resemble Teddy.

"Does he match any of the missing persons reports you've found?" she asked.

"Nope. Closest is some trust-fund type reported missing a few months ago in Boston. But the geography and timing are all wrong. He wasn't reported missing until April. And there's no reason to think he'd have been anywhere near here. Plus, whoever our guy was, I don't see him as well off."

"You didn't land in Coral Cay until after all this," Ben continued, waving a hand toward the page. "No idea who he might be?"

Kate shook her head, hoping they were wrong about Teddy. Should she ask him? Or was it better to wait until they had some proof?

"I'm going to swing by and show this to Maxi and Peter later," Ben said. "To see if any of these gentlemen might look familiar. And if you want to share them with your buddy Manny, I wouldn't object."

Kate flinched. So much for her stealth investigation skills. "What did Carl say, exactly?" she asked, chagrined.

Ben smiled and plucked two more cookies out of the box, placing one squarely on the desk in front of Kate and palming the second for himself. "That the guy is a right royal pain in the posterior. But he's not bad at his job. Look, I'm not proud. And I have precious little to go on right now," he said, nodding toward the sheet depicting the many faces of Alvin. "So if I can get a few leads, at this point I don't care where they come from."

Chapter 34

As soon as Kate got back to the bakery, she picked up the phone and dialed the flower shop.

"Flowers Maximus, this is Maxi."

"How would you like yet another job?" Kate said. "The bad news is that there's plenty that could go wrong. The good news is I can pay you in cookies."

"Kinda sounds like all my other jobs," Maxi said. "Except for the part about the cookies."

Kate peeked around the corner, eyeing the crowd in the shop. "I need someone to help me carry the doghouse over to Oy and Begorra. I can't exactly deliver it on the bike. And the bakery's been slammed all day, so Sam's got his hands full. I wanted to get this thing over there early. So they'd have it for the start of the party."

"I could use a break. I've been working with flowers all day. You know, between watching the guys stick cameras in the yard. By the way, those carrot cake things were a hit. I think they actually might have prevented war from breaking out."

"Nah, I talked to Ben. I suspect Manny's starting to grow on them."

"The only thing I saw him growing on was Carl's last nerve. So when do you want to move your house? 'Cause I got something I think might help."

"Anytime you have a minute. I figure if I can get it over there early, then I can show up later, after I've locked up and started some of the baking for tomorrow. I'm opening in the morning, so I can't stay late."

"Me either. Parent-teacher conferences at Javie's school. Come to think of it, I might steal a box of cookies for the teacher. My little guy can be kind of a handful."

"You got it. Oh, and Ben gave me a picture of Alvin," Kate whispered into the phone. "What they think he might have looked like. I didn't mention Teddy. I figured you look at it first. If he looks familiar, then we talk to Ben."

"In that case, chica, I'll be right over."

Chapter 35

In the bakery kitchen, Maxi lounged against the counter while Kate leaned in and examined the shiny stainless-steel cart her friend had just wheeled through the back door. It was about three feet high with two shelves—the top one padded with a black rubber mat.

"OK, that is more than slightly brilliant," Kate said, grinning from ear to ear.

"Yeah, I kinda thought so my own self," the florist said.

"And it will actually fit," Kate said, looking back at the doghouse in question. "I don't believe it. How on earth did you come up with this?"

"I use it when I'm putting together some of the really big flower orders. Sometimes for deliveries, too, if they're close enough to walk. Best of all, it means we don't have to wrestle your cookie casa in and out of the Jeep. I even wiped it down good so it would be shiny and super clean."

"I love this," Kate said. "Where can I get one for the bakery?"

"Hey, I can hook you up with my supplier. He'll be happy to sell you one."

"I'm going to take you up on that," Kate said, marveling at the contraption. "So why didn't you tell me the resorts were cutting back on their orders?"

Maxi frowned. "Corizon, it's just a little blip. Business goes up, and sometimes it goes down. You're already helping me with Alvin. And so is Ben. And Manny. But the flower shop? That's my thing. It's like my garden. I may have to water and weed and plant. But if I care for it—watch over it—it'll blossom again. It won't always be perfect all the time. But I'll have a super beautiful garden."

Kate paused, torn. She wanted to help. But she didn't want to push.

"OK, that's fair," she said finally. "So tell me about Pirate Night Dinners."

Maxi shook her head. "Ay, to me, the best part of the festival. Although the parade is pretty good, too."

"I heard you were supposed to host this year."

Maxi smiled ruefully. "I know it sounds kinda silly now. Especially with Alvin and everything. But I was really looking forward to it."

"Well, Sam and I wanted to know if you'd like to borrow the Cookie House?"

Maxi looked up hopefully. "It's a lot of work. You don't know what you're getting into."

"So show me," Kate said, smiling. "It's my first festival. Besides, you're hosting. I'm just helping. And don't forget, I used to work in restaurants."

Maxi's face bloomed. "Except for a few feet and a fence, it's almost the same location. All of the advantages without any of the Alvin problems."

"Actually, this might be better," Kate said. "It'll be a lot less work with the two of us than it would be for you alone. And if we have a big group of people over here, we can kind of keep an eye on your place, too."

"The best part is the hosting business brings dinner and does all the cleaning up," Maxi said excitedly. "And we all take turns. Everyone does a different night. Although, the first night is a barbecue. You know, to kick off the festival."

"So who decides who's cooking which night?" Kate asked.

"Officially, the Coral Cay downtown business group. Unofficially, Barb. She keeps the list and organizes everybody. Sometimes we have too many volunteers. Sometimes not enough. But La Presidenta makes sure it comes out OK. Even if she has to twist a few arms to do it. And she makes a great pot of chili, too. Picante y delicioso."

"What about tables and chairs and linens?" Kate asked.

"Our business owners group pays for that. Barb rents them from a service. Kinda like you do for a wedding. Are you sure you want to do this? Sam is gonna hate it."

"It was Sam's idea. Well, him and half of Coral Cay."

"Yeah, 'cause the other half thinks I planted Alvin," the florist said lightly.

"They do not," Kate said, giggling. "But they might believe you already have too much on your plate."

Maxi beamed. "Well, then please tell all of them *muchísimas gracias!*"

Chapter 36

Kate and Maxi carefully maneuvered the cart—with a large box on top covering its precious cargo—through the front door of Oy and Begorra.

While it was late afternoon, well before the dinner rush, the pub still enjoyed a smattering of customers. Mostly tourist families grabbing a hearty lunch.

"Hey, guys!" Andy Levy called from across the gleaming wood bar. "Is that what I think it is?"

"If you mean, is it a super large doghouse made of cookies, then, yes," Maxi said.

"We also brought a few dozen of some of the other varieties, for the party," Kate added, pointing to the white bakery boxes stacked on the lower shelf of the cart.

"Ex-cell-an-tay. Bridget's in the back getting things set up now. And thanks for the balloons," he said to Maxi.

"*De nada*. It's not a party without balloons."

"True," Andy agreed, nodding. "And this party's gonna be great. Doctor Jack won't know what hit him.

Hey, you wanna hear something cool? Those key lime tarts are totally on fire. We're sold out again. Any chance we might be able to get a few more?"

"We're fresh out now, but I'm baking more tonight," Kate said. "I can drop some off tomorrow morning after I take the rolls over to Sunny's studio. Will that work?"

"Oh yeah! We just need them for the lunch crowd. And probably the dinner crowd."

"So what's this Dr. Scanlon like?" Maxi said. "I haven't met him yet."

"He eats a lot of his meals here. Mostly, takeout though, 'cause he's getting his clinic set up. I know he's crazy for Bridget's Irish stew sandwiches, he's from Denver, he likes to ski, and he loves the ocean. So far, that's about it."

"I hope he likes to water ski, 'cause there's not much snow around here," Maxi said.

"I kinda got the impression he's not a big fan of frozen winters," Andy said, lowering his voice. "Oh, and Sunny's trying to recruit him to take a yoga class."

"Sunny's trying to recruit everybody to take a yoga class," Maxi said. "No news there."

Kate nodded. "When he was in Coral Cay last month house hunting, he mentioned he was really looking forward to a little beach weather. Speaking of coming here to escape the cold weather, do you remember Amos's nephew, Teddy?"

"He bought the old Henderson place!" Andy said suddenly, snapping his fingers.

"Teddy?" Kate and Maxi asked in unison.

"Doctor Jack," Andy replied. "Hey, whatever happened to Teddy? Wasn't he gonna move here?"

"That's what everybody thought," Maxi said, sliding an eye toward Kate.

"Do you remember his last name?"

"I thought it was Tully," Andy said. "I remember Amos said, 'Meet my nephew Teddy,' and we shook hands. Maybe I just sorta filled in the blanks. Man, that guy could eat. He used to come in here and put away two meals in one sitting. Wonder where he got to?"

"Oh, I heard he just went back home," Kate said, vaguely. "Now, where can we set up this doghouse?"

"So where's this picture of Alvin?" Maxi said, as the two of them walked back down Main Street.

Kate swung the backpack off her shoulders and retrieved a manila folder. She carefully extracted a sheet and passed it to Maxi. "They don't know about hair and eye color—or hairstyle, either," she explained. "So they kind of guess and draw a few different versions."

The florist gripped the photocopy in both hands, studying the illustrations.

"Do any of them look like Teddy?"

"I don't know," Maxi said, shaking her head. "This one could be him, if the face was a little fuller. Plus Teddy has a beard and a mustache. And his hair is kinda shaggy. It's hard to tell."

"Ben said that Alvin had a broken arm, probably as a child. And he'd had his nose broken in the past few years. Also that he did a lot of walking. Would any of that fit?"

"I don't know about the broken stuff, but I remember he didn't have a car. He walked everywhere, kinda like we all do. And I was standing in front of Amos's store when he arrived in Coral Cay. He climbed out of a taxi."

"Amos is going to be at the party tonight," Kate said. "Maybe we can casually ask him about Teddy."

"'Casually' means we can say, 'Hey, have you heard from Teddy—what's that scamp up to?' Maxi said, shaking her head. "Not 'Has someone ever poked him in the nose—and can you show us some nice X-rays?'"

"I realize that, believe me. Ben already knew I was getting these pictures for Manny."

"What did he say?" Maxi asked.

"Believe it or not, he's glad for the help. It sounds like they've hit a real dead end."

Maxi suddenly froze.

"What is it?" Kate asked.

"When Teddy got out of the taxi? He had a bag kinda like that one," she said, pointing to Kate's black backpack. Only it had the big metal rack on it that hooked around his shoulders."

"Oh geez," Kate said, feeling a familiar knot in her stomach.

"When Ben came to see us, he talked about those little dents in Alvin's shoulders," Maxi recalled, eyes widening. "Ben thought it might be because Alvin carried something super heavy for work. But what if it was from all the time lugging around a super big backpack?"

Chapter 37

Later that evening, just half a block from the pub, Kate stopped short and took a deep breath. For some reason, she felt like she'd been running—and running late—all day. And this was exactly the mindset she'd wanted to leave behind in Manhattan.

Moving to Coral Cay, she'd vowed to live in the now. She slowed to a stroll and soaked up the scene around her. Jasmine and salt brine on a stiff breeze off the bay promised rain before sunrise.

Just before the cool of the evening, tourists ambled down both sides of the street—a number of them carrying ice-cream cones or boxes of colorful saltwater taffy. Many of the locals, she suspected, were already packed into Oy and Begorra.

She hadn't seen Manny staking out their block when she'd locked up at the bakery. It was possible he could keep tabs remotely now that Carl's cameras were in place. Or maybe he'd show up later tonight. Hopefully with John Quincy in tow.

For his part, Oliver was spending the night with Maxi and her family. The florist had given the pup a ride when she'd gone home to change earlier.

"Mr. Oliver travels light," her friend had reported by phone. "Just grabbed his purple disc thing and hopped in the Jeep."

From the sound of it, Michael, Javie, and Elena had been overjoyed at the prospect of their furry four-footed overnight guest.

Kate lingered in front of As Time Goes By. It seemed the antiques dealers weren't immune to pirate fever, either. In one window, a black pirate hat rested next to an antique spyglass. In front of them, a heavy gold-chain necklace spilled out of a palm-sized wooden treasure chest, along with a lovely long strand of pearls. A man's gold signet ring rested, as if tossed casually, next to it.

The pirate hat reminded her of tricorn cookies she'd made with jam filling. And it gave her an idea.

She pulled a tiny notepad out of her purse, and smiled as she sketched the hat. Satisfied, she tucked the pad into her purse, took one last look at the display, and strolled down the block.

Minutes later, as Kate pushed open the pub door, she could barely hear over the steady thrum of conversation, punctuated by laughter. While diners polished off their dinners in one half of the pub, the other side—centered around a polished oak bar with gleaming brass fixtures—played host to the gathering that included most of the downtown business owners of Coral Cay.

Maxi's banner of red balloons arched over the bar. Beneath that hung a yellow sign proclaiming WELCOME DR. JACK SCANLON in big red letters.

Kate took two steps and ran smack into Evan Thorpe.

"Hey, we were wondering when you'd arrive," he said, leaning over and giving her a quick peck on the cheek.

"Can I get you a glass of champagne or some lemonade? They've got a big pitcher of the stuff next to your dog-house."

"No thanks, I'm just going to circulate a little first," she said, heading to where Maxi was chatting with Annie Kim and Rosie and Andre Armand.

"Corizon, you look *muy bonita*," Maxi said happily, a champagne flute in her hand.

"So do you," Kate replied. "I love that sundress. And you two look great."

"Yeah, we Coral Cay girls clean up nice," Annie said grinning.

"I saw the big old mosquito take a nip," Maxi said, nodding her head in Evan's direction. "Say the word, and I'll swat him with a rolled up newspaper."

"I honestly believe that boy has been lurking by the front door since this thing started," Rosie drawled, taking a sip from her glass. "Now at least we know why."

"So where's the man of the hour?" Kate asked, eager to change the subject.

"Missing," said Annie.

"He had an emergency at the clinic," Maxi said. "Not even open yet, and he's already making like a doctor and saving lives."

"Gosh, I hope nobody's hurt," Kate said.

"One of Delores Philpott's cats is having kittens," the florist explained. "I gave Delores a ride into town. And we almost didn't make it. That little tabby nearly gave birth in the back of my Jeep. No telling what Mr. Oliver's gonna think of that the next time he hitches a ride."

"Look out, she'll be trying to find good homes for all of them," Annie warned, teasingly.

"Not at my house, she's not. I love the little things, but mi amor is allergic. And so is Miguelito. Besides, thanks to Delores, I think we've exceeded the maximum cat capacity on our block."

"What do you think, Rosie? A little tabby to keep us company at the shop?" Andre asked lightly.

Rosie tilted her head. "That's not a bad idea," she said smiling. "So how's Oliver? I saw him trotting down Main Street today looking very full of himself."

"He's spending the evening with mi niños," Maxi replied. "When I left, they were tearing around the backyard like wild things."

Kate sensed something and glanced across the room. Harper Duval was staring at her. He raised his glass.

She nodded and looked quickly back to Maxi.

"Well, you'll be happy to know that Oliver came by the pharmacy on his own this morning," Annie said. "Seriously, I wish all my customers were that good with their meds."

"Maybe if human medicine tasted like food . . ." Kate started.

"Tell me about it," the pharmacist agreed, smiling.

"It should taste like cookies," Maxi said. "Then they'd be lining up around the block, just like they are at the Cookie House."

"And how is your wonderful contest progressing?" Andre asked. "I myself may have added a suggestion to your jar. Buttery madeleines like my dear *grand-mère*, my grandmother, used to make. Dipped in the richest dark *chocolat*."

"Oh, that sounds wonderful," Kate said. "If we don't select them for the contest, I'd like to make them anyway."

"I heard from Mitzy that you guys actually had a fight break out over those icebox cookies," Annie said.

"It wasn't a fight exactly," Kate said. "More of a very spirited disagreement between two true aficionados."

"That's a fight," Rosie said, laughing.

"But it is good news for the bakery, no?" Andre asked.

"Very good. Sam's pretty pleased with the way things are going. And so am I. Hey, there's Amos. Maxi, do you want to come with me to say 'hi'?"

"Admit it, you just want me around to swat that big mosquito," her friend replied.

"You're not wrong," Kate admitted.

"That doghouse of yours is really something," Amos said between sips of lemonade. "A pup could almost move right in. 'Course, nobody knows what it tastes like. Don't want to touch it 'til Doc Scanlon arrives. Where is he, anyway? Late for his own party? That's not good."

"He had a veterinary emergency," Kate explained.

"So what have you heard from Teddy lately?" Maxi asked out of the blue. "What's he up to these days?"

Amos stopped mid-sip and shrugged. "This and that. The usual, I guess."

"He sounds like a nice guy," Kate said. "I'm sorry I didn't get a chance to meet him the last time he was here. Will he be visiting again over summer break?"

"Boy's got plans for the summer," Amos said. "There's Sam. Got to say hello."

With that he took off across the room.

"Ay, that was weird," Maxi said.

"Him or us?" Kate replied. "He probably thinks I'm angling for a date with his nephew."

"Yeah, corizon, because you don't have nearly enough prospects here already. Your ex and Harp have been circling like sharks ever since you arrived."

"I was kind of hoping that was my imagination," Kate admitted.

Maxi shook her head.

The door banged open, and when Jack Scanlon walked in, a cheer went up from the crowd.

Tall with an athlete's build in a crisp blue dress shirt and jeans, Jack Scanlon could have passed for a tourist. Or a ballplayer. When he grinned, Kate noticed a slight tan and the dimple in his cheek.

"Sorry I'm late to my own party," he announced above the din. "But you'll be happy to know, it's a girl, and a girl, and a girl, and a boy. Mom and kittens are doing fine. And if anyone's looking to adopt, Delores Philpott would love to talk with you."

Andy Levy pumped the veterinarian's hand and guided him to the bar where they'd set up punch, champagne, nibbles, and Kate's doghouse. "Let me get you a drink, Doc. What'll it be—beer, lemonade, champagne, or something else?

"Well, since I'm officially off the clock, I wouldn't say no to a beer, thanks. I can't believe you guys went to all this trouble."

"No trouble, Doc," Bridget said, pouring him a frosty mug. "We're really glad you're here. Just warning you though, Barb is going to want to make a speech."

"I am not," Barb said, laughing. "I'm just going to say welcome to Coral Cay, and I hope you enjoy it here as much as we do. And if you ever need anything, we're all here for you."

"See, that wasn't so bad," Barb declared to Bridget, who slapped the bookstore owner on the shoulder and handed her a glass of beer.

"Wow, is that a gingerbread doghouse?" the vet asked, pointing at the corner of the bar.

"The house is gingerbread, the yard is shortbread," Kate said. "And the decorations are icing and marzipan—so all completely edible."

"Did I mention I missed lunch?" he admitted. "Let's tear into this thing."

"Shouldn't we save it for later?" Evan asked, suddenly appearing at Kate's elbow. "It's a party decoration."

"No, it's party food," Kate corrected. "It's meant to be eaten. Like birthday cake."

"Sounds good to me," Jack said, breaking off a big corner of the yard. "I'm going to start with the short-bread. C'mon, everyone, dig in!"

Evan turned on the 500-watt smile and extended his hand. "I'm Evan Thorpe."

"Jack Scanlon," the vet said, shrugging, as he put his beer on the bar and offered a strong hand in return. "You live here in town?"

"Just getting settled. I'm with the Thorpe Family Foundation. We're funding a historical project in Coral Cay. And Kate here's my . . ."

"Ex-girlfriend," Maxi interjected. "Longtime ex. She dumped him."

Evan's mouth fell open. He recovered almost instantly. But his eyes were hard. And the smile had vanished. "I see someone I really must speak with," he said stiffly.

"Nice to meet you," Jack called after him, nonplussed. "See you around town."

"Did I say that out loud?" Maxi asked Kate under her breath. "Ay. I really shouldn't drink champagne on an empty stomach."

"You promised to swat the mosquitos," Kate said softly. "And I think you did great."

"Some shindig, no?" Gabe Louden said. "'If more of us valued food and cheer and song above hoarded gold, it would be a merrier world.' 'Course Tolkien never tasted gold doubloons. Those things are first-rate. I want a heads-up when they hit the shelves."

"I told you the man loved biscuits," Claire said.

"I'm waiting until I have the chocolate ones to go with them," Kate said. "And I'm still perfecting that recipe. When it's closer along, you guys can be my taste-testers, if you're up for it."

"Brilliant! I always fancy a little chocolate," Claire said. "So how are you enjoying the saga of the Blys?"

"It's fascinating. Every time I uncover a little corner, I realize how much more I want to learn."

"I know," Claire said. "I so wish you could see their home. Some of the pieces they've collected are truly amazing. But the stories that go with them are even better."

"You had mentioned the portrait of Sir George—the one in the side room?" Kate said.

Claire nodded.

"I'd love to see what he actually looked like," Kate continued. "His brother, Henry, too, if there's one of him. Do you think someone there might be willing to email photos of their portraits?"

"That's a splendid idea! Nothing brings it home like a few snaps. And if we're searching for Gentleman George, we should have his picture. Sophie lives on the estate. I'll contact her straightaway."

"Do you think the family would be all right with that?" Kate asked.

"I don't see why not," Claire said emphatically. "That's why people of the period dressed to the nines and paid a positive fortune to have the best artists come and paint them. The likeness was meant to be shared. And, of course, it was also a bit of showing off."

"Tudor selfie," Gabe summarized.

"Quite," Claire agreed.

Minutes later, Kate sidled up to Sam and Amos. Abruptly, the grocer excused himself to refill his glass.

"Do you know anything about Teddy?" she asked. "Teddy Tully?"

"Don't think his name's Tully," Sam said. "He's Amos's sister's boy. Don't remember his surname, though. Don't know that I ever heard it."

"Just 'Teddy,'" Kate said, resigned.

Sam nodded.

"Any idea where he lives?"

"Family's from Vermont. Don't know where Teddy settled. Thought he was gonna move here."

"So did everyone else. Everyone except Teddy, apparently."

"Probably just as well," the baker said. "Boy's got wanderlust. Could see it in him. Didn't shy away from a fight, either. Told me he was a bouncer. One of those clubs in Atlanta. Before he came here."

"He didn't happen to mention breaking his nose, did he?" Kate asked, holding her breath.

"Yup. Said he zigged when he shoulda zagged. Lucky punch."

Chapter 38

Her morning baking done, Kate poured a cup of coffee, added a little cream, and headed out to the front porch of the Cookie House. The sun was just coming up, and the sky was a watercolor wash of pink, orange, and blue.

Stepping outside from the warm bakery, she shivered in the cool morning air. The grass was still damp with dew and last night's rain. Small birds of different colors hopped across the lawn. The purple, pink, and white flowers in their yard, which Maxi had planted and tended so carefully, had enjoyed a nice long drink, she mused. Everything looked fresh and new. Clean.

She looked up to see something low and fast barreling down the sidewalk on Main Street. An oatmeal-colored streak.

She set her coffee on the bench and jogged down the walkway. Oliver paused at the street, flipped his head quickly to and fro, then charged across.

The half-grown pup had built up so much momentum that when they collided he very nearly knocked her over.

"I missed you too," she said, scratching behind his ears and ruffling his hair, as he put his paws on her legs and looked up at her with big saucer-like eyes. "I know you were really taking care of Maxi's family. But I'm so glad you're back."

She knelt down and rubbed the puppy's back, and when he rolled over, she patted his pink tummy and gave it a good long scratch. Kate patted his side and smoothed the fluffy hair on his head, before finally standing. "Come on, little guy. Time to get us both some breakfast. Then you can come with me on my bike deliveries."

As they walked into the bakery, the phone rang.

Kate grabbed the handset from the kitchen wall. "The Cookie House, this is Kate."

"I've got some news on Teddy," Maxi said.

"Me too. But it's not the kind of thing I should share on the phone. You want to stop by?"

"Ay, I'm still at home. I've got to meet with Javie's teacher this morning. But first I have to find Mr. Oliver. He was just here. Now he's disappeared—poof! It's like he's the little bunny in the magician's hat."

"He's over here—running around in the backyard."

"I thought he got enough of that last night," she said, laughing.

"Hey, how about a couple of key lime tarts for Javie's teacher? I just baked them this morning. They smell great. And Andy Levy says they're on fire."

"I hope that's a good thing," Maxi said. "I need a new dictionary just to understand half of what that boy says. But you got yourself a deal. Put the coffee on—I'll be right over."

Chapter 39

"OK, I can't be my usual lazy self," Maxi said, topping off her coffee mug. "I gotta get out of here soon, 'cause I can't be late to Javie's school."

"Since when have you ever been lazy?" Kate said. "You never stop moving long enough. And why are they having conferences during the summer?"

"Ay, I know. The kids got their room assignments for next year already. So the teachers want to meet the parents, and get them signed up for clubs and room moms and field-trip escorts and stuff. Teachers are super organized. And mi amor has been taking off at dawn lately and coming home late. So he can't go."

"How's everything going there?" Kate asked quietly.

Maxi shrugged.

"You still think he's hiding something?"

"I don't just think it," she said, exhaling. "I know it."

Kate paused, remembering her conversation with Manny. Could Peter be cheating? Or did he know more about Alvin than he was letting on? Somehow, the second option seemed more plausible. But if that was the case, wouldn't the state attorney's office have offered the family more protection? Unless, maybe, there was a secret Peter was keeping from them, as well.

"OK, so what did you discover about Teddy?" Kate asked, hoping that somehow it would cancel out what she learned from Sam.

"Teddy's last name is Randolph," Maxi said, as she pulled up a chair at the kitchen table.

Kate poured cream into her own mug. "How did you learn that? I talked with everyone at that party last night. Even Sam didn't know his last name."

"Annie."

"You're kidding."

"After you left, I was chatting with Annie and Sunny. I mentioned Teddy, and it turns out Annie had filled a prescription for the guy. He was fighting off some kind of bronchitis or something when he first arrived. That was January, and it was still super cold most everywhere else."

"Oh, I remember," Kate said, recalling her last frozen winter in New York, and the banks of gray snow that seemed to line both sides of the street for days at a time.

"So what did you learn?" Maxi asked, setting her coffee mug on the table with a *thunk*.

"I'm really afraid Alvin is Teddy," Kate said. "That's why I didn't want to say anything on the phone. Since you actually knew him."

"Nooo," Maxi said. "Why do you think it's him?"

"Remember how Ben said Alvin had broken his nose sometime in the last few years?"

Maxi nodded.

"Well, Sam remembered that Teddy worked as a bouncer. And that he'd gotten his nose broken on the job."

"Dios mio, what are we going to tell Amos?"

"I've been weighing that one, too. And I think we take the information to Ben. It's not much, really. More of a possible lead than anything else. But he's got the resources to follow up and find out if it really is Teddy. Because it's also possible that Teddy's safe and sound somewhere else."

"That would be really good," Maxi said hopefully.

"Now that you've given us Teddy's last name, I think I know how we can find out where he is. But we'll have to wait until you get back, because we're going to need your computer."

Chapter 40

The bakery had been jammed all morning, as word of the cookie contest had spread. Even the vacationers made a point of stopping by to sample the winners and take a chance that theirs might be the next entry pulled from the oversized yellow cookie jar on the counter.

"That doghouse was a work of art," Rosie Armand said as she stepped up to the counter, after the shop had finally cleared. "Andre was fascinated just trying to figure out how you constructed it and kept it standing."

"Edible duct tape."

"Really?"

"Almost as good," Kate said grinning. "Sugar icing is a wonder. But I always kind of hold my breath when I'm first putting them together. Hey, while you're here, I'll select tomorrow's contest winner. If I have a witness, then everyone knows I'm not cherry-picking them."

"I wouldn't care if you were," Rosie said. "I've tried every one so far, and they're all amazing."

Kate looked up and saw Sam Hepplewhite coming through the front door.

"Thought you might need lunch," he said, holding up a white paper shopping bag from Oy and Begorra. "Special today's lasagna. Got two of 'em. Figure we can eat in the kitchen."

"Sounds great, I'm starving," Kate called over her shoulder, as she handed a wax bag to Rosie, along with two small bakery boxes. "OK, here's the focaccia. And a half dozen of the campout cookies—today's winner thanks to Javie and Michael Más-Buchanan. And I also included a box of those anise and almond ones you like."

"Those are my favorite—thank you!" Rosie said, handing her a twenty. "I'm thinking I just might stop for some of that lasagna for my own self."

After handing Rosie the change, Kate lifted the cookie jar carefully from its spot on the counter, reached in, and gave the entries a good stir. Then she plunged her hand to the very bottom and snagged a three-by-five card.

Unfolding it, she read aloud, "Praline sandies."

"Ooh, my mom makes those," Rosie said. "Pralines are an old New Orleans specialty. Every family has a recipe that uses them in one way or another. My mom makes praline sandies—and hers are wonderful. Little flaky, buttery cookies with a thick layer of caramel over the top. And in the middle, a single candied pecan half. They are scrumptious."

"They sound great," Kate said. "And I'm open to any baking hints you want to share."

"Oh, that's not my recipe," Rosie said, pointing to the paper card in Kate's hand. "I wouldn't dare. Andre is stuffing the ballot box for his grandma's madeleines— but don't tell him I told you."

"So if this is a popular New Orleans treat, that probably means the winner is"—Kate looked down at the paper and flipped it over in her hand to read the back— "Harper Duval."

Chapter 41

With Sam manning the counters, and the first batch of sandies cooling on a rack, Kate decided it was time for a break. From the front porch, she could see Maxi's Jeep in the driveway of the flower shop.

"What say we go for a little visit?" she said to Oliver, who was stretched out on one of the two white benches that flanked the bakery's front door. "I'll take her some campout cookies for Javie, and Michael, and Elena. And you can run around her backyard. But no digging," she warned him, playfully. "Definitely no digging."

Oliver scrambled to his feet, executed his own version of a downward dog, and hopped off the bench. When she returned with a large bakery box just a few minutes later, he held the purple Frisbee softly in his mouth.

As Kate walked through the door of Flowers Maximus, Maxi was on the phone. "OK, so you want two large pirate boots with silver buckles and one pirate ship? Oh sure, I can do that. No problem. No, that's fine. We'll just bill the resort. How about some balloons?"

She turned, saw Kate standing there, pointed to the phone and flashed a thumbs-up. "We can do bunches, or an arch, or singles. Uh-huh, an arch is very festive. Well, if you want it to look like the ocean, we can mix blues and greens. Of course! OK, so I'll add two arches to the order."

Maxi held up a hand to indicate she'd be just a minute. "A pirate treasure, too? Have you got a cake? 'Cause a pirate treasure cake would be exquisite. And I guarantee you, no one's ever had one of those before. Uh-huh. Well, I know a pastry chef who could. Trained at the CIA and just moved here from Manhattan. Beautiful stuff. Mmm-hmm, well, normally yes, but she owes me a favor," Maxi said, winking at Kate. "What's your budget? OK, let me make a call, and I'll get right back to you. And the flowers and balloons will be delivered to the resort the day after tomorrow. Of course, and thank you for calling."

Grinning, Maxi hung up the phone. She scribbled something on a piece of paper and handed it to Kate. "A couple with mucho bucks is celebrating their tenth anniversary. They honeymooned here during the Pirate Festival. So he wants to give her a pirate-themed anniversary costume party. Which means I'm making a big ol' pirate ship out of carnations."

"You got a resort order?"

"I got a resort order," she said happily. "See, my flower garden business is blooming again."

"Sounds like you're going to need a lot more flowers," Kate said.

"Si, but my next stop is the library. If I'm gonna build a giant ship out of flowers, I gotta see what a real pirate ship looks like."

"You already promised him you could do it, no problem," Kate said, grinning.

"I *can* do it no problem. I just gotta see what it is first. Corizon, when you run a shop, you learn on the job. And lesson number one is you never turn away business. Ay, I've been hanging out with the teachers too long."

"So what was the bit about a cake?"

"He needs something that looks like pirate treasure, and he also wanted a big glitzy anniversary cake. So I advised that a treasure cake would be perfect. Naturally, I recommended this New York pastry chef I know. Booked solid, but probably willing to squeeze them in for the right price."

"Are you sure Sunny is the only one descended from a pirate?" Kate said.

"Hey, those guys were all over the Caribbean. You never know."

Kate shook her head, laughing. "So what's the job?"

"A big fancy cake to serve twenty-five people the day after tomorrow. The good news is he's a smart guy and he knows it's a rush job, so he's willing to pay *mucho dinero.* This is his name, cell number, and budget."

Kate looked at the paper and her eyes went wide. "OK, so I'm making a treasure cake. Thank you."

"De nada. Besides, if I gotta work late, you gotta work late."

"I was so worried about the Alvin stuff earlier I forgot to give you the good news," Kate said, presenting the large bakery box. "Javie and Michael won the cookie of the day contest today. This is their prize."

Maxi cautiously opened the lid. Her face lit up. "Campout cookies. This will make my little pirates so happy. But this looks like a lot more than a dozen."

"Don't tell anyone. I gave them a dozen each, and threw in another twelve for Elena. And I might have added a few for you to nibble before you get home. It sounds like parent-teacher conferences are a little stress-ful."

Maxi shook her head and grinned. "You have no idea," she said, reaching in and delicately lifting a cookie out of the box. "When someone tells you you have a bright, energetic little boy—that's code for 'the little imp talks all the time and won't sit still.'"

"Gee, I wonder who he gets that from?" Kate said.

"I know, right? Oh, chocolate. This makes it all bet-ter." She held out the box to Kate, who took one. "So what's this idea you had to find Teddy, like, right now?"

"I thought we'd search for his social media accounts. If we find them—and if he's been posting recently—then we pretty much know Teddy's all right, and Alvin is someone else.

"OK, that's a super smart idea."

"That's just the sugar rush talking."

"*Esta volao*," Maxi said between bites. "I'd forgotten just how good these are."

"May I do the honors?" Kate asked, gesturing at Maxi's desktop computer, set up against the wall on what looked like a small white antique desk.

"If that means I get to sit here and eat cookies, *por supuesto*—of course," Maxi said happily. "Try his Face-book account first. Mi mami loves Facebook. That's how she and her ladies stay in touch—and share pictures of all their grandkids."

Kate seated herself in the desk chair and started typ-ing. "R-a-n-d-o-l-p-h? And I'm going to try Teddy, The-odore, and Edward."

"Theodore A.," Maxi said. "I don't know why, but I'm betting the 'A' stands for Amos."

"Wow, when you set out to get information you really get information."

Maxi smiled.

"Hey, here's something. And the pictures look exactly like you described him. Shaggy dark hair, full beard, and more than a passing resemblance to a teddy bear."

Maxi pulled her chair around so that she could see the screen. "That's him," she said, pointing. "That's Teddy. So when's the last time he put something on his wall?"

"Let me see," Kate said, scanning the page. "Huh, that's weird. All of these posts are old."

"How old?"

Kate scanned the page with her left index finger, while she used the mouse in her right hand to move around the page.

"February," she said finally. "The last post he made was on February fourteenth."

Chapter 42

Maxi's face fell. She dropped the remains of her cookie into the wastepaper basket by her feet. "So what did he say? When he posted?"

"'Something big going down. And no shortage of the Benjamins! More later.'"

Kate stared at the screen. "There's a selfie, too. It looks like it was taken here in Coral Cay. Look," she said, "you can just make out Amos's store in the background."

"So he was here on Valentine's Day, and then nothing," Maxi said dejectedly. "Did anybody respond to his post?"

"A string of heart emojis and a couple of flower emojis. And a couple of thumbs-up signs. And one of an arm making a muscle." Kate shook her head. "The guy has an insane number of friends, though."

"It's not his friends I'm worried about," Maxi said. "Try Twitter. Maybe he gave up Facebook for a while."

Kate typed silently for a couple of minutes. "Here we

go. @TeddyBearDolph. Wow—over twenty thousand followers. Oh, geez. Nothing since February fourteenth."

"What did he say then?" Maxi asked.

"Well, that day he only tweeted twice. The first one says 'send big hearts & good luck 2 ol T-bear—could really use it.' And there's a fingers crossed emoji. Then later, he tweets 'sweet! big changes coming. can't wait. stay tuned . . .'"

Kate shook her head. "That's his last message."

"Any photos?" Maxi asked hopefully.

Kate nodded somberly. "A close-up of a hundred-dollar bill."

Chapter 43

As Kate drizzled caramel over the first batch of sandies, she kept a close eye on the stainless-steel pot on the stove. Candied pecans could go from buttery to burned in no time flat. And another batch of chocolate crinkle cookies was cooling on the rack—just awaiting a last-minute dusting of powdered sugar.

After Twitter and Facebook, the two of them had scoured a host of other social media platforms—everything from Instagram and YouTube to Tumblr and Pinterest. Teddy was active—and outrageously popular—on all of them. But from what they could find, he hadn't posted anything anywhere after Valentine's Day.

Maxi wanted to march straight over to the Coral Cay police station the very minute they discovered that Teddy Randolph had disappeared from social media the same day he disappeared from Coral Cay.

Kate reasoned that they could give it a few more hours. And that it might be better to chat with Ben in a less formal setting.

Like a bakery.

She almost didn't care if he took them seriously. She was more worried about Amos. He was obviously close to Teddy.

Kate didn't believe for a minute that the grocer could hurt a fly. But there was clearly something going on there. Otherwise, why did he act so strange every time his nephew's name came up? Had they had a disagreement and parted on bad terms? That would explain why Teddy just took off.

Or, with the description of Alvin now circulating around town, had Amos begun to suspect that maybe something had happened to Teddy?

The phone rang. Kate jumped.

She grabbed a towel, lifted the candied pecans carefully off the stove, and poured the pan's contents onto a baking sheet. She dropped the hot pot into the sink and snatched the phone off the wall.

"The Cookie House, this is Kate."

"Ben's car is coming up the block, and I'm on my way over," Maxi said.

"If you want to steer clear, I can handle this end of it," Kate offered.

"Nope, we're in this together. Besides, I want to hear what else he's learned about Alvin. Now that I'm pretty sure he's not going to arrest me."

Kate snatched the shaker of powdered sugar and gave the crinkle cookies a generous coating. Then she arranged them on a platter and set the table with three clean mugs, plates, and white paper napkins.

Somehow, she had a feeling that she and Maxi wouldn't be eating.

Her friend walked in the back door at the same moment she heard the shop bell.

"You're just in time," she whispered, as Maxi settled herself at the table.

"Hey, Sam." Kate heard Ben's booming baritone as she slipped the tray of pecans into the oven. "I'm supposed to meet Kate and Maxi to talk about a case. And I'd like to buy a loaf of the sourdough, if you've got any left."

"Think I can find one," Sam replied. "You want that sliced?"

As the men chatted—Kate caught a reference to the Marlins game—she filled the mugs with steaming coffee.

"Corizon, do you know what you're going to say?"

"Pretty much. Keep it simple. This is just a tip. Nothing more."

"What's a tip?" Ben said, appearing at the kitchen door with a large wax-paper bag in one hand.

He removed his Panama hat. "Ladies."

"We already poured you a cup," Maxi said.

"And there are some cookies on the table," Kate added.

"Why do I have the feeling this is a setup?" Ben Abrams said, surveying the neatly laid table with a skeptical eye.

He put his hat and bag on the table, relaxed into a chair, took a sip of coffee, and let out a long sigh. "First time I've had a chance to sit down all day. OK, ladies, shoot. What is it? Because right now, you're both making me very nervous."

"We might have a tip on the identity of Alv . . . I mean, the skeleton from the backyard," Kate said.

"I'm listening," the detective said, reaching for the closest cookie on the platter.

Maxi slid the platter down the table directly in front of him.

"We're afraid it could be Amos's nephew, Teddy," Kate said.

"Oh geez," Ben said, putting down the cookie before it even reached his mouth. "Why do you think that? Is this something Stenkowski came up with?"

"No, Manny had nothing to do with this," Kate said. "We just happened to notice that Teddy left town about the same time you think that skeleton was probably buried. And Teddy Randolph was very active on social media. I mean, he literally has accounts and tons of followers on every platform you can think of—even some of the really obscure ones. But he hasn't posted to any of them since February fourteenth. And Teddy used to work as a bouncer. That's how he broke his nose. He didn't have a car—at least, not recently. So he walked everywhere. And he had one of those big backpacks with a metal rack on the back that he used to haul around his stuff."

"The shoulder grooves," Ben said, nodding. "What's Amos say?"

"Amos thinks Teddy just cleared off. But we're afraid that something might have happened to him."

"Have you learned anything new about Alvin?" Maxi pleaded. "Anything that might mean he's not Teddy?"

"Alvin?"

"Peter refers to the skeleton as Exhibit A," Maxi explained. "Like part of a legal case. So I call him Alvin."

"I like that," Ben said. "More personal. Truth is, I'm taking a second look at the missing guy from Boston. Had a nice chat with one of the detectives there. Money or not, it turns out the guy might be a closer match than we first thought."

"Can you tell us anything?" Kate asked.

"The man who went missing was a trust fund baby. But it turns out he's been living rough for a very long time. No need to go into the details. Suffice it to say, he also had a backpack."

"But I thought you said the timing was wrong. That no one reported him until a couple of months ago?" Kate asked.

"April. That's true. But the man who reported him missing wasn't a friend or a family member. He never even met the guy. He just managed the family trust. They'd had an appointment, and when ol' Joel didn't show up, he felt like he had a fiduciary duty to file a report. Detective said that's the exact phrase the money manager used. Fiduciary duty."

"So he could have easily gone missing a lot earlier," Kate concluded.

"Yup. Thing is, I called the money manager. He thinks the guy was finally getting his act together. And said he'd mentioned wanting to visit a sister in Florida. Manager's new on the account. Didn't know if she lives here or is vacationing here. But he's going to look it up and get me a name and address. So now I've gone from having no possible leads on an ID to having two strong leads. And one of them's from right here in Coral Cay."

Chapter 44

Kate vowed that if she ever did cherry-pick the cookie contest winners, praline sandies would never make the cut. It wasn't that the recipe came from Harper Duval. In fact, the idea of smoothing things over actually seemed like a good idea.

No, it was more because praline sandies involved a lot of very intricate, labor-intensive steps. And, with almost every single one, a knife-edge in timing separated a perfect batch from disaster. Every family in New Orleans might have a recipe for pralines, just as Rosie had said, but Kate was willing to bet they only broke it out for very special occasions.

Still, when she finished the first batch and tasted it, she felt a huge sense of accomplishment. And relief.

The second bite was just as good. Decadent and delicious. And just enough salt in the cookie—and the candied pecan—to complement the caramel.

Sam dubbed them "real good," before taking two more off the plate and disappearing into the shop.

High praise from a man who hadn't even wanted cookies in his bakery.

As she rolled batch number two into the big oven, it hit her that she didn't have that much time to start planning her pirate treasure cake. And Maxi was right. A little reference material really would help.

Time to hit the books.

"Sam, I have to go over to the library for a little while. I need some pictures for that big cake I'm making for the resort party. You want anything?"

"Give my best to Effie," the baker said. "Wouldn't hurt to take her some a' those peanut butter cookies with the chocolate chips. She likes those."

"That's a great idea—thanks. Oh, and the next batch of sandies will be up in about fifteen minutes."

"Yup. Got that. Ask Effie if they have any Westerns I haven't read. Louis L'Amour and the like. She knows."

Kate emptied out her small backpack, and repacked it with a notebook, a couple of pens, and—of course—a box of peanut butter chocolate chip cookies. She zipped the sack, threw it over one shoulder, and looked around for Oliver. But the pup had vanished.

When she sailed through the front door of the bakery, there he was. Sitting patiently on the front porch, the handle of his blue leash in his mouth.

"Admit it, if I wasn't here, you'd be totally fine walking yourself, wouldn't you?"

He looked quickly away, an innocent expression on his face. But the black eyes were full of mischief.

As Kate and Oliver strolled down Main Street, he stopped to sniff various bushes. Some scents elicited an enthusiastic tail wag. Others, just a small wave. And with some, no reaction at all.

As thin clouds trailed high in the turquoise sky, a warm breeze carried the tangy smell of salt—and the beach. Kate marveled at the profusion of colorful flowers, spilling out of the oversized planters that dotted the street.

"Kate! Hullo!"

She turned and saw Claire's smiling face, waving from two stores down.

"Claire, how's it going?"

"Marvelous, thank you. And you're just the person I wanted to see. Well, you and this fuzzy little one," she said, giving Oliver a chuff under the chin. "Sophie emailed those portrait photos. I printed them out, and I'm giving them to everyone in the book club. I've got the stack in the shop, if you want."

"I'd love it, thanks," Kate said, as they all ducked into Wheels. "We were just heading over to the library."

"Well, tell Effie I said hullo. Oh, and tell her we got in that new basket for her bike. All right, check this out," she said, handing Kate a sheet of paper. "Is he a handsome gentleman or what?"

Even in a photo of a flat painting, Sir George Bly seemed to inhabit three dimensions. With a hand on the hilt of his sword, a smile on his lips, and a devilish glint in his eyes, he was poised to leap off the page and into the room.

"You weren't kidding," Kate said, absorbing the dashing figure. "The ladies must have loved him."

"All but the one he was madly in love with. I haven't found much yet. All I know is her name was Jayne. Jayne Bly, the Duchess of Marleigh, after she married his brother."

"Ouch, that had to hurt," Kate said. "Wait a minute, there was a letter from Henry to his wife, Jayne. In the book of family correspondence you lent me."

Claire nodded. "I know. Sounds like they were a real love match. So while poor Sir George was out fighting to save the kingdom on the high seas, Henry wooed and wed the only woman his brother ever loved."

"I wonder if that had anything to do with the estrangement between them."

"I wondered the same thing," Claire said. "But it was Henry who won the fair maiden. You wouldn't think he'd be the one to hold a grudge."

"I know. And at the time of the letter, George was already dead and it sounded like Henry really missed him. I wonder what happened? Jayne married the stay-at-home brother who inherited the estate and the title. Could she have secretly carried a torch for the pirate bad boy?"

Claire laughed. "I'm telling you, it's a sixteenth-century soap opera. And it will pull you right in. Any new clues from your detective chappie?"

Kate startled. For a split second, she thought the bike shop owner meant Ben. And the mystery of Alvin's real identity. Then she realized that Claire was talking about Manny and the search for Sir George Bly's final resting place. Not to mention, his treasure.

Kate shook her head. "Nothing yet. But right now, I think he's just trying to take in the source material and learn the local terrain."

Not exactly a lie, she reasoned.

Come to think of it, where *was* Manny? Kate hadn't seen him in a couple of days. Though Maxi's back garden had been mercifully quiet and prowler-free. She had a feeling that must have been Manny's doing.

A pair of tourists walked into the shop, sporting matching pink camp shirts, white Bermuda shorts, and blue fanny packs. "Is this where you rent a bike?" the man asked.

"It certainly is," Claire said with a bright smile.

"Trike, Harold," the wife said, testily. "I want one of those big three-wheeled trikes. Like the one Marsha has back home. With the flag on the back. I don't want to fall over and crack something."

"We have an excellent selection of those," Claire said. "Are you looking for something to ride down on the beach or more for around town?"

Kate waved goodbye, and she and Oliver were out the door.

The Coral Cay library was built in the Old Florida style. A two-story white wooden structure with a tin roof, it looked like a large home. Set off by itself, the building was rimmed with lush red and pink hibiscus. The expansive rolling lawn even boasted a smattering of coconut palms. Beyond the manicured carpet of green, the land on either side was so wild it might as well have been jungle.

Kate already knew from her neighbors that the long, wide front porch was a favorite spot to host library activities for children and adults alike. And, just as with almost every other business in Coral Cay, a dog bowl full of crystal clear water sat just outside the front door. This one was pink plastic.

"OK, it looks like you're welcome here, too," Kate said to Oliver.

The pup enjoyed a good long drink. Satiated, he licked his chops and walked right in the front door.

Across the library, Kate saw movement. A pretty, petite African American woman of about sixty was fast-walking toward them.

"Uh-oh," Kate said under her breath to Oliver. "Is it possible that welcome only extends as far as the porch?"

When the woman got within range, she bent over and

reached out both hands. "Ol-i-ver," she sang, beaming, as she stroked the fuzzy, wheat-colored flanks. "How's my sweet puppy today?"

Oliver scooted toward her and sat up a little straighter, basking in the attention.

"You must be Kate," the woman said, finally standing. "I'm Effie. Effie Parker."

Kate put out her hand. "Kate McGuire."

"Oh, I know your work," she said, grinning. "Every time Sam comes over here lately, he somehow manages to smuggle me some cookies. Not that he's bragging on you, or anything."

"Which reminds me," Kate said, reaching into her satchel to retrieve the bakery box. "Sam sent these with his compliments."

"Isn't that man a dear," Effie said, taking the box. She flipped up the lid. "Oh, these are my favorites. Salty and sweet. A glass of milk, a few of these, and a good book? Heaven.

"Now what brings you here today? Don't tell me that you came all this way just to deliver these? Because, between you and me, I need the exercise," she said patting a wide hip and smiling broadly. "You definitely don't."

"I have a pastry research project," Kate said. "I'm supposed to create an anniversary cake that looks like a pirate treasure."

"For the Pirate Festival?"

"Not exactly. The couple who commissioned it honeymooned in Coral Cay. And they love the festival. This year they're celebrating their anniversary with a theme party at one of the resorts. I'm getting the idea they want something big and splashy. And I'm looking for a few photos to give me some ideas."

"Oh, this will be fun. I have some beautiful reference

books. We can make color copies of anything you want from those. And I also have some history books that you can check out and take with you."

Effie Parker's hands flew when she spoke. Oliver watched, mesmerized, as the women chatted.

"That sounds perfect," Kate said, relieved. "Thank you. This library is beautiful. I've only been in town a few months, and I'm still getting settled. This is my first trip."

"We'll get you all signed up for a library card, then. You're from Manhattan, I understand?"

"Yes, I am," Kate said, surprised.

"Ah, they have some wonderful libraries there. Some good book stores, too," the librarian said with a wink.

"They really do. Oh, and before I forget. Claire asked me to tell you that the basket for your bicycle arrived. And Sam wanted to know if you might have any Westerns that he hasn't read?"

Effie Parker smiled widely. "That is good news about the basket. And don't worry. I'd never let you leave here without a couple of good Westerns. I swear, that man gobbles them down like peanuts."

An hour later, armed with a stack of books and a folder full of color copies, Kate carefully packed up her sack. Oliver, who had been plied with treats, dozed at her feet.

"These are for Sam," Effie said, appearing with three spotless paperbacks. "Thought they'd be right up his alley, so I put them on hold for him. Is it true you're working on the project to find Sir George Bly?"

"Yes, but right now it's just at the research stage. Do you have anything in the library that would give us some background on him or the Bly family?"

"Actually, yes. We have some very old books in the permanent collection. Nothing contemporaneous, obviously. But a few things from the late 1800s and early

1900s that mention Gentleman George and some of the legends. I haven't been through it all. Let me take a look and see what I can find that might be useful. It's too bad Caroline's not in town these days. She has quite a few books on the local pirate legends. Well, she loves books, period. She and her husband both."

"To be honest, I'm kind of more interested in Sir George's personal story," Kate confessed. "I think there might have been some kind of a love triangle between him and his brother, Henry, and the woman Henry later married. Jayne was her first name. Spelled with a 'y.'"

"Oh, you are hooked," the librarian said, obviously delighted. "I'm just happy you're more interested in the history than that mythical treasure. Although I do understand that the legend of Gentleman George's hoard does bring people to our island."

"Actually, there's something you might want to see," Kate said, reaching for her backpack. She pulled out a file, opened it, and handed the top sheet of paper to Effie Parker. "This is Sir George Bly. It's a portrait that hangs in Marleigh Hall. Claire had seen it when she was there once, and she asked a friend of hers to take a picture and send it to us."

Effie took the page carefully by the edges and studied it. "My, he's quite the fellow, isn't he? Very charismatic. You can see where he might be able to convince a band of men to climb into a tiny wooden ship and set off into the unknown."

"And this one is his brother, Henry," Kate said, handing her the second page.

The portrait depicted a middle-aged man, fashionably dressed in an opulently furnished private office, holding an open book carefully in both hands—as though the viewer had walked in and surprised him in his study.

The librarian sighed, shaking her head.

"At least he's a reader," Kate noted.

"Yes, although at that time, books were incredibly expensive," Effie said. "Owning them was a status symbol. So he might have just been showing off. Hmm. Very similar features. Older, of course. Not quite as hale and hearty, though. Not as lively."

"And yet Sir George died young, and Henry lived to be a hundred and one or a hundred and two."

Effie shook her head. "Well, I have to admit, now I really want to know a lot more about both of them. And the mysterious Miss Jayne with a 'y.'"

As Kate gathered the rest of her materials, she glanced over at the wall above the copier. Several large framed photos showed groups of people in elegant costumes.

"Oh, that's right, you weren't here then," Effie said, following as Kate walked over to the wall to get a closer look. "That was our last fundraiser. Harper and Caroline used to throw a huge party on Valentine's Day. Those two spared no expense. And we were so grateful, believe you me. Those parties raised a lot of money for this library."

As she spoke, Kate was mesmerized by the colorful costumes. Apparently, the guests had gone all out, too. A man with a cowboy hat, chaps, and a lariat looked like he'd stepped off the MGM lot, circa 1950. His companion was dolled up as a PG version of a Las Vegas showgirl. Standing next to them, dressed as a flapper, was Sunny Eisenberg.

In the center of another photo, Harper Duval had his arm around a tall, beautiful woman. Caroline was a flawless Marie Antoinette, right down to the beauty mark on her cheek—and Harp her unfortunate Louis XVI. They were flanked on either side by people Kate didn't recognize—a saucy parlor maid and Sherlock Holmes. Standing at the very edge of the photo, almost out of the frame, was Teddy Randolph. He was dressed as a French Royal musketeer—complete with cuffed black leather boots fitted with shiny silver buckles.

Chapter 45

The next morning, before the shop opened, Kate grabbed the glass cleaner and wiped down the bakery cases and the countertops. Then she attacked the shop windows.

"You know, if you scrub any harder, you're gonna rub a hole in that glass."

Kate looked up. Manny Stenkowski was standing in the bakery shop. He was wearing a red Hawaiian shirt open over a white T-shirt, khaki board shorts, and his fishing hat.

"Your partner let me in the back door. Can't stay long. Got John Quincy outside. Wasn't sure about bringing him in here. With the old guy and everything."

"Are you hungry? Sam just baked up some cheddar biscuits and I've got some lemonade in the fridge."

"I could eat," he admitted.

"I'll bring everything out to the porch. Just give me a minute to wash up."

"So what's eating you?" Manny asked, grabbing a biscuit from the basket, breaking off half, and placing it in front of John Quincy. The beagle sniffed the offering, then scarfed it down in one bite. He looked up at Manny and wagged his tail.

The P.I. put the other half of the biscuit in front of him.

"What makes you think something's wrong?" Kate asked.

"When my Margot starts scrubbing things like that, it means she's angry. Usually at me."

Kate sighed. "I'm afraid we might have figured out who the skeleton is. And he's family of a friend."

"Aw, geez. I'm sorry."

Kate shook her head. "So how are the cameras in Maxi's yard working? No more prowlers?"

"Yes and no. Cameras are great. Your friend Carl did a first-rate job, even if he is a putz. I've been keeping tabs on the yard at night from the hotel. You know, the part of this island with working Wi-Fi and cell phones."

"Not to mention room service."

"Hey, one of the perks of the job. And when you're up all night watching live feeds in black and white, anything that keeps you awake is a plus. This lemonade is good. Lately, I been drinking coffee by the gallon."

Kate smiled.

"Had a band of would-be treasure hunters last night. Your friend Buchanan is gonna break the news to his wife. Cops have the guys down at the jail now. Same deal as before. Trio of twentysomethings read about it on the Internet. Figured it was an easy score. So they jumped in their truck with a couple of shovels and a dream. Definitely not criminal masterminds. I don't think they're killers, either. Anyway, that covers my nights. During the day, I've been taking a closer look at that yard crew your friend hired."

"The ones who laid the sod?"

Manny nodded.

"When do you sleep?"

"Late afternoons, early evenings. Right now, my body clock's all messed up. Comes with the job. Good news is, I think we can cross them off the list. Company's a family outfit, and they're all squeaky clean. Only staff they added back in February was a son who joined the crew for two weeks when he was home for college break. And that wasn't 'til almost March."

"So we're back to it being someone from Coral Cay."

Manny nodded. He took another biscuit, broke it, and put half in front of John Quincy. "This is your last one."

The beagle looked up at Manny with liquid eyes, as his tail beat a staccato rhythm.

"Hey, I know they're good. But we can't have you getting a paunch."

The P.I. shook his head and grinned. "He's like me that way. Can't say no to the good chow. Anyway, as far as your friend's yard is concerned, I'm recommending we hire a couple of security guards. Low profile, no uniforms, 'cause that just feeds the conspiracy nuts. They think we have something 'to guard,'" the P.I. said, using air quotes. "Basically, you just want someone camped out in the backyard at night to call the cops the minute these idiots show up. We do that a couple a' times, word gets out, and they stop coming. 'Cause the easy score ain't so easy."

Kate smiled. "You make it sound so simple."

"Hey, it ain't rocket science. If it was, I wouldn't be in this business."

Chapter 46

While Sam manned the store, Kate finished her plans for the pirate treasure cake. Getting the shape would require multiple cakes and a little bit of engineering. And the icing work would be intricate.

Once the chocolate sponge cakes were cooling on the racks, she double-checked her sketches and set about mixing up a luscious buttercream frosting.

When she looked up, Ben Abrams was standing in the doorway. "Mind if I come in?" he asked, removing his hat.

"Of course," Kate said, smiling. "Coffee's on the counter, if you like."

"Didn't see Oliver out front," Ben said, pouring himself a mug. "You know where he might be?"

"Probably over at Maxi's. He's been spending a lot of time there recently. Why? Is everything all right?"

"That's a good place for him right now. I guess you heard about the treasure hunters over there last night?"

Kate nodded, as she put some extra muscle into mixing the icing.

"I thought you bakers used the electric appliances," Ben said.

"We do. Every day. But sometimes hand mixing gives me a better feel for the consistency. And for this cake, that's going to be really important."

Ben nodded.

"So why were you asking about Oliver?"

"I was hoping I might borrow him for a little while. I've noticed he has a calming effect on people. I wouldn't mind having you and Maxi on hand, either."

"On hand for what?" Kate asked, puzzled.

"I'm afraid I need to have a little chat with Amos about Teddy," Ben said. "And I thought it might help the guy to have a couple of friendly faces in the room."

Chapter 47

As Ben, Oliver, Maxi, and Kate trooped through the doorway of Amos Tully's market, Maxi shivered.

"I'm not so sure about this," the florist said. "I want to help, but what can I do?"

"This is Ben's show," Kate said softly. "Well, Ben and Oliver. We're just here for moral support."

"Next time I decide to start a side business, please stop me. You hear about those bobos who tried to jump the fence last night?"

Kate nodded.

"Okeydokey, I'll let you know when that special cleanser comes in," Amos said, as he handed a woman her change. "Between you and me, it'll get anything out."

As the customer left the store, Ben stepped forward. "Amos, need to have a quick word. Can we go into the back?

Oliver, Kate noticed, had been glued to Ben's side. It

was almost like the pup knew that he'd been comman-
deered. And he knew who was leading the mission.

Amos Tully's back room wasn't elegantly furnished
like the Kims', but it was neat and tidy. In one corner
were a couple of cozy chairs and two low tables—the
second one supporting a small old-fashioned box-style
TV.

Ben gestured for Amos to sit, and took the chair opposite. Kate and Maxi leaned against the walls, while
Oliver planted himself at the grocer's feet.

Almost instinctively, Amos reached out and stroked
the pup's head. The grocer looked over at Ben and
blinked a couple of times. "So what's all this about?" he
finally said.

"When's the last time you heard from Teddy?" the detective asked gently.

"Why does everyone keep asking about Teddy? I told
you before, he went home."

"No, Amos, he didn't. Do you know where he is right
now?"

Amos shook his head. "Nothing strange about that.
The boy's off doing his own thing."

Ben nodded. "When's the last time you actually saw
him? In person."

"When he left town," Amos said. "Why?"

"I just need to know where he is right now. To rule
out a few things. I wouldn't ask if it weren't important."

"He's off on a job. A good opportunity, too. But I
can't talk about it."

"What kind of opportunity?" Ben asked.

"Can't say," Amos said, clamping his mouth shut,
while rhythmically petting the soft hair on Oliver's back.

"OK, do you remember the date he left Coral Cay?
The exact date?"

Kate exchanged a look with Maxi. She was amazed at the detective's patience.

Amos nodded. "February fourteenth. He came home from that big wingding at Harp and Caroline's place and grabbed his stuff. I called him a taxi."

"Where was he going?" Ben asked quietly.

Amos shrugged, looking away. But he continued patting Oliver's silky flank.

"Amos, I need to know. I wouldn't be here if I didn't."

"Bus station in Hibiscus Springs. He was catching a bus to Orlando."

"What's in Orlando? Why was he going there?"

Amos turned his full attention to Oliver, refusing to meet Ben's eyes.

"OK, let's go another route. On his way out of town, could he have stopped somewhere? To see someone?"

Kate remembered the library photo. Teddy in a musketeer costume.

Amos shook his head. "Cab was late. 'Cause the driver got lost. Teddy had to get going. He was afraid he'd miss his bus."

"What was he wearing when he left?" Kate asked softly.

Amos looked genuinely perplexed. "Same thing he always wore," he snapped. "Jeans and a sweatshirt. Had some kinda raincoat, too."

She remembered the look on Teddy's face in the photo. Embarrassment. Something clicked.

Kate looked over at Ben, a question in her eyes. He nodded.

"Teddy wasn't at the party as a guest, was he?"

Amos shook his head tersely. "'Course not. He was parking cars."

"So the costume was whose idea?" she asked.

"Caroline insisted," Amos said. "All of 'em had to wear costumes. The boy hated it. But that was the job. And he'd agreed."

"When did Caroline ask for help?" Kate pressed.

"Two nights before the party. Calls me and says they need one more kid to park cars. Wants to know if Teddy would help. A hundred, plus whatever he made in tips. Teddy was always looking to pick up extra cash. He said sure."

Ben rubbed his chin. "Amos, I'm worried that skeleton from the backyard of the flower shop could be Teddy."

Amos looked shocked. "That's why you're all here?"

Ben nodded gravely.

Amos's face relaxed. "It's not him."

"I know," Ben said. "That's not what I want, either, but I have to check out every possibility. Since that night, his phone's been off, he hasn't been using social media, and he hasn't touched his bank account."

"No," Amos said emphatically. "I'm not spouting some touchy-feely claptrap. I mean it's not him."

The grocer closed his eyes tight, opened them, and seemed to reach some sort of decision. He stood suddenly and stepped over to an old battered metal filing cabinet next to his chair. Opening the top drawer, he pulled out a file, and handed it off to the detective.

"He was going to the Orlando airport. Flight to Atlanta, then on to San Francisco. From there, he caught a plane to Australia."

Ben opened the file and read the document on top. He flipped the pages. "This is some kind of employment contract."

Amos nodded. "And a non-disclosure agreement, too. Ironclad. All nice and legal. That's why I'm not supposed to yak about it. Teddy signed it that night. Before he left. Asked me to keep a copy for him. It's for one of those big reality TV shows. Teddy's not your skeleton. Teddy's a contestant on *Insanity Island*."

Chapter 48

During the afternoon lull, Sam took a break to run errands. And Kate returned to her anniversary cake. As she picked up the icing bag, the phone rang.

"The Cookie House, this is Kate."

"This is Emily Nelson with The Caullet Group. I'm calling for Kate McGuire."

Celebrity chef and restaurateur Jean-Marie Caullet ran a string of upscale dining spots in New York, Boston, and Provincetown. In an era when a lot of establishments were struggling to keep seats filled and doors open, his places boasted six-month waiting lists. The man had become a synonym for culinary success.

"This is Kate McGuire," she said. "What can I do for you?"

"Well, you can come to work for us."

"Excuse me?"

"Chef Caullet has an opening in his Williamsburg eatery. Ambrosia. He needs a pastry chef. He wants you."

"I'm sorry," Kate said. "I think there must be some mistake. I didn't apply for a job. I mean, I did, but that was at a different restaurant in his group. And it was a couple of years ago."

"Chef Caullet is a big believer in the right person for the right job," Emily said brightly. "Sometimes he keeps a résumé on file for years before he hires someone for a spot. But he recently sampled your desserts at . . . let's see"—she paused—"Soleil. Back in March. Now that he has an opening for a pastry chef, he'd like to offer you the position. Are you interested?"

Kate looked around the bakery. Sunshine flooded the sparkling kitchen, which smelled of chocolate, candied pecans, and fresh-baked bread. The chocolate treasure chest, awaiting its frosting makeover, was ready to go on the counter. And she could just make out the edge of Oliver's purple Frisbee under the kitchen table.

"Please convey my thanks to Chef Caullet for the wonderful opportunity," Kate said, taken aback by just how much she had changed her life in a few short months. "But I've taken another position. I'm now a partner in a bakery in Coral Cay, Florida. And I love it here."

Chapter 49

Andy Levy came through the door of the Cookie House and skidded to a stop. The place was packed.

Kate looked up and recognized the panic in his eyes.

"Hang on a sec," she said to Minette Ivers. "What's up, Andy?"

"Any chance you have some more of those tarts? You'd really be saving my life."

"Sure, how many do you need?"

"A half dozen would do it for now. But a dozen would be great."

"I just took a batch out of the oven, so if you need a few more . . ." Kate started.

"Two dozen."

"No problem. You want to wait in the kitchen? You can grab some coffee, and I'll be right in." To Minette she said, "Now, I've wrapped the focaccia in wax paper. So it will stay nice and fresh until Carl puts it on the grill. And I threw in a few of those icebox cookies you liked."

"I have to hide those," Minette said, giggling. "Otherwise, they're going to disappear like the last batch. Carl swore he didn't know where they went. But he had chocolate on his breath when he said it."

Ten minutes later, she'd finally cleared the shop. Unfortunately, she'd also cleared most of the contents of the cases, too. They'd need another batch of oatmeal cookies, pronto. Along with some icebox cookies. They were perilously low on peanut butter chocolate chip. And the only sandies she had left were in the box she'd earmarked for Harp—his prize for winning the cookie of the day contest.

When she walked into the kitchen, Andy was sitting at the table, sipping coffee and conversing with Oliver, who seemed to be listening intently.

"So that's when I said, 'What the heck.' And now look at us."

"If he ever answers you back, let me know," Kate said.

"I know, right?" Andy said, reaching out to ruffle Oliver's hair. "He'd make a great shrink. Thanks again for the tarts. We have a Brownie troop in there now. Late lunch. Twelve nine-year-old girls. Bridget says a dozen girls that age can never agree on anything. Well, she's wrong. They all wanted key lime tarts. And we only have six left."

"Pastry emergency."

"You know it," he said, checking his wrist. "Oops, that's the Fitbit."

He quickly consulted the other arm. "At this rate, I'll make it back just in time for dessert. A dozen different lunches. 'Hold this, skip that, can I have this on the side?' And all of them ordered exactly the same dessert. How does that even happen?"

"Hot new trend?" Kate suggested lightly.

"On fleek, definitely," Andy said, taking two large

bakery boxes from her hands. "Thanks again," he called, as he went through the door. "And you too, Oliver!"

Kate walked back into the shop to take a quick inventory. Oliver followed her. As she walked around the cases, noting what they'd need and jotting it down, he dogged her every step.

"Woof." A soft bark. Just to get her attention.

The shop bell rang.

Kate looked up. Harp.

On the bright side, he wasn't carrying a bouquet. Decked out in a starched white Oxford cloth shirt, chinos with sharp creases, and leather loafers, the wine shop owner seemed upbeat and relaxed.

She quickly put on her game face. "You may have already heard, but you won the cookie of the day contest. Your prize is a dozen praline sandies. And from what our customers are telling me, they're pretty good. We're actually sold out—your box is the last one in the shop."

"Then it's fortunate I happened by," he said, smiling. "I haven't had sandies in ages. Since my mother used to bake them. A little taste of home. Oh my, you weren't kidding about being sold out. You're like poor Mother Hubbard—the cupboards are nearly bare."

"I'm just restocking now," she admitted. "I've got some of Sam's sourdough in the back. And the sourdough rolls are pretty popular too."

"Sourdough would be lovely, and you don't have to slice it. And that focaccia looks wonderful—I could use one of those. So how comes the progress with Mr. Bones? I heard the local gendarmerie caught a trio of scamps last night?"

"Scamps, yes. But they're probably not responsible for the skeleton."

"Do the police have any idea as to his identity?" Harp asked.

Kate wasn't about to share what Ben told her and Maxi in confidence. Besides, they really didn't know who Alvin was. Not yet.

"Not in the slightest," she said. "Was there anyone you remember who was here in town in February? Someone who just sort of vanished?"

"That would describe every tourist who comes into my shop," Harp said casually. "They all vanish."

"Hey, do you remember Amos's nephew, Teddy?" she asked.

"Not really," Harp said. "I think I saw him around Coral Cay a few times. Shaggy gent, from what I recall."

Kate nodded, as she pulled the focaccia from the case. "He went to your Valentine's Day party."

Harp grinned. "Half of Florida did, apparently. But that evening is a bit of a blur. So much to do behind the scenes. And seriously, what I do recall, I wish I could forget. Caroline was rather displeased that night. It seemed nothing was quite up to her standards. Including me."

"I saw the photos at the library," Kate said. "The party looked spectacular. And everyone was so glamorous. I noticed that Teddy was dressed as a musketeer. I was wondering if you might know where he got his costume?"

"No idea," Harp said. "Everyone supplied their own. And Caroline procured ours. I remember that because I never would have chosen Louis XVI. The Sun King, perhaps. He had much more fun. So how goes the search for Gentleman George?"

"We're plodding along," Kate said, smiling. "It really is a fascinating story."

"That's why I'm here, actually. I fear I was a bit churlish at the book club meeting. And I must admit more than a dollop of that was a certain animosity toward your friend from New York. I wasn't at my best. I'm truly sorry."

Behind the counter, Oliver inched over and stepped on her foot. When Kate looked down, the pup gazed up at her, concern in his dark eyes.

"Anyway," Harp continued breezily, "I'm given to understand that the Gentleman George project is particularly near and dear to our illustrious leader. And Barb does so much for Coral Cay. So I want to volunteer my services to help. Whatever you need."

"That's great news," Kate said, relieved. "And I'm sure Barb will be glad to hear it, too. I was wondering if you might have any books on Sir George or anything that might reference the local pirate legends?"

"Honestly, that was more of my ex's bailiwick. And I wouldn't exactly feel right rifling through her things."

"No, of course not," Kate agreed.

"I'll tell you what," Harp said, snapping his fingers. "Let me look on the bookshelves in our library. That part of the house is community property, so to speak. So she can't very well begrudge me access to that. Especially for such a worthy cause. Besides, Caroline always did appreciate a good treasure hunt."

Chapter 50

Kate had just gotten the first layer of icing onto the treasure chest. The shape was perfect. Now with a layer of what she liked to think of as "primer" in place, she was ready for the fun part.

She retrieved her sketches—as well as some of Effie's photocopies—from the kitchen table.

That's when she heard the shop bell. And prayed it was Sam. She'd gotten the cases restocked, and in between her cake work, she'd even managed to bake up more cookies. But they could use breads. And those were Sam's specialty.

"Hey there, Katie, it's me. And someone out here wants to meet you." Evan.

Kate sighed.

"Don't tell me you had a sudden craving for cookies?" she said, barreling through the shop door.

When she saw Evan, she stopped cold. The man she kept hoping would disappear from her life was standing in the bakery cradling a small, fluffy white and black puppy.

"What are you doing?" Kate asked astonished.

"Hi there, Katie-pie," Evan said, using the puppy's tiny paw to wave at her. "Is he adorable or what? He doesn't have a name yet. I figured that was something for his new lady. At the pound, they're pretty sure he's something called a 'Parson Russell Terrier.'"

"You adopted a dog?"

"Not a dog. A puppy. And this one doesn't hate me. You know, like that other one."

"Oliver. His name is Oliver. And what are you going to do with a dog?"

"It's not for me," he said, turning up the wattage on his smile. "It's for you. A present."

To the puppy he said, "Aren't you?"

Evan held the dog up in front of Kate. "Tell me this isn't the cutest little face you've ever seen."

"Evan, I can't keep a dog. I have a dog. And he's housebroken. Wait a minute," Kate said, as a stray thought struck her brain like a lightning bolt. "How did they get this number? When I applied, I put my cell number on my résumé. But they called the bakery. And there's no way they'd have this number. Or even know I was here. It was you!"

"What was me?" To the puppy he said, "She's crazy, but she loves you. She really does."

"The job offer from Caullet," Kate said, feeling her face go hot. "That was you. Admit it."

"You got a job offer from Chef Caullet? That's great, honey. That's always been your dream."

"Don't call me 'honey.' And it *was* my dream. Before. Now, *this* is my dream."

"Not too late for a mid-course correction," he said, looking around. "Look, the truth is, the Thorpes have spent enough on food and drinks with Caullet to earn a couple of favors. So yes, I cashed one in. For you. To make your dream come true. And I never knew you liked dogs. But now I do. And that other thing is too big for our Manhattan penthouse. Especially with your hours. But this little guy," Evan said, hoisting the puppy up over the counter.

"Our Manhattan penthouse?"

"Yeah, didn't I tell you? I snagged us the top spot in the Excalibur. Got a really sweet deal, too. I already took care of the closing, and we can move in whenever we want."

"I don't want. And what was with telling everyone in town that you were buying a house in Coral Cay?"

"Hey, we can do that too, if we see something we really like. Nothing wrong with having a winter place. Now look at that fat little tummy. Tell me you don't want to give him a good home?"

"Yes, of course I want to give him a good home," Kate said, tearing around the counter and lifting the small creature carefully from Evan's hands. "But I don't want to give you a good home. Not anymore."

Shielding the puppy with her body, she felt the urge to protect him from the world. And especially from Evan Thorpe.

"Look, I don't expect you to understand," she said, lowering her voice so that she didn't scare the furry little bundle in her arms. "But I am happy here. I'm not going back. To Manhattan or to you. So if that's the only reason you're here, you need to go home now."

Chapter 51

"OK, but you gotta admit, this beats flowers," Maxi said, as she sat on the sofa of the flower shop holding the drowsy puppy in her lap. "I mean, it's not like you can refuse delivery or regift him."

Maxi stroked the puppy's pink tummy, and he wriggled happily.

"Score one for Evan." Kate said grimly.

"Where did he get him?"

"Evan said he was from the pound. The truth is, I have no idea."

"OK, maybe we could find him a home," Maxi said. "We could talk to Dr. Scanlon. He could put out the word."

"Actually, that's a great idea. But what do I do with him tonight? I have one night to make a chocolate cake look like a treasure chest. And I have to finish tomorrow's baking. And I'm pretty sure this sweet little thing violates just about every bakery health code there is."

She looked over at the furry little creature and felt her heart melt. "Why does he have to be so cute?"

"It's a trap," Maxi said. "Like babies. Face it, these little ones? They need you to do everything for them. All they've got is cute. And they use it to their advantage. It's their superpower."

Kate sat on the sofa, reached over, and rubbed the puppy's back. He let out a long, contented sigh.

"Look, corizon, the treasure chest thing's my fault," Maxi said, stroking the puppy's head with one finger, as he answered with a soft mewling sound. "I could take him to my house. Just for the night. We can run him to Dr. Scanlon's office in the morning."

"I can't ask you to do that. This isn't your mess, it's mine."

"Hey, it's at least half mine," Maxi said, grinning. "Gimme some credit. Besides, watching mi niños play with a puppy? Best night ever."

Chapter 52

Just as Kate was finishing wiping down the bakery counters, the phone rang.

"The Cookie House, this is Kate."

"Oh my gosh, Katie, how are you?" her sister Jeanine asked.

"Doing great, Jeanine. How are you guys?"

"Oh, you know how it is. I've just been so busy. So very busy. It's not easy having not just one, but two tremendously gifted children. Billy's teachers absolutely insisted that we feed his exploding intellect with a complete slate of educational enrichment during the school break. His little mind is just thirsty for knowledge."

Summer school again. Kate felt for the poor kid. Only in the third grade, and Billy was three for three. On the bright side, if they kept him busy, he had less time to blow things up—which seemed to be his favorite hobby.

"And of course Wendy just got back from violin camp. She's so musical. It just pours out of her."

As if on cue, Kate could hear the screeching start up

in the background. It sounded like a cat yowling on the back fence. How could someone play for two and a half years and never improve?

"She's a natural talent, and it's up to us, as her parents, to help her make the most of it. Of course, that means a lot of sacrifice," Jeanine said, sighing. "You wouldn't know anything about that. But hopefully, someday soon. Right?"

Jeanine was the only person Kate had met who made motherhood sound both awful and inevitable. Admittedly, until recently, none of Kate's close friends even had children. So until she'd met Maxi—and seen a very different approach—she'd all but written it off. But now, Kate had to admit, she saw the appeal.

"Not in the immediate future," Kate said carefully.

"Well, of course. You want to have some time together as a couple first. That's true. I'm just very happy to hear that you and Evan are patching things up. That boy is good for you. And he truly loves you. You know, you're not going to find another one like that."

"I hope not," Kate said lightly.

"Well, no. He's your one and only. Now, I was thinking. For Thanksgiving this year, I'd like to host. Take the heavy lifting off your shoulders. All you two have to do is show up. And we definitely want to invite his folks. It's high time the two families met . . ."

"Jeanine, Evan and I aren't getting back together. We broke up months ago."

"Every couple has spats. Believe me, I know that. But you came to your senses. That's what's important. Dave and I like Evan, Katie. We approve of him."

"Jeanine," Kate said quietly, "what on earth makes you think that we're getting back together?"

"Evan has told me how much he loves you. Do you know he actually cried when you broke off the engagement? He called me on the phone, and he cried. It broke my heart, Katie. Just broke my heart. As a happily married woman, I'm telling you, you'd be a fool to pass up a man who loves you that much. And you are a lot of things, Katie McGuire, but you are no fool. Look, you threw your little tantrum and ran away from home. But he's willing to be the adult in the relationship. He came after you and proved that. Now it's time to be a big girl and come home."

"Jeanine, you're my sister and I love you. But I don't love Evan. We weren't right for each other. And I'm not going to marry him. But if you guys want to come down here for Thanksgiving, that would be wonderful. You can see my bakery, and I'll show you around Coral Cay. And you can meet my friends. I hope you consider it. I'd love to see you all."

"I'm afraid that simply won't be possible," Jeanine said frostily. "And all I can say, Katie, is that you certainly have a lot of growing up to do."

Chapter 53

As Kate put the finishing touches on the treasure chest cake, she glanced at the clock on the stove. Almost two in the morning. Oliver was snoozing under the kitchen table. She could hear the soft snuffle sounds as his fluffy chest moved rhythmically up and down.

In the old days, when Sam ran the place by himself, he'd have just been showing up at the bakery about this time. But between the two of them that evening, they'd managed to whip up enough breads, rolls, and cookies to restock the shop for tomorrow.

She hoped Sam was getting a good night's sleep. He'd earned it. And if the morning's traffic was anything like yesterday's, he was going to need it. As she touched up the chocolate treasure box—as she'd come to think of it—that reminded her that it was past time to bake up more doubloons. And that led her mind right back to Gentleman George. Something was bothering her. But it just wouldn't come.

She leaned over one side of the cake, to even out one

of the "brass" straps on the chest. But she couldn't quite reach the spot. She sighed and turned the cake stand to get a better angle. It would be so much easier if she were ambidextrous.

That's when it hit her.

Kate dropped the icing bag on the counter and reached into the cupboard for her backpack. She lifted out the file folder for the book club project and opened it. The portrait of Gentleman George was right on top.

It was exactly as she remembered. The sumptuous uniform, the devil-may-care grin. But one detail hadn't registered. Until now. It was the pirate's right hand that rested lightly on his sword—a sword that he wore on his right side.

Kate grabbed a clean butter knife from the drawer. She tucked it carefully into her right jeans pocket. Then she tried to draw it out quickly with her right hand. Awkward. And with a long blade, like a sword, it would be even more impossible. But with her left hand, the move was easy.

So if the old pirate wore his scabbard on the right, that could only mean one thing: Gentleman George Bly was left-handed.

She looked at Henry's portrait. The man clutched his book with both hands. And while there was a scattering of objects across the desk, absolutely nothing in the painting gave any indication of whether he wrote with his left hand or his right.

She recalled the cramped writing from his letter to Jayne. She ran upstairs, pulled the correspondence book from her bedside table and opened it carefully, turning pages until she reached Henry's letter.

The small writing, even the ostentatious signature—it all slanted to the left. And there was a telltale smear—where the side of his hand dragged across the ink before it had completely dried. Henry Bly, like his brother George, was left-handed.

Not an earth-shattering discovery, she realized. Not treasure or even history. But a little personal detail. Like she was somehow getting to know the real George Bly across a four-hundred-year divide.

It probably wouldn't rate a thumbtack on Barb's pirate history display board. But Kate felt a spark. Like she understood the old pirate just a little better. And there was one less secret between them.

Chapter 54

The sun was just beginning to climb in the sky, as Kate walked barefoot along the beach. Oliver padded along beside her, his purple Frisbee in his mouth.

The morning air was still cool. A stiff breeze blew in off the Gulf. Just off the shore, seagulls skimmed the waves, plucking morsels from the water for their breakfast.

"If you want to toss a Frisbee, Oliver, this is definitely the place to do it," Kate said, brushing sand from the front of her shorts. "What say we give it a shot?"

The pup dropped his prize in the sand and stood at the ready, vibrating with excitement. Kate flung the disc and watched it sail.

But a flying disc was no match for a flying dog. Time and time again, the poodle mix chased down the toy and snatched it out of midair.

Off in the distance, Kate spotted someone, moving at a good clip on the wet sand. A runner. And something about him seemed familiar.

As he got closer, Kate realized it was Jack Scanlon.

Disc still in his mouth, Oliver reversed course and headed for the vet. The pup ran past him, circled around and dropped the Frisbee at his feet. Then he planted his front paws in the sand and ducked his head. An invitation to play.

"Is it my imagination, or is he actually running rings around me," the vet said, smiling.

"Puppy energy," Kate said. "There's nothing like it."

Jack picked up the disc and let it fly. Oliver was off and running. He neatly snagged his quarry, landing gracefully in the sand.

"He's really good at this," Jack said. "Did you teach him?"

"No, he just started doing it one day. It's possible someone else in town taught him. He's very social."

"I can see that," Jack said, laughing. "But I've never seen a poodle do that—catch a disc. Got to be the golden in him. Great exercise, though. Do you guys come out here every morning?"

"No, I'm still getting settled in," Kate said. "I hate to admit it, but right now there's no such thing as a regular morning. I put in a late night decorating a cake, and this seemed like a good way to shake things up this morning."

"I'm in pretty much the same boat," Jack admitted. "Now that the clinic's open, there's no such thing as an average day. It's always different. But I figured I'd take a little time this morning to enjoy the beach."

"Now you're thinking like a native," Kate said. "One of the first things I learned when I arrived—the tourists have sunburns, the locals don't. They hit the beach in the early mornings or the late evenings. Usually with a hat."

"You do the same thing in the Rockies, believe it or not," he said. "Glare. For me, it's not just about the exercise. Or even the scenery—although this is hard to beat. I need to familiarize myself with the island—and the beaches." He looked over at her, and down at the sand. "Keep a secret?"

"Of course," Kate said, intrigued.

"I didn't relocate just to get away from the frozen winters," he said, cracking a smile. "Although, that was part of it. I'm taking classes in marine biology. I want to lend a hand with some of the local conservation efforts. Helping animals that are displaced or relocated. There are a lot of good people doing some important work here. I want to be part of it. It's why I became a vet."

"And you can't exactly do that from Denver," Kate said softly.

"No, you can't. So how did you end up here? You're a pastry chef from Manhattan. And I hear you pretty much turned that bakery around. And now you own it. But why did you move here in the first place?"

"The town turned the bakery around," Kate protested. "I was just a witness. And Sam wanted someone to share the work, so he made me a partner. *Junior* partner."

"Right. But what brought you here?"

"It wasn't that I didn't like Manhattan. I did. But I didn't like the way I was living there. The only time I saw the sun was on my way to work. And all I did was work. I'd heard so much about Coral Cay. The food. The island. The people."

She recalled the tattered file folder she'd kept for years. With magazine and newspaper clippings. Anything related to the island, the resorts, the restaurants, or the food. Too nerdy? Definitely.

"I wanted to come here on vacation and see it," she continued. "Maybe move here later if it turned out to be everything I believed it was. Then one day I realized that that magical someday vacation was never going to happen. If I ever wanted to see Coral Cay, I was just going to have to drop everything, get in my car, and drive there."

"And you did, and the rest is history," he said, smiling.

"And I did, and my car broke down on Main Street," she countered. "And then the rest is history. So, you know, basically your typical relocation story."

"Somehow, Ms. McGuire, I don't think anything about you is typical," he teased.

In spite of the cool breeze coming in off the water, Kate could feel her face go hot. And she could smell his aftershave. Citrus with a hint of spice. Masculine and warm.

"It's funny I should run into you," Kate said finally. "Maxi and I were planning on dropping by the vet clinic this morning."

"Wellness visit for young Oliver?" he asked.

"Trying to re-home a puppy," Kate said. "A little Parson Russell Terrier. We were wondering if you might know of someone looking for a dog who could give him a good home?"

"How old is the little guy?" Jack said. "And do you know the reason he needs a new home?" The knit of his brow and tone of his voice told Kate she'd touched a nerve.

"No idea how old he is—I'm guessing about three months, maybe. A friend of mine got him at the pound. For a gift. It's kind of a long story."

Jack shook his head. "I always hate to see that. Surprising someone with a living creature as a present. Not a good way to go. Better to get someone a gift certificate to a local shelter. That way, they can go down, meet the cats and dogs themselves—and see if they bond with one. Tell you what, bring the little guy in this afternoon. I can give him a quick exam to make sure he's healthy—on the house. And I can probably give you an idea of just how old he is, too. Then we'll see what we can do about finding him a home. A good home."

"That would be great. I really appreciate it."

"So, if you don't mind my asking, who is this person who's going around gifting animals? Because I wouldn't mind having a friendly chat with them. Just to make sure this doesn't happen again."

"This was just a one-time aberration," Kate said. "And you'd only be wasting your breath. I can guarantee you this is someone who honestly never listens to anyone."

"Yes! Even no two recipes are alike. Remember I said every family has its own way of fixin' pralines?"

Kate nodded.

"One of my cousins puts hot pepper in hers. Just a little, mind you. Gives 'em a kick and takes the edge off the sweet. But that's *her* thing, and nobody else makes 'em like that."

"But the cookies I baked from Harper Duval's recipe," Kate said, "which is really his mother's recipe . . ."

"Look and taste exactly like the ones my mom makes. I mean exactly. Would you mind if I checked out the recipe? I mean, does that violate some kind of baker's code?"

"I think I can make an exception," Kate said smiling. "Besides, now you've got me curious. Come on into the kitchen. You can pour yourself a cup of coffee, and I'll pull the recipe out of my file box."

"At least Harp's come around on the Gentleman George project," Kate said, as Rosie settled into a chair at the bakery's kitchen table. "When he stopped in here yesterday to pick up his contest cookies, he told me he wants to help. He's even going to see if Caroline might have left behind any history books that could be useful."

"I found a little nugget on George my own self," Rosie said, grinning. "Annie is great with genealogy, and she'd gotten a document dump from the area that includes Marleigh Hall. And it is a pile. So we split it up. Anyway, in my stack there was a reference to George Bly's birth year—1559. I realize it's not much. But I'm insanely proud that I found it. I got to make my own little mark on Barb's Gentleman George board."

"Rosie, that's fantastic," Kate said. "And you have every right to be proud. Claire gave me a book of family correspondence that was assembled at Marleigh Hall. In the front there's a family tree. And even that doesn't give his birth year. Or his death year. Just question marks for both. Henry, on the other hand, lived a very well-documented life."

"Hey, I guess that's what happens when you're sailing the high seas," Rosie said. "No time for paperwork."

"OK," Kate said, pulling a three-by-five card from a small white metal recipe box. "Here we go. He actually included a recipe—some of them don't—and this is it. It was on the back of his entry. I recopied it onto this card, so that I have it for the bakery. But I didn't change anything."

Rosie frowned as she scanned the card. "This is it. This is my mother's recipe. Word for word. Ingredients, instructions—everything the same."

Kate paused, perplexed. She worked in food. Similarities in recipes were common. And cooks and chefs bickered constantly—and bitterly—about who developed popular dishes first. Or whose version was superior. But exact matches? Those were rare. And suspicious.

"Could he somehow have gotten it from her?" Kate asked finally.

Rosie laughed out loud. "Sorry, you don't know my mom. If you did, that would be funny. No, she definitely wouldn't share. I've made these with her for years. And I had to practically get down on my knees and beg her for a copy of this. But she finally wrote out the recipes to some of her specialties for me. In a little yellow address book—about yea big," Rosie said, holding her hands about half a foot apart. "It's one of my prized possessions."

"Could she have gotten the recipe from Harp's mother?" Kate asked. "Maybe they knew each other."

"No, Mom got this one from her mother," Rosie said, taking a last glance at the card and handing it back to Kate. "Thanks for letting me look, though. Even if it didn't really answer my question. I guess it's just going to remain one of life's little mysteries."

Chapter 56

When she finally had a break between customers, Kate walked into the kitchen and topped off her coffee. Then she grabbed the phone and dialed the flower shop.

"Flowers Maximus, this is Maxi."

"Good news on a couple of fronts," Kate said. "I finished the treasure chest cake, and it looks awesome. Like something straight out of a pirate legend. I even topped it off with doubloon cookies, foil-wrapped chocolate coins, and a couple of those lollipop rings that resemble rubies—so it looks like there's treasure spilling out of the top. If you want, I can come with you to the resort to help with the party delivery. And I ran into Jack Scanlon this morning. He's willing to give the puppy a wellness check and help us find him a new home."

"The checkup would be a good idea, but I don't think we're going to need to find him a home," Maxi said, yawning.

"Why not? What happened?"

"Here's something I didn't know. Bringing your

family a puppy makes you the best mom ever. Taking that puppy away from them the next morning? Not so much."

"Oh geez," Kate said.

"Peter and I were up all last night talking about it. He fell for the little guy pretty hard, too. And we'd been considering getting the boys a dog for a while. Now that Elena's getting bigger—and she understands the need to be gentle with a little puppy—we think we're ready. So we're keeping him."

"Maxi, that's wonderful! I'm so happy for you. Now Oliver will have a little brother."

"You haven't heard the best part," the florist said. "My little pirates put their heads together on a name. They want to call him George."

Chapter 57

That morning, as a steady stream of customers poured into the Cookie House, Sam worked the counter, while Kate decided it was time to give the kitchen a good scrub. "Cleaning therapy," one of her CIA instructors called it.

So when the phone rang, she was more than ready for a break. She half expected it to be the resort. She just hoped they didn't need pirate cookies to go with the pirate cake. Or that they hadn't cancelled the party altogether.

"The Cookie House, this is Kate."

"Find my heart, and you will spy my treasure."

"Harp?"

"Supposedly the last words of our pirate friend. All oral history, apparently. But that's the line that launched the age-old search for his lost treasure. This particular nugget is from a dusty little tome entitled *Gentleman George's Lost Hoard*. I found a couple of Caroline's books, but this one from the 1890s is particularly illuminating. Apparently, in the early seventeen hundreds, they even turned his story into a drinking song. Performed in only the best establishments, of course."

"Well, of course."

"Anyway, I brought the books over to the shop intending to drop them off at your bakery. But I haven't been able to put a foot out the door all morning. For reasons beyond my comprehension, my store has been deluged with customers."

"I know what you mean. We've been swamped, too."

"Pirate fever, I'm afraid. Anyway, I can't get away. But if you happen to be passing by, you could pick them up."

"Sam's working the counter. As soon as I finish in the kitchen, I can take a break. I'll be over within the hour. While I'm at it, do you need anything for the shop?"

"Two loaves of Sam's sourdough would be lovely. And a few of those sandies, if you have any left."

Kate remembered her visit from Rosie this morning. Should she ask Harp about the recipe? Perhaps that was a question better posed in person. When she could gauge his reaction.

"Don't worry, I think I can find some. See you soon."

Chapter 58

Harper Duval was right. Tourists were out in record numbers. The normal end-of-season push? Or had word of Gentleman George's lost treasure spread more quickly than they'd anticipated?

There were so many people on the sidewalk, it was difficult for her and Oliver to walk side by side. At one point, the dog simply stopped, stood stock-still, and let the crowd flow around him.

At the doorway of In Vino Veritas, the pup hesitated. He looked up at Kate, a question in his eyes.

"Just for a minute, I promise. We have to drop these off," she said softly, balancing the bags of bread on the box of cookies, to reach for the door handle. "Then we're out of here. I promise."

Was it her imagination, or did Oliver look doubtful?

"Honest. Come on."

Harp's shop was, as promised, full of people. But it was still less crowded than the sidewalk out front. Seeing her, the proprietor rushed over and rescued the parcels from her arms.

"This way," he said. "It's a little less crowded toward the back. And I can set you up with a good cup of coffee for your troubles."

Despite the throng, Oliver remained quietly Velcroed to her side.

Harp looked down as he passed an antique china cup to Kate. The aroma gave it away: chicory coffee.

"I'm sorry I don't have any refreshment for the little fellow. I could get him some water, if that might suit."

"Don't worry," Kate said hurriedly. "We're in the middle of his walking time. We'll be out of here in a few minutes."

"Let me just nip into the back and get you those books."

On the floor, Oliver stretched out, relaxed, by her feet. The door opened, and Kate looked up to see Ben Abrams at the front of the store. She waved, and he returned the gesture.

The brawny detective was surprisingly graceful at cutting through the crowd.

"Is it always like this right before the festival?" Kate asked.

"Not like *this*," Ben said. "Pirate fever. Isn't a metal detector available for sale or rent within fifty miles. Your friend Gentleman George made the national news. You know anything about that?"

"No. Why would you think that?" Then it hit her. "Oh no, Evan."

Ben nodded. "Can't prove it. He denies it, of course. But the smarmy smile says otherwise."

"Ben, I'm so sorry. I had no idea."

"Don't apologize. It's not your doing." The police detective shook his head. "That ex of yours is a real piece of work. Just to be on the safe side, we're stepping up patrols past the flower shop, in addition to your friend Manny's security guys. And the CCTV. But if you see anything, even if you're not sure, don't hesitate to phone it in. I'd rather err on the side of caution."

Kate nodded. "Of course. I'll let Sam know, too."

"Good. Hey, is Harp around? I needed to have a quick word."

"In the back, getting me some books. On Gentleman George, ironically."

Ben grinned.

Seconds later, the shop owner appeared, carrying a stack of books. "Some of these are a bit tattered, I'm afraid, but they came that way. And this one on top is the one I was telling you about." He stopped short when he noticed Ben Abrams.

"Harp, I need to speak with Caroline," Ben said quietly. "Do you know how I can reach her?"

"What's this all about, Ben?"

The detective looked around the crowded store. "Maybe we should step into the back."

Harper Duval went still. "All right," he said finally. "This way. Kate's my guest—she comes, too."

Kate felt that familiar knot in her stomach. She didn't really want to be part of the conversation. But she remembered the exchange with Amos. Maybe Harp needed a friendly face there, too.

"Would that be OK?" she asked Ben.

He nodded.

They walked into Harper Duval's back room, which was almost like an extension of his store. Same dark wood, marble counters, and brass fixtures. Same smell of sandalwood and spices. The shop owner slipped a pocket door closed, giving them a modicum of privacy.

But to Kate it felt claustrophobic. Oliver's shoulder, tight to her knee, was comforting.

Ben leaned against one wall, his arms crossed. "Do you know a man named Joel Drummond?" he asked.

"Of course, he was Caroline's brother," Harp said, turning to face him. "Why?"

Ben focused on Harp, softening his tone. "It's possible that the skeleton found behind the flower shop is him. I need to inform your wife and arrange for some tests to prove it one way or the other."

"But it can't be him," Harp said, startled. "Joel died years ago. Like my wife, he had problems with alcohol. But unlike Caroline, he never managed to beat it."

The detective cocked his head to one side. His manner and body language telegraphed "relaxed and friendly." But he was laser-focused on Harp. "Well, a man claiming to be Joel Drummond approached the family's trust fund manager just after the New Year. He said he was on his way to Florida to visit his sister. But when he got back to Boston he wanted to come in, meet with the manager, and reassert his claim to a share of the trust. They scheduled an appointment for April, but Joel never showed."

"So the manager never met him?" Harp asked.

Ben shook his head. "Nope."

"If he had, he'd have discovered that the gentleman was a fraud. And I'm guessing your con man got a very understandable case of cold feet. We've had quite a few 'Joels' pop up over the years. Though none of them has ever been audacious enough to go directly to the trustee. That's a nice touch."

"Either way, we have to rule Joel Drummond in or out. Which means, I need to talk with Caroline."

"You do realize this little maneuver will be the end of my marriage?" Harp said glumly.

"How so?" Ben asked curiously, shifting his weight from the wall.

"Caroline knows her brother is gone," Harp said. "She'll think I cooked up this whole plot in an attempt to force her back to Coral Cay. Back to me. And she'll be so angry that she'll take that opportunity to finalize our divorce. I don't want that.

"I know I've been a bit of a mess lately," the shop owner said, more to Kate than to Ben. "But I have to admit, her attitude—and the speed with which she left— well, my ego took a pummeling. But I've had time for reflection. I'm not blameless in this, either, let me assure you. And I want my wife back. I want my marriage back. And I'm hoping that if I just give her a little time and a little space, she'll come back. On her own. But it has to be her idea. If you do this, if you force the issue, that's it for us. She'll end it."

"We need to find out who this guy is, Harp." Ben's gravel voice sounded tired. Kate could see the fatigue and long hours in the shadows under his eyes. "Whoever he is, we owe him that. And when I talk with Caroline, I'll leave your name out of it. This is on me."

Harp shook his head sadly. "It won't matter. She'll believe that I engineered this. As an attempt to clip her wings. And the more you insist that I had nothing to do with it, the more she'll believe that I did."

"Well, we're at an impasse then," Ben said quietly. "Because I have to do my job."

Harper Duval sighed. "When my wife left for rehab, she took a few suitcases with her. The rest of her things are still at the house. And will remain there until she makes up her mind about us. What if you came by and collected whatever you need to make a DNA comparison? I give you my blanket permission as the homeowner to take whatever you require. That way, you wouldn't have to contact her unless you're positive it's him. And I can guarantee you, whoever that body is, it's not Joel Drummond."

Ben sighed. "Eventually, to confirm his identity officially, we'll need a swab taken directly from Caroline."

"Understandable. And if it does turn out to be Joel, you contact Caroline, break the news, and do what you need to do. But, seeing as how her brother's been gone for at least a decade, I can assure you that won't be necessary. This way, you get to rule out Joel—and I get the chance to save my marriage."

Ben shook his head. Kate could tell he was wrestling with his conscience. "We'd need something of hers that has DNA on it—like a hairbrush or even a hat. And if it comes back a match, Harp, my hands are tied. I'll have to ask her to come back to Coral Cay to make a formal identification. And get an official confirmation from our lab."

"Of course," Harp said, obviously relieved. "And thank you. I'm truly grateful. My lady has at least a dozen hairbrushes. Along with an extensive collection of millinery. Come by anytime, and please take whatever you like."

Chapter 59

As Kate curled up in bed that night in her room on the second story of the Cookie House, Oliver snoozed at her feet.

Treasure hunters or not, she felt safe and secure. Between the police, private security, cameras, and her vicious golden doodle guard dog, there was nothing to fear. Oliver rolled over in his sleep, exposing his pink belly. His legs jerked. Wherever he was, he was running. Still chasing the purple disc? Then he smiled and sighed.

Kate patted his shaggy flank. His hair was silky and clean. She'd given him a thorough brushing when they'd returned from the beach, and the pup had loved it.

She returned to her book. Caroline's book. She marveled at Harp's one-eighty. He'd gone from bon vivant almost-bachelor to worried husband in the course of a few short days.

But breakups did play havoc with the emotions. She knew that was true. And sometimes a little time to think could give you a whole new perspective. In her case, it had given her a whole new life in Coral Cay.

She hadn't seen or heard from Evan since he'd shown up yesterday with little George. Had he finally gotten the message? Or was he just off making mischief somewhere else?

She resumed her reading. Finally she came to the scant phrases that inspired the legend—and the looters. "Mark me well. Find my heart, and you will spy my treasure. Riches beyond imagining."

Kate reread the passage three times. Just as she had with each of the books stacked up on her bedside table. Each retelling of the story was slightly different. Perhaps they had originated from different narrators—the recollections of various members of Sir George's crew. Or, as the legend was told and retold over the years, the storytellers might have embroidered it with their own flourishes.

Likewise, each book had a slightly different take on Sir George Bly's last words. But the gist was the same. Find him, find the treasure.

Suddenly, she remembered something. Rosie learned that Sir George had been born in 1559. Kate reached over and lifted the Bly family book from the table. She opened it to the front and looked for the family tree. She found poor George's entry, with nothing but question marks for his birth and death dates. Then she slid her finger over to the entry for his older brother, Henry.

Lord Henry Bly, Duke of Marleigh, b. 1559–d. 1661

Were the two brothers less than a year apart in age? Or had they actually been twins?

Chapter 60

Kate rolled a rack of cookies out of the oven, as a blanket of heat enveloped the kitchen, along with the smell of cinnamon and orange zest.

The sun was just up, and Oliver was gallivanting around the backyard. Kate planned to join him as soon as she loaded another rack into the big oven.

The Pirate Festival started today. And Kate wanted to be prepared. She'd been baking half the night. Now it was time to get some coffee and stretch her legs. And definitely toss a Frisbee.

Suddenly, the phone rang. Simultaneously, someone pounded on the front door of the shop.

"Delivery!"

"Just a sec!" she called, grabbing the phone from the wall. "The Cookie House, this is Kate."

"The guys with the tables and chairs for the pirate dinners are coming early," Maxi said, breathlessly. "Super early. Their dispatcher just called, and they're gonna be there any minute."

The man pounded on the door. "Hey, delivery here! You want these things or not?"

"They're here," Kate hissed. "Hang on."

She opened the door to a crew of three, one carrying a clipboard, the other two lugging folding tables and stacks of chairs. A big red supply van was parked at the curb.

"Just take them past here, through the kitchen, and out the back door," Kate said, pointing the way, as she reverted to restaurant mode. "We're setting up in the backyard."

She stepped back, and the two men hauled their cargo through the shop toward the kitchen. The first man stepped up and shoved the clipboard at her.

"Just sign here," he insisted.

"After they're set up, and we do a quick count," Kate said. "When you're done, I'll get us all some coffee and fresh pastry. In the meantime, I'll be in the kitchen if you guys need anything."

Picking up the phone she'd hurriedly dropped on the counter, Kate half-expected a dial tone. But instead, she heard her friend's voice. "That's very good, Mr. George. *Eres un perrito tan inteligente!* Yes, you are! A super good boy!"

"What did the super good boy do?"

"He used *el baño* in the yard this morning. And we are very proud of him. Extra treats for Mr. George."

"We're good on the delivery," Kate said. "The guys are here, and they're setting up out back."

"Sorry, corizon, I scheduled all our deliveries for this afternoon. But apparently pirate fever has hit big-time. The dispatcher said they were swamped with orders, and it was now or never. I'll be there in a couple of minutes. But if anybody shows up with a mountain of tablecloths or a big giant tent, just open the door and say 'gracias.'"

"Aye aye, captain," Kate said lightly. "Don't worry about a thing. I've got the coffeepot going and some pastry coming out of the oven. Like Sunny says. 'Just relax and breathe.'"

Chapter 61

By nine, the rest of the deliveries had arrived. And an hour later, the backyard of the Cookie House had been transformed.

As Kate and Maxi put the small flower arrangements on the tables, Carl Ivers and two of his helpers finished stringing lanterns and winding fairy lights around the tent poles.

"We only need the tent top if the weather gets bad," Maxi explained. "Otherwise, you want to eat under the sky. Like the pirates. But the poles are up, just in case. For now, the guys are going to use them for the lights. Then, if we get a rainy evening, we just attach the cover, and we're ready to go. In the meantime, I've got it stashed in my shop."

"That works," Kate said. "So you said the first night's a barbecue," Kate said. "How does that work, exactly?"

"Well, mi amor and a couple of the guys from the firehouse will be working the grills. And everybody brings something good for them to cook up. Veggies, corn on the cob, steaks or burgers or hot dogs. Whatever you like. Last year, somebody brought a pot of soft-shell crabs. Yum! Amos and Harp usually supply the condiments— ketchup and mustard and chutney and stuff. But Carl has this special mayonnaise he likes, so Minette brought a whole tub of it."

"Well, we've got rolls and desserts covered," Kate said, grinning.

"We're all done here," the hardware store owner declared. "Should be good to go tonight."

"How about some iced tea?" Kate asked.

"Love to, but we've got to get back," Carl said, taking off his white painter's cap and mopping his brow. "Because of the festival prep, everybody in town is needing something. And Minette's holding down the fort at the shop."

"Then how about a few cookies for the road?" Kate asked. "I've got some of the chocolate icebox ones she likes."

"You got yourself a deal," he said. "And I'd like to buy a box each for these two."

"No charge," Kate said. "Thanks to you three, this place is officially ready for the pirate festival. Come on into the bakery, you can pick out whatever you like."

A short while later, as Kate shut the industrial oven and headed for the back door, Bridget O'Hanlon stuck her head into the kitchen.

"I brought some stuff for the barbecue. Is it OK if I come through?"

"Of course," Kate said cheerfully. "We're just taking a break and enjoying the atmosphere."

Bridget stepped into the backyard and looked around in wonder as she set a large market bag onto one of the tables. "This is perfect," she said, in a hushed voice. "If you aren't careful, you might get stuck with this permanently."

"I love it," Maxi said dreamily. "I'm just glad someone else does too."

"Hang on, girls, I've got something you might want to try," Kate said, disappearing into the kitchen. She returned a few minutes later with a tray. On it was a pitcher of iced tea, three glasses, and a platter heaped with chocolate-coated cookies.

"Time to celebrate," Kate announced, as she poured the tea.

Maxi absentmindedly picked up one of the cookies. "These look like little pirate hats."

"Exactly," Kate said.

"Oh my gosh, they really do," Bridget said. "How did you do that?"

"Remember the display in Rosie and Andre's window? The one with the pirate hat? It reminded me of an old recipe I used to love making. Tricorn jam cookies."

"Wait a minute, there's jam in these?" Bridget asked.

Kate nodded. "But I needed them to look like pirate hats. So I had to exaggerate the shape just a little. And since everyone thinks pirate hats are black, of course I had to dunk the whole thing in dark chocolate."

"Well, if you absolutely had to," Maxi said, plucking one off the platter. "Oooohhhh, this is good!"

Bridget took a bite and closed her eyes. "It's orange and chocolate and cookie," she said happily.

"I got the idea from Gabe. Remember at the book club dinner? How much he loved Andy's spiked orange pancakes with Andre's melted chocolate sauce? But I made these with a sour-orange marmalade. That way, when I add the bittersweet chocolate, it's not too sweet."

"Yeah, it's got a nice tang," Bridget said, reaching for another.

"They go into the shop today. And you guys are the first ones to taste them."

"So how goes the search for Gentleman George?" Maxi asked. "I've been so busy with pirate nights, I haven't had time to add anything to Barb's board. Or even research anything to add to Barb's board."

Bridget looked down at the ground.

"What is it?" Kate asked. "Is something wrong?"

"Promise not to tell?" Bridget asked, dropping her voice.

"Por supuesto," Maxi said, putting her hand on her heart. "To the grave."

Kate nodded in agreement. "Definitely. What's up?"

"Well, it started when Andy and I called one of the maritime museums in Boston. They'd put on a pirate exhibit a year or so ago. And we wanted to see if there was anything they might be willing to share. Not artifacts, but research. Or stories. Maybe some interesting little tidbits of information. Anything that might shed some light on Gentleman George or what life was like for pirates back then."

Bridget paused. "Barb is gonna hate this," she said finally.

Kate and Maxi looked at one another.

"Barb wants to find the truth," Kate said gently. "Whatever it is."

"She's still gonna be really upset," Bridget said. "One of the curators emailed us some stuff. A few research papers that mention some of the pirates of that era. But nothing about George. Then there was a page from a letter. Most of it you can't even read. It's four hundred years old. And it's in pretty sorry shape. So you can only see a few words here and there. And those are in another language. Latin. It was written by a priest. Or he might have been a monk. I'm not really sure. Anyway, he was aboard one of the ships that Gentleman George and his men raided. And apparently, he survived and wrote all about it in a letter."

"What did he say?"

She shook her head. "From the fragments that survived—and that's not much, believe me, just a few phrases here and there—the guy is clearly not a fan. He calls George Bly 'a sinister swordsman and sailor.'"

"Sinister?" Kate asked, her eyes wide. "Are you sure?"

"That was one of the few parts I could actually understand. The word is the same in English and Latin. So this priest didn't just doubt that George was a gentleman. He thought our pirate founder was evil incarnate."

Chapter 62

Kate glanced over her shoulder into the backyard. Maxi was right. As soon as the tables went up, people started arriving—bringing food, drinks, and gossip. Some were looking to help set up for tonight's barbecue. Others just wanted to escape the crowds—and their shops—for a few minutes to regain their equilibrium.

Kate was afraid Oliver might be upset at losing the yard. But instead, the pup acted as the unofficial greeter—spreading his own special brand of calm. She also noticed that, from time to time, he managed to encourage a few of the kids and teenagers to toss the purple Frisbee around on the front lawn.

For her part, Kate was doing good just to keep up with the crowd that poured into the bakery. At first, she and Sam were taking turns. But after a while, it was all hands on deck. And the customers just kept coming. At this rate, Kate didn't know if they'd even have time to make it to the barbecue. Even if it was just a few feet from the kitchen door.

"Not usually like this," Sam said brusquely, as they passed each other in the kitchen. "It's all that Gentleman George nonsense."

"Yes, but on the plus side, we're sold out of pirate bread, pirate hat cookies, and both flavors of doubloons. Andy and Bridget need more key lime tarts for the pub. And two of the resorts called asking for treasure chest cakes."

"You don't say," the baker replied, cracking a wry smile. "Might just have to go easy on the old salt then."

All afternoon, Kate noticed a certain reverse symmetry between the crowds in the store and the shopkeepers congregating out back. As the bakery emptied out, the backyard would fill up. And vice versa.

Until, by six or so that evening, the backyard of the Cookie House was teeming with familiar faces, while the shop itself was nearly empty. And the bakery cases had been picked clean.

Through the open back door, Kate could smell the familiar mix of charcoal, starter fluid, and meat—the scent of summer—as steaks, burgers, and hot dogs sizzled on a half dozen different grills.

Still, she was surprised to see Sam amble up to the front door, flip the OPEN sign to CLOSED, and turn the deadbolt.

"Out of almost everything anyway," he explained. "Might as well enjoy the party. Besides, it's your first Pirate Festival."

And with that, he disappeared into the kitchen.

As she crossed the backyard, Kate spied Sunny Eisenberg chatting with Mr. and Mrs. Kim.

"So how's your mom, Sunny?" Kate asked. "Will she be here for the festival?"

"I think Mom will be finished bedeviling my brother about the same time the festival and the tourist season wrap up," the yoga instructor cackled. "She'd rather face down a hurricane."

"Your mother is a very smart lady," Leonard Kim said.

"We've been slammed all day," Kate said. "You guys, too?"

Margaret Kim nodded. "They come in wanting pirate this, and pirate that. What they really buy? Sunblock, stomach medicine, aspirin, and earplugs."

"You could wrap them together in a pack and call it the pirate special," Sunny cracked.

"You laugh, but it's true," Leonard Kim said, shaking his head. "And the resorts would love it. One in every room."

"Why earplugs?" Kate asked.

"Why, dear, haven't you heard?" Sunny asked. "Tonight the festival kicks off with fireworks."

"Could I ask you one super big favor?" Maxi asked, as the two of them were refilling pitchers of tea and lemonade in the kitchen.

"Does it involve sunblock, stomach medicine, aspirin, or earplugs?" Kate asked.

"Close. A small puppy and your upstairs room. Peter and mi mami and the kids are on their way, and they're bringing George. We don't want to leave him home alone. Especially when the fireworks start. But it's way too loco for the little guy out there with the grills and the smoke and the people. Do you mind if we settle him upstairs where it's quiet? Peter's bringing the little doggie bed. And Mr. George has been running around all day, so I'm hoping he's going to be sleepy."

"Of course you can. I just heard about the fireworks. Any idea how Oliver will react?"

Maxi shook her glossy bob. "He wasn't here for the

last Pirate Festival. So this is his first one, too. We could ask Dr. Jack."

"That's a great idea," Kate said. "Do you have his phone number?"

"No need, corizon," Maxi said, grinning. "Just like everyone else in Coral Cay, he's out in the backyard. He just arrived."

"I know you probably get this all the time, but could I trouble you for a little professional advice? If it makes it more palatable, I can pay you in bread or cookies."

Jack Scanlon smiled warmly, and Kate could feel herself doing the same.

"I've been paid in everything from skiing lessons to fresh goat cheese," he said. "And, for what it's worth, I'm always available for advice. That's why I became a vet."

"Goat cheese?"

"Little farm outside of Denver. Beautiful place. Bruce, their border collie, needed stitches. Got into it protecting the flock from some mountain cat. Some of the best cheese I've ever tasted."

"Later tonight, the island puts on a fireworks display to kick off the festival," Kate said. "Oliver's never been around fireworks. At least, not that I know of. And George—Maxi's new puppy—he'll be here, too. Anything special we should do?"

"You're in good company," Jack admitted, glancing around the yard, as he swirled the ice cubes in his glass. "I've been getting that question all day. And from what I gather, the pros they have doing this will actually be setting them off from the mainland. Which should help a bit, as far as the noise. I'd keep an eye on the little guys. If they start acting nervous or afraid, take them inside, get them settled in familiar surroundings. With a favorite blanket or toy. Inside closets or bathrooms are good spots—that minimizes the noise. Just be sure to puppy-proof the place first. Get rid of the toilet paper, cleaning products—things they can get into. Oh, and anything with electrical cords. Dogs are like humans—when they get nervous, they like to chew. Then you should be good to go. And if you have any problems, say the word. Barring any emergencies, I should be around. Except for the crowds and the traffic, I have to say, I'm kind of enjoying this whole pirate thing."

"So where's your fiancé tonight?" Mitzy Allen asked, as she balanced a plate loaded down with a hamburger and roasted potatoes in one hand and a glass of iced tea in the other. "Did you guys find a house you like yet?"

"He's not my fiancé anymore," Kate explained patiently. "He's just in town for the Gentleman George project. And I already have a home. I live over the bakeshop."

Mitzy winked conspiratorially. "I get it. But don't tell Sam. I don't know how he'd feel about a couple of newlyweds living over the store." And with that, she waltzed across the yard and pulled up a chair next to Annie Kim.

Maxi appeared at Kate's side wearing a barbecue apron and brandishing a set of stainless-steel tongs. "You OK, corizon? You got a funny look on your face."

"I've been talking to Mitzy Allen . . ."

"That would do it," Maxi said. "Hey, good news. Mi amor is here, and he's grilling up hot dogs. And mi mami brought some of her mango coleslaw. Salty and sweet. You wanna hear something weird, though?"

"Does it involve rumors that Evan and I are secretly married and living over the shop?" Kate asked, shaking her head in wonder.

"It involves Harper Duval," the florist said. "He dropped off a couple of bags of goodies this afternoon, while Sam was here. Stuff for the cookout. And he said he'd be here tonight. But he hasn't shown."

"Maybe the store is swamped. That tourist crowd was pretty intense today."

"Nope. Rosie passed by his store on the way here. It's dark. Closed and locked."

"He's smoking again, I know that," Kate said. "So he's definitely stressed."

"So's mi amor," Maxi admitted. "But instead of smoking, he cleaned out the garage. Totally organized the whole thing."

"Isn't that a good thing?" Kate asked cautiously.

"It's a wonderful thing," Maxi said, sighing. "*Realmente fabuloso.* And I've only been begging him to do it for a whole year. So why am I so freaked out?"

Chapter 63

As the moon rose into the sky, the lanterns and fairy lights seemed to take on a magical glow. The denizens of Coral Cay filed in and out of the yard, but the thrum of conversation, punctuated by laughter, was constant.

"Hey there, Katie, how's it going?"

Kate looked up to see Evan barreling toward her across the yard. Just as suddenly, Oliver was at her side.

"It's OK," she crooned softly to the pup. "Just a minor annoyance. Like sand fleas."

To Evan she said, "We're doing great, thanks. Nearly sold out of everything. Are you enjoying the Pirate Festival?"

He was dressed casually. A spotless white golf shirt and a pair of immaculate jeans. His sunglasses were pushed casually on top of his head. "You know, I really am," he said, amping up the grin. "Did you know they're going to have a boat parade later this week? The Pirate Flotilla. Some of the vessels are really modeled on the old ships. You know, like they used to sail back in the day. But they invite anyone with a boat to join in. And a lot of us will be flying the Jolly Roger, just for the occasion. I was wondering if you might want to join me? We could invite some of our new friends. Break out the good French champagne. I thought they might enjoy it. And it would be fun. You know, in the spirit of old Gentleman George."

"Sorry, but I'm going to be busy," she said breezily, as she passed him heading for the kitchen.

"Doing what?" he called after her.

"Anything but that," she sang out without turning.

As she ducked into the kitchen, she spotted Maxi and Peter in the yard. Whatever was going on at home or with Peter, outwardly the family appeared content.

Esperanza held Elena, who in turn cradled George. Grandmother and granddaughter whispered back and forth. Sharing secrets.

Peter took a bite of something from Maxi's plate, and they both laughed.

When Kate reappeared from the kitchen with a basket of warm challah rolls, she found Manny standing by the back gate. "You OK with one more? Three more, if you count John Quincy and his appetite."

Kate glanced down, and the beagle looked up hopefully. She bent and gave him a friendly scratch behind one ear. He licked her hand politely.

"I was actually supposed to meet your ex," Manny said quietly. "He wanted to talk business. Said he'd be here tonight. You seen him?"

"I know he's somewhere," she said. "Beyond that . . ."

"Got it," Manny said knowingly. "So do I need to buy a ticket or something?"

"Nope, just come on in," Kate said happily. "The more the merrier. And, for what it's worth, this will be going on every night this week. You and John Quincy can come by anytime. It's called 'Pirate Night Dinners.' Apparently, it's a festival tradition. And this first night's a barbecue. So you-know-who might be able to snag himself a nice juicy steak."

John Quincy sniffed the air pointedly and licked his chops.

"Wouldn't mind a little of that my own self."

"Pull up a chair. You're just in time for the fireworks. And if the little one gets skittish, say the word. You can take him upstairs."

"He's fine around loud noises," Manny said. "That was part of his police dog training. As long as he has some good chow in front of him, he'll be just fine."

As Manny made his way toward one of the grilling stations, Kate spotted Claire and Gabe coming toward the fence and waved. "How are the Treasure Island Tours?"

"Wonderful," Claire answered enthusiastically. "And our guests are loving them. But this one was MIA," she said, pointing a thumb at her boyfriend.

"I spent the day answering auto emergencies," Gabe said with a wry smile. "A few overheated engines. A dead battery. One poor fool didn't seem to realize that 'E' on the gas gauge meant 'empty.' And another who got stranded trying to drive his pickup truck onto the beach."

"No," Kate said. "What did you do?"

The mechanic shook his head. "Kyle Hardy called me. The guy was stuck in the sand but good. Worse than that backhoe next door. Took me forever to get him out. Driving on the beach is a kind of jerk move. I hate to say it, but I was glad Kyle Hardy gave him a ticket."

"Wait, what?" Kate asked.

"I still can't fathom why it's actually allowed in some parts of the state," Claire fumed. "It's barbaric."

"At least it's not legal on Coral Cay," the mechanic said. "And we've got the giant signs everywhere to prove it. Kyle took his photo in front of one of them. Actually asked the man to smile. Then he wrote out the ticket. Don't think the driver will be contesting that one."

"What did you mean about a backhoe?" Kate said, frantically trying to rewind the conversation.

"Few months back," Gabe said, shaking his head. "One of the hardest jobs I've ever had. Just next door. Lawn crew was laying sod. They brought in a backhoe to pull out some old stumps and tree roots. Used to leave it on the property every night. Too much work to load it on and off the truck every day. And frankly, who's going to steal a backhoe? But sure enough, one morning they came in and someone had moved the thing. Crew chief believed it was probably teenagers. But in the process of playing with it, they damaged it. One of the treads had slipped off. And it took four of us working in tandem for two solid hours to get it back on. The bard said 'No profit grows where is no pleasure ta'en.' And I truly love what I do. But not that day," the mechanic added mournfully.

"Wait a minute," Kate said suddenly. "They parked a backhoe on the site and just left it there? Did they lock it up or anything?"

"Chain with a flimsy little padlock. Like you'd put on a high school locker. But the lock was long gone when they showed up for work that morning. Luckily, the keys were still there. They kept them under the seat. Can you believe that? Big piece of expensive equipment, and they stick the keys under the seat. I wouldn't do that with a golf cart."

Suddenly, Kate understood exactly why Alvin had been buried on Maxi's property. Not only were the florist and Sam out of town. But with a backhoe, digging a grave would be a piece of cake.

She looked over at the happy Más-Buchanan family, giggling and enjoying the celebration.

Not tonight, she decided. Alvin had kept his secret for months. He could keep it for a little while longer.

A sudden bang, followed by a pop got everyone's attention. Almost everyone looked up, as an orange and yellow explosion lit up the sky.

"Gabe, look, it's started," Claire said, laying a protective hand on his arm.

"Nice one!" he said appreciatively. "Let's go grab a seat."

But Kate's attention was elsewhere. Under the glow of the lanterns, she could see Oliver stretched out lazily in the grass between Michael and Javie.

Nearby, drowsy George dozed blissfully in Elena's lap. And, just as Manny predicted, John Quincy, busy working on a steak, didn't seem to mind the commotion.

That's when Kate noticed that Jack Scanlon was doing the same thing she was. Checking on the animals. She smiled and looked away quickly—up into the night sky.

Chapter 64

Over the next week, the crowds continued to flood into Coral Cay to enjoy the festival. Publicly, the downtown business owners rejoiced, welcoming every last visitor. Privately, many of them just wanted life in Coral Cay to return to normal.

Parking spots were at a premium. And one enterprising group of college students was cashing in by running a shuttle service—using an abandoned mall in Hibiscus Springs and a couple of rental vans.

But interest in the backyard of the flower shop had finally waned. While there had been several more attempts—mostly on one very busy festival night—the trespassers were caught each time and heavily fined. And Manny had been right. That seemed to do the trick.

"Too bad we can't just say we found him, and send everybody home," Maxi said, during a rare coffee break in the kitchen of the Cookie House. "I actually feel sorry for Barb. The Gentleman George project was her idea, and I know this wasn't what she wanted."

"I know," Kate said, as she took a batch of key lime crisps out of her test oven. "Is Ben any closer to figuring out Alvin's real identity?"

"Nope. He got the DNA test back, and Harp was right. It's not a match to Caroline. I was wondering if it meant that maybe they had different daddies. But Peter said it wasn't even close. They don't know who Alvin is. And I'm beginning to wonder if they ever will."

"At least now we know why Alvin was in your yard," Kate said, using a spatula to gently loosen the cookies from the baking sheet. "And that takes some of the heat off of you."

"I can't believe I didn't know about the backhoe," Maxi said.

"Gabe said he felt stupid for not putting two and two together. But, to be fair, the machine wasn't left anywhere near where we found Alvin. It was pretty much right where the crew put it the day before. Gabe and the lawn guys just assumed that whoever tried to swipe the thing wrecked it before they could go anywhere."

"Sounds like they broke it when they were putting it back," Maxi said. "And they had to put it back. If you want to hide a body, you can't leave a big backhoe standing next to it. That's like a neon sign that says, 'Hey, guess what's under here?'"

Kate studied the cookies as she set the sheet on the counter. "The texture is right. And the color is good. Now I just need to see what they taste like. And that's why you're really here. I need an honest opinion."

"Awful, horrible, yucky," Maxi said, grinning. "Sorry, just practicing."

Kate saw motion to her left and looked up. "Andre, come in. Would you like some coffee?"

"Ah, thank you, but no. I cannot stay. I am hoping perhaps you can help me with a small problem?"

"Of course," Kate said, wiping her hands on her bakery apron and turning to face him. "Just tell me what I can do."

"My Rosie is very upset. A book that is very special to her, it has gone missing. We have been through the house everywhere. But it seems it is gone."

"It wasn't about pirates, was it?" Maxi asked. "'Cause this whole island is losing its pirate mind."

Andre shook his head. "No, no, nothing like that. It is not valuable, this book. It is sentimental. And my wife, she is inconsolable."

"Not her mother's recipe book?" Kate breathed.

"Yes," he said, nodding sadly.

"She told me about that—about how much it meant to her. I'm so sorry. How can I help?"

"I know that it seems small. But one recipe that she loved—she said you had a copy? From the contest? I thought perhaps—until we find the book—if she might have that?"

"Of course," Kate said. "I don't have a photocopier. But you can have my recipe card. I can use Harp's entry later to write out another one."

She walked over to the counter and riffled through the small metal box. She pulled out a card and handed it off to him. "I know this isn't much compared to what she's lost. I'm so sorry."

"*Bon*," he said simply. "It is, as they say, better than nothing."

"Just out of curiosity, when's the last time Rosie remembers having the book—or seeing it around?"

"Ah, let me see. Ah, yes. It was just a few days before *la Saint-Valentin*. The day of Saint Valentine. She used it to make a big batch of her mother's famous bonbons. *Magnifique!*"

After he left, Maxi looked at Kate and shook her head.

"I know from the look on your face, there's a story there. Spill. And why is Harp entering Rosie's recipe in the cookie contest?"

"That's what I'd like to know," Kate admitted. "I started to ask him last week. But that's when Ben showed up with the news that Alvin might be Harp's long-lost brother-in-law."

"Yeah, I guess after that, you can't say, 'Oh and by the way, are you stealing cookie recipes?'"

"Pretty much," Kate said, shaking her head. "But that's the part that doesn't make any sense. I mean, it's not like you have to be a good baker to win the contest. You don't even have to have the best recipe. It's a drawing."

"What?" Maxi said. "You've got that look on your face again. The one that means trouble."

"Have you noticed that whatever questions we have lately, all the answers keep coming back to Valentine's Day?"

Chapter 65

"I can't believe the festival is over," Kate said, as she carried a tray with two stacks of cups, a glass carafe of coffee, and a plate of cookies to a table in the backyard of the Cookie House.

In the cool of the morning, some of the shopkeepers had taken to meeting for coffee at the Cookie House. Oliver, who'd just finished a rousing game of catch the disc with Gabe, was stretched out on the grass.

"Like the man says, 'Fish and visitors stink after three days,'" Gabe said, taking a sip from his mug.

"That old Ben Franklin knew a thing or two," Amos said. "It's like family. Happy to see 'em come. And happy to see 'em go home." He clinked cups with Gabe.

Sam grinned, refolding the newspaper in front of him. "Speakin' of family, you heard anything from Teddy?"

"Now you know good and well I can't talk about that. Even if I am very proud of the boy. Very proud."

"Hmm, put a five-spot on Teddy to win *Insanity Island*—got it," Gabe said, rubbing his chin.

"So when they gonna pick up these tables?" Amos asked.

"Today, this afternoon," Kate said.

"Don't let 'em dillydally," the grocer said. "They'll try to charge you for another day."

"Girl knows what she's doing, Amos," Sam said, not even looking up from his paper. "She's a partner in this place."

"I'm just sayin' sometimes people try and take advantage, that's all."

"Hey, guys," Bridget said, from the kitchen door. "Kate, I brought that letter you wanted to see. You know the one I mean?"

"We're having some coffee," Kate said. "Join us. Believe me, we've got plenty."

"I could use a break," Bridget said, pulling out a chair. "We're having a little lull in the breakfast traffic. But it's gonna pick back up again pretty soon."

Kate poured coffee into a mug and handed it over to her. "You guys still haven't . . . um, said anything?"

Bridget shook her head.

"Talk to the guys," Kate said quietly. "They can help."

"You think?" she asked, reaching over to pat Oliver's fluffy back.

"Definitely," Kate said, encouragingly. "Besides, it doesn't make sense with everything else we've been learning about Gentleman George. He seemed to be a pretty decent guy."

"Pirate gossip? Pray tell," Gabe said, palming a cookie from the plate.

"I discovered something about George Bly," Bridget said, wrapping her hands around the cup. "And I don't know how to tell Barb."

"I didn't realize it, but there's a lot about that man to be admired," the mechanic said. "Everyone who worked for him got paid an equal share. And crew membership was strictly voluntary. In those days, that actually made him a pretty decent boss."

Bridget hesitated and put the paper on the table in front of Sam and Amos.

"What's this?" Amos asked.

"A letter. From a monk—or he might have been a priest—Father Alfonso. He was on a ship that George's crew attacked. Afterward, he wrote about it. And he claims George Bly was evil."

Amos picked up the paper, put on his glasses and examined it. He passed it over to Gabe.

"What?" Sam asked.

"I don't read Latin. Or chicken scratch. Man's handwriting is worse than Doc Patel's."

Gabe studied the page.

"Sinister," Bridget said. "He called George 'sinister.' And in those days, that meant 'really bad.' Like devil bad."

"He does use that word," Gabe said cryptically.

"Is there anything else it could mean?" Kate asked.

"Well, possibly," Gabe said. "But we'd need to learn a bit more about George."

"Like what?" Bridget asked.

"Well, it could also mean left-handed."

"George was left-handed," Kate said quickly.

"How do you know that?" Amos asked.

"The portrait. The one Claire had emailed to us from Marleigh Hall. George is wearing his scabbard on his right side. And you'd only do that if you were left-handed."

Gabe beamed. "That would explain it."

"What do you mean?" Bridget asked.

"Well, at the very least, we know George and his men let Father Alfonso live," Gabe said. "Because Father

Alfonso was able to sit down later and write this letter. And that tracks with what little we've been able to glean about George and his crew so far. And second, Alfonso was a priest from an enemy ship, probably Spanish. I don't think he was commenting on George's character. I think he was giving the folks back home a little insider information. He'd seen George fight. He was telling his countrymen that when the battle got up close and personal, good old Gentleman George favored his left hand. He was trying to tell the Spanish how to beat him."

Chapter 66

"That's the last of 'em for today," Sam said, locking the door to the bakery. "Gonna make an early night of it. Want to scoot by the library real quick. Pick up a couple more books."

"Tell Effie I said 'hi,'" Kate said. "And you were right. She loves those peanut butter chocolate chip cookies."

"Never doubted it," Sam said, holding up the bakery box in his hand as he motored out the back door.

Just as he left, Kate heard a loud knock on the front door. She looked out to see Manny and John Quincy on the front porch.

"Hey, are we early?" the P.I. asked.

"Early for what?" Kate replied, puzzled.

"Your friend invited us for a home-cooked meal. She said to just show up here around closing."

"That works," Kate said, as the phone rang. "Come on back—I have to get that."

She ran and grabbed the handset from the wall. "The Cookie House, this is Kate."

"How would you like to go to a cookout at my house?" Maxi said.

"Manny just showed up with John Quincy. He said something about a home-cooked meal. You didn't have enough to do during the Pirate Festival?"

"It's kind of a belated welcome party for Mr. George. So we're inviting a couple of the dogs we know. Plus, Manny needs a good meal. He's been eating resort food and junk food for too long. I think those pirate dinners were the only real food he's had since he got here. And thanks to him, no more bobos in my back-yard."

"So basically, I'm Oliver's plus-one?"

"Yup."

"What would you like me to bring?"

"Three dozen of those challah rolls. And I'll pick up all four of you out front."

"So what's with the backpack?" Maxi asked, as Kate climbed into the back seat with Oliver on one side and John Quincy on the other.

"Books," Kate said. "I need to run a quick errand. Any chance we could make a stop at Harp's place on the way home?"

"Does this have anything to do with that recipe book?" Maxi asked.

"As far as he's concerned, I'm just returning Caroline's pirate books. And it won't take long, I promise."

"Which one is Harp?" Manny asked.

"He runs the wine shop," Kate called from the back. "I don't know if you've met him."

"Nice work if you can get it," he said.

"Wait 'til you see his house," Maxi said. "He's loaded."

"So is he the new boyfriend?" Manny asked.

"No!" Kate and Maxi said in unison.

"OK, OK, I'm just askin'," Manny said, putting up both hands.

"He loaned me some books for the Gentleman George project," Kate said. "I just want to get them back to him."

They bounced along, enjoying the sunshine, until Maxi turned down a road that ran along the bluffs. "And we're almost there," Maxi promised.

"Man, that salt air is great," Manny said, inhaling deeply. "That's something you don't get in Orlando. We're landlocked. Air just sits on you. In the summer it's like wearing a wet sweater."

Behind him in the back seat, John Quincy had his nose out the window, floppy ears blowing in the breeze.

"This is the place," Maxi said, as she turned the Jeep up the wide driveway toward the Duvals' palatial home.

"Man, you weren't kidding," Manny said. "This guy must sell a lot of wine."

"It's family money," Kate said. "He and his wife both."

"Figures," the P.I. said. "That's what Margot and I had in common, too. Our bank balances. When we got hitched, neither one of us had a dime."

"What do we do with you-know-who?" Maxi asked, as she shifted the car into park.

"I was going to leave him in the car," Kate said.

"Hey, I'm sittin' right here," Manny said.

"Not you. Oliver," Kate explained. "For some reason, Harp doesn't like dogs. And Oliver doesn't like Harp."

"So the three of us can stay in the car," Manny said. "No problemo. Better yet, we can stretch our legs. It's not like your friend has a shortage of grass out there."

"Perfect," Kate said. "I owe you one."

"I got one word for you," Manny said. "Gingersnaps."

"Done," Kate said smiling.

As she and Maxi started up the walkway, Kate swung the backpack onto her shoulder. When she looked up, Oliver was galloping toward her.

She bent and ruffled the soft hair on his head. "You've got to wait here this time. I'll be right out. I promise."

But Oliver, glued to her leg, ignored her.

Kate looked back at the car. Manny shrugged.

"He's got a purple Frisbee in the backseat," Kate called. "If you offer to throw it, he'll come running."

Manny leaned into the back seat, grabbed the disc, and waved it out the window.

"Look, Oliver," Kate said. "Manny's got your Frisbee. You want to play Frisbee?"

Oliver looked up at her with a serious expression and fixed his eyes on Harp's imposing oak door. He refused to so much as look at the purple toy.

"So it looks like Mr. Oliver is coming with us," Maxi said. "What's the plan?"

"It's a slim yellow volume, about this big," Kate said, holding her hands about five inches apart. "I was going to distract him. And I was hoping you could slip into the kitchen and see if you see it."

"Sure, 'cause if you steal something, you just leave it lying around."

"I don't think Harp necessarily stole it. The book disappeared back in February. I was wondering if maybe Caroline took it."

"Why?"

"I don't know. Maybe for the party. I don't think he'd have entered that cookie recipe in the contest if he'd known it was Rosie's."

"So why did he say it was his mother's?"

"No idea," Kate said as the three of them stepped up to the front door.

"OK, showtime," Maxi said, reaching out to ring the bell.

"Ladies," Harp said, opening the thick oversized door. "And Oliver. To what do I owe this most delightful surprise?"

"We were on our way home, and I wanted to return your books," Kate said. "And you were right. They had some fascinating information."

"Well, please come in," he said, glancing down the driveway. "Would your friend like to join us? I can pour us all a nice glass of Merlot."

"Don't mind him," Maxi said, exchanging glances with Kate. "He's expecting a call. Some kind of business thing."

"By all means come in, and I wasn't kidding about that Merlot."

"Well, I wouldn't say no to sitting in the air-conditioning for a few minutes," Kate said, fanning herself with her hand. "That car was a little on the warm side. And I'd love to share what I found out about Gentlemen George."

For his part, Oliver remained almost surgically attached to her leg. But his focus was on Harp. Kate was relieved to see the pup wasn't displaying the open disdain he'd expressed toward Evan.

This was something very different. But at least he was polite and well-behaved.

"I'm driving, so no wine for me," Maxi said. "But could I possibly use your powder room?"

"Of course, you know where it is. Since we're talking books, let's go into the library," Harp said to Kate genially. "I was just sitting in there myself."

He led them into a large two-story room that was flooded with light. And Effie was right. These people obviously loved books.

Floor-to-ceiling shelves lined the room in wood so pale it appeared almost golden. A rolling ladder offered access to every shelf.

The floor was terra-cotta tile, interspersed with colorful glazed tile squares. Sunlight streamed through windows that stretched the full height of the walls. Behind a messy antique desk, Kate spotted a lush potted lemon tree that rivaled the two Maxi kept in front of her shop.

"This is fantastic," Kate said. "It's absolutely beautiful."

"I think it's my favorite room, really," Harp said, smiling modestly. "Well, that and the wine cave, naturally. I designed both of them myself."

Harp reached into a small refrigerator behind the wet bar and pulled out two small bottles of spring water. He handed one off to Kate.

"To recover from your journey," he said.

"Thank you," she said.

Harp took the second bottle, poured half of it into a saucer and sat the dish in front of Oliver.

The dog turned away sharply.

"He's been a little off today," Kate said, embarrassed by the snub. "He may need to see Dr. Scanlon."

"I think the crowds on the island lately have been getting to all of us," Harp said lightly. "I believe that's why I enjoy this room so. Just peace and quiet."

"We missed you at the Pirate Night Dinners," Kate said, catching the lingering scent of cigarette smoke.

"Ah, yes. I have to say, I'm afraid I would not have been good company this week," he said. "I haven't exactly been in a celebratory mood lately. But I'm quite glad this year's festival was a rousing success. That helps all of us."

Arrrrroooo-ar-ar-ar-arrrrroooooo!

"What the deuce!" Harp exclaimed.

"It sounds like a howl," Kate said.

Immediately, she thought of John Quincy. Was the dog injured? Was Manny hurt?

She went running to the front door and collided with Maxi, who was jogging back from the direction of the kitchen.

"You were right," the florist stage-whispered. "I found it, and it's in my purse. But what the heck is going on outside?"

"I think it's John Quincy," Kate said, panicked. "Something's wrong. Really wrong. We've got to find them."

Kate looked out the tall front windows. But neither man nor dog was in the Jeep. Or even within sight of the car. They had vanished.

The gut-wrenching howl continued without stopping. If anything, the din was getting louder.

Arrr-oooo! Arrrr-ooo! Arrr-arrr-arrr-oooo!

Harp sprinted past them toward the back of the house. When Kate, Maxi, and Oliver followed, they found him looking out through a glass wall into his expansive back-yard.

But the wine shop owner wasn't taking in the million-dollar ocean view. He was fixed on something a little closer to home. Literally.

Kate watched the color drain from Harp's face. He sagged until he was sitting on the floor.

Off to one side of the yard, John Quincy had planted himself by the Duvals' ornate white gazebo. Head thrown back, he howled for all he was worth. Next to him, Manny Stenkowski knelt, wrapping his left arm around his four-legged friend. He spoke animatedly into a phone in his right hand.

Maxi was nonplussed. "Must be the big, important business call he was talking about," she said to Harp. "It's a wonder he can hear anything over that racket."

Kate strode across the backyard with Oliver matching her steps. She reached Manny just as he clicked off his call. He slipped the phone into his pocket and turned his full attention to John Quincy.

"Does this mean what I think it means?" Kate asked.

"Yup," Manny said, with a hint of pride. "John Quincy may have left the force, but he hasn't lost his touch."

"The police?"

"On their way. I called your friend Ben. Not a bad guy, once you get to know him. We've made our peace."

He rubbed John Quincy's sides. "OK, we're done here, buddy. Good job. Good job. You're a champ, you know that? Time to get you back to the car. Then it's burgers for both of us."

John Quincy kept howling.

Off in the distance, Kate heard a chorus of sirens.

Oliver padded over to the obviously stressed beagle, standing directly in front of him. For a split second the howling dog stopped and lowered his head. Oliver leaned in and bumped noses.

Then Oliver trotted back to Kate. She reached down and gave him a comforting pat. But in that moment, she wasn't quite sure who was reassuring whom.

Quiet now, John Quincy blinked and looked up at Manny with soft liquid eyes. Manny scratched him behind one ear and took the beagle's lead in his hand.

"I wanna get this little guy out of here," the P.I. said. "I'm takin' him back to the car. I'll talk to your friend when he gets here."

Kate looked at Maxi, who had materialized beside her, then down at Oliver. "We'll come with you."

Just inside the house, Kate could see Harper Duval, sitting on the floor, staring into his backyard with glazed, unfocused eyes.

Chapter 67

After disappearing into Harper Duval's house for what seemed like an eternity, Ben Abrams finally sauntered out and ambled down the long driveway.

Kate, Maxi, and Manny—along with Oliver and John Quincy—were sitting under one of the pin oaks in the Duvals' front yard. They'd spoken to Ben earlier, after which he'd instructed them to stay put.

"Something tells me we're not getting that home-cooked meal tonight," Manny said, as the police detective approached.

"I'd like to invite you folks in for a comfy sit-down, but the whole blasted house is a crime scene," Ben said. "I've got your preliminaries. But I need you all to come in and give formal statements first thing in the morning. If you promise to do that, I can let you go for tonight. OK?"

All three of them nodded in unison.

"Who was it?" Kate asked quietly. "Under the gazebo?"

Ben sighed. "It was Caroline."

"But that's not possible," Maxi said. "She's in Europe."

Kate patted her friend's shoulder.

"She didn't have a drinking problem," Ben said. "She never went to rehab. And it turns out she wasn't even Caroline Drummond. She was a con artist name Peggy-Ann Moffat. She'd replaced Caroline Drummond—the real Caroline Drummond—long before she met Harp or moved here."

"How?" Kate asked. "Did Harp know?"

"He did," Ben said removing his hat and rubbing his forehead. "And that's a very long story. The short version is Peggy-Ann befriended Caroline Drummond about fifteen years ago. The Drummond kid had lost her family—and was more than a little lost herself. Peggy-Ann cozied up to Caroline—adopted her wardrobe, aped her look. When Caroline died in a car accident about a year later, Peggy-Ann just stepped into her shoes. The two were riding in the same car. And they looked enough alike. Plus Caroline didn't have any close family left. Just Joel. And everyone assumed he was dead."

"So who's Alvin?" Maxi asked.

"Joel Drummond," Ben said. "The trustee was right. He'd finally gotten his act together. And after he'd been clean for a while, he decided to look up his sister. But when he showed up here, instead of Caroline, he found Peggy-Ann."

"And she killed him?" Maxi asked softly.

Ben nodded. "That's what Harper claims. And I have to say, so far I believe him. What he's telling us fits the evidence we have currently. She stored the body in one of the outbuildings here. On the edge of the property. Padlocked, so no one would find it."

"That when she did her bit trying to age it, too?" Manny asked.

Ben nodded. "Chemicals. And I have a couple of crime-lab folks who'd have loved to see her do jail time for that alone. Gave 'em a devil of a time."

"But why did she bury the poor guy behind the flower shop?" Maxi asked. "She has a beautiful big yard."

"She didn't want Harp to find out," Ben said. "The morning after the party, Harp left town. Some wine symposium in Orlando. Didn't get back until Sunday night."

"Can you prove your guy Harp was really there?" Manny asked skeptically.

Ben nodded. "We tracked his phone. And there were enough people who remembered him there throughout the event. He's pretty popular among that crowd, too."

"So by the time he got home . . ." Kate started.

"My yard had a new occupant. And because it was all one big dirt pile anyway, no one noticed."

Ben nodded, leaning back against the side of Maxi's Jeep. "Over the next few days, your lawn service covered it with sod and no one was the wiser."

"Cold," Manny said. "That lady was stone-cold."

"For what it's worth, I think the fault lines in that marriage were real," Ben said. "And it only got worse over the next week."

"What do you mean?" Kate asked, concerned.

"We think the confrontation with Joel was Wednesday," Ben said. "Probably afternoon. Friday night, Peggy-Ann is throwing her big party. And she has no way of knowing if Joel was alone. Or who he might have told he was coming here. She'd eliminated one problem. But she knew it might not be the last."

"Everyone said she was pretty high-strung the night of the party," Kate said.

"Sunny told me she'd been bawling out the help all

night," Maxi added. "Said she should have been riding a broom instead of wearing a crown. After that night, I think everybody in town kinda felt sorry for Harp."

"Well, she had practically everyone in Florida coming to that bash," Ben said. "Including some pretty big names in state law enforcement."

"When did Harp find out what had happened?" Kate asked.

"A week or so later, when Caroline tried to kill Maxi," Ben said somberly.

Maxi's eyes went wide. Her mouth dropped open, but no sound emerged.

Kate reached over and patted her shoulder. Oliver, wedged between them, nuzzled Maxi's cheek. She stroked his head rhythmically.

"Why?" the florist finally asked.

Ben went silent. Kate could tell he was weighing his words.

"Did it have something to do with the flower?" Kate asked. "The long-stemmed red rose?"

Ben nodded. "Before Joel went to his sister's house, he stopped off at the flower shop. He wanted to bring Caroline red roses. Apparently, they were her favorite. Peggy-Ann realized the flowers were evidence, so she got rid of them. Threw them in with everything else. But she was worried. She knew how friendly you were, Maxi. You talk to everyone. And she was afraid Joel might have shared something with you while he was in your shop. Why he was in town. Who he was visiting. She was convinced you were a loose end."

Maxi shook her head in disbelief. "Caroline and I— we weren't super close," she said softly. "But I thought she was my friend."

"Right after you guys returned from Miami, Harp caught her putting something in your drink at a party.

So he knocked into you and spilled the drink out of your hand," Ben said. "Made it look like an accident. Later, he doctored Peggy-Ann's drink with some meds he had for his back. The effect had her stumbling around like she'd had a few too many."

"I remember that whole evening," Maxi breathed. "Not a fun party."

"Was he trying to make her sleepy, or get her to tell him why she did it?" Kate asked.

"Both," Ben said. "And that's the night he learned about Joel."

"Talk about having your shorts in the wringer," Manny said, shaking his head.

"By this time, Harp was frantic," Ben said. "He couldn't let Peggy-Ann out of his sight, for fear of what she'd do. But he wasn't ready to come to us yet, either."

"She'd have claimed he did it," Kate said quietly.

Ben nodded. "And Peggy-Ann wouldn't tell him where she put the body. She was taunting him with it."

"So why did everyone in town think Caroline had a drinking problem?" Kate asked.

"From there on, Harp was keeping her drugged," Ben said. "Just enough to make her woozy. To keep her at home. And prevent her from hurting anyone. And he was checking on her constantly. Even so, she managed to get out once or twice. I'm guessing at this point the guy was pretty much sleeping with one eye open."

"It's awful, but I don't remember Joel," Maxi said. "That was right before we left for Miami. I was running around getting ready. So most of the time, there was someone else at the counter."

"For what it's worth, I'm pretty sure this wasn't just about you," Ben said gently. "When Harp saw how easily Peggy-Ann dispatched Joel, and how little it bothered her to try it a second time with you, I think the penny finally dropped."

"That Caroline Drummond's car 'accident' was no accident," Manny murmured. "Your friend Peggy-Ann did it."

Ben nodded. "Harp had always known Peggy-Ann's real identity. And where her money—their money—came from. I think the guy had some romanticized notion that they were a couple of fun-loving grifters living on found money. The real Caroline Drummond hadn't had any relatives, and she was gone. I think he rationalized that all that wealth would have just been sitting in a bank vault somewhere gathering dust."

"And interest," Manny said.

"Well, to give the man credit, living on found money was one thing," Ben said. "Killing for it was another. After he learned the truth, our friend Harp began to crack."

"At one point, he started smoking again," Kate said. "I remember that."

"A couple of times," Ben confirmed.

Manny shook his head. "Stress."

"But what happened to Caroline?" Maxi asked, softly. "I mean, Peggy-Ann. How?"

"Harp says that he'd finally come to the conclusion he had to turn her in—turn them both in. He tried talking with Caroline—sorry, Peggy-Ann—one last time. To reason with her. Turns out she'd caught on to the sedatives. And she'd managed to avoid the last few doses. So she got the drop on him. Brained him with a lamp and made a run for it. Now, the rest of this is just Harp's story. He says he caught up with Peggy-Ann just as she reached the staircase. Grabbed her shoulder. She wrenched free. But the momentum carried her right down the stairs. And that tumble killed her."

"You believe that?" Manny asked.

"Absent concrete evidence, I'm reserving judgment," Ben said evenly. "Let's see what we learn in the next few days."

"So he still didn't know where Joel was?" Kate asked.

"Not a clue," Ben said. "Even after you guys found the skeleton, he wasn't sure. I mean, no reason Joel would have been wearing high black boots with silver buckles. Or pirate clothes. Plus, you two discovered an actual skeleton—what appeared to be an older burial. Then he remembered those costumes that his wife had rented for the party. And I think he figured out the rest."

"So by the time the Coral Cay Irregulars met to talk about Gentleman George . . ." Kate started.

"The last thing he wanted was hordes of people digging up the island," Ben finished. "He wanted the whole thing to go away."

"And all this time he covered Caroline's disappearance by saying she'd gone to rehab," Maxi said. "And then later that she was traveling through Europe."

Ben shrugged. "I think some part of his brain hoped that everything would just go back to normal."

"That explains why he played the suitor with me," Kate said. "If he'd been successful, Evan would have left Coral Cay a lot sooner. And taken the Thorpe Family Foundation funding with him. And without Evan stoking the frenzy over Gentleman George, interest would have naturally waned."

Ben grinned. "Uhh, I don't think that was the total reason for that. Do I think he wanted to distract you from nosing around the burial in Maxi's yard? Oh yeah. But the guy had it bad long before that. It was all over his face whenever you were around. Grifter or not, that was one true thing he couldn't hide. And, I believe that some part of his brain realized that it was now or never. So he was pulling out all the stops."

Kate looked down at the grass. Maxi patted her back.

"Wait a minute—that's why the DNA didn't match," Kate said. "Joel was Joel. But Caroline wasn't the real Caroline."

"Exactly," Ben said. "And don't I feel like a schmuck for trying to cut the guy a little slack to save his marriage."

"Happens to all of us," Manny said, stroking John Quincy's side as he leaned back against the tree.

"Why dress him like a pirate?" Maxi asked.

"I think I know the answer to that one," Kate said. She looked up at Ben, who nodded.

"She didn't," Kate said. "She threw Teddy Randolph's party costume into the hole, hoping to implicate him, if the remains were ever found. He didn't have a steady job. He moved around a lot. He'd already gotten in a few scrapes."

"So when I saw those silver buckles and thought of Gentleman George Bly . . ." Maxi started.

"A totally unforeseen complication," Kate said. "As was our Oliver digging deep enough to find the bones in the first place. And I'm guessing Harper Duval isn't really from New Orleans?"

Ben shook his head. "His name isn't even Harper Duval. Grew up dirt poor in Alabama. Somehow, after Peggy-Ann Moffat became Caroline Drummond, these two found each other. And they've been living high off of Caroline's trust fund for ten years. It wasn't hard. The Drummond family's gone. They thought Joel was gone. And the trustees overseeing the account have changed a few times over the years, as the original bank was acquired and merged and changed hands. No one had any reason to believe that Caroline wasn't really Caroline.

Harper and Peggy-Ann were even smart enough to move to an out-of-the-way spot where no one knew either of them—or the real Caroline Drummond."

Ben studied each of their faces in turn. "So what exactly were the three of you doing over here tonight?"

"I was promised a home-cooked meal," Manny said.

"Returning books," Maxi said. "Pirate books."

Ben looked at Kate. "And you, Little Miss Innocent?"

"It was a cookie recipe," she said simply. "Peggy-Ann discovered that Rosie Armand had a trove of authentic New Orleans recipes. Stuff that had been passed down in her family for generations. So she stole it. I'm guessing she'd have used it here and there over the years to bolster Harp's claim of a long New Orleans pedigree. Unfortunately, shortly after she took it, she died.

"Then when Harp needed a recipe for the cookie contest—one with a distinct New Orleans flavor, in keeping with his persona—he copied one out of the book," she continued. "He had no idea Peggy-Ann had stolen that book. Let alone that she'd stolen it from someone right here in Coral Cay. He just picked something that looked good and entered it in the contest—claiming it was his mother's own recipe.

"But Rosie recognized it," Kate added. "Then she realized her family cookbook was missing. I was just here trying to get it back."

Ben smiled and shook his head. "A long con that went on for a dozen years or more. Drained millions out of one of the biggest banks in Boston. Fooled countless law enforcement pros, including yours truly. And you're telling me it all unraveled because of a couple of cookies?"

Chapter 68

As the sun climbed in the blue South Florida sky, the morning air was cool and moist.

"I can't believe Sunny is doing this," Maxi said, as she maneuvered the Jeep over the washboard road and around a hairpin turn. "You think in spite of everything, she really wants to know what happened to Gentleman George?"

"I think she already knows," Kate said. "But I wouldn't mind finding out the truth. Speaking of which, are you doing OK with the whole Harp thing? You haven't said much about it this past week."

"I'm not sure how I feel exactly," Maxi admitted. "Part of me wants to say 'thank you,' and the other part of me wants to kick him in the shins."

"That seems fair. He did kind of save your life."

"That's what mi amor said. Then he recused himself from Harp's case. I know one thing. Whatever the guy's real name is, to me he'll always be Harper Duval."

"Did you ever find out what Peter was hiding?" Kate asked.

"His boss is retiring. And the guy wants Peter to run for state's attorney."

"Maxi, that's wonderful!"

"Yes and no. Right after that, we found Mr. Bones. So Peter didn't know if they'd still want him. And he was worried that maybe his job was somehow the reason we got Alvin in the first place. Plus, the new job would be a big change. A lot more hours. A lot of time campaigning. And we're really happy right now."

"So what did he decide?"

"He hasn't. But I told him the same thing he always tells me—whatever you want, I'm all for it. And I mean it."

"Have you noticed the tourist crowds really are thinning out?"

"It's the annual cycle, corizon. Treasure fantasies or vacations, sooner or later people got to get back to their real lives."

"Speaking of which, Evan finally left town this morning," Kate said.

"Are you sure? 'Cause that boy seemed pretty set on taking you back to Manhattan with him."

"Officially, the Thorpe Family Foundation believes that the Gentleman George project can be better supported remotely by its New York offices due to economies of scale."

"And unofficially?" Maxi asked.

"Evan got bored and wanted to go home."

"Sounds about right. At least I got a puppy out of the deal. OK, I think this is the turnoff to Iris's place."

From the road, it was marked by a barely visible gap between overgrown bushes. But once they made the turn, they could see a little cottage at the end of the gravel lane.

To Kate, it looked like a scene from a fairy tale. Or something she might create out of gingerbread. A snug little house with a slate roof surrounded by a beautiful garden. Everything seemed to be blooming at once.

"This is incredible," Kate said. "Does Iris do all this herself?"

"Yup," Maxi said, as she shifted the car into park. "She lives here by herself, too. You should see the back. It's on an inlet that goes out to the water. Really pretty."

"Hey, there's Sunny," Kate said, waving.

Sunny Eisenberg, clad in a brown silk T-shirt with a matching wrap skirt and sandals, waved back from beneath a rose trellis heavy with large pink flowers.

"You girls must have found it on your first pass," she said, as they trundled up the walkway. "Most people run past it a couple of times—even when they've been here before."

"Sunny, your mom's place is beautiful," Kate said, astonished.

The air was cool, and the gentle breeze smelled of roses mingled with salt water.

"It's a nice spot. And the home's been here a long time. Rumor has it, this is the site where Gentleman George and his men camped. Later, someone put up a cabin. Then it became a cottage. And now here we are. But we don't want that to get out," she said, putting a finger to her lips.

"Mom's still in the Poconos tormenting my brother George," she confided with a grin. "But she had a couple of boxes that she thought might be useful. I'll get you set up, then I have to take off for the studio. Just lock up when you're done, and you can drop off the key."

Everything in the cottage was neat and sized to fit, Kate noticed. Like a dollhouse. And it smelled faintly of lavender.

"I've put everything out on the back porch," Sunny explained, leading them out to a bright screened enclosure that looked out onto the water. "It's nice and cool, even without air-conditioning. And I thought a pitcher of iced lemonade might hit the spot."

Iris's porch functioned more like an outdoor room, Kate noted—with cozy chairs and a big central table holding stacks of books and, on this occasion, a collection of boxes.

Off to one side, there was a small flowered sofa with two more chairs. A conversation nook. She could easily picture curling up on the couch with a good read and a cold drink on a warm afternoon.

"Well, I'll let you girls get to it," Sunny said. There's a phone on the table in the living room if you need anything."

"We'll be fine," Kate said. "And thanks again for this."

"Anytime," she said with a wink. "Besides, it was mom's idea. She's a bit more sentimental."

After Sunny left, Kate poured them each a glass of lemonade and they got to work.

"This is where I want to live after my own little pirates move out," Maxi said, looking around.

"I know," Kate said. "I wonder what it would take to put a sun porch on the Cookie House."

"No more projects," Maxi said grinning. "And no digging. That's how we got into this mess."

In hushed silence, they pored through the trove. Notes, family letters, and the odd bill or two. Kate could hear a pair of doves calling to each other in Iris's backyard.

Then she glimpsed it. An old, yellowed photocopy slipped into a protective plastic sleeve. The cramped handwriting was eerily similar to the letter she'd read from Henry. But these letters slanted to the right.

Marleigh Hall
23 April, 1609

My dearest brother George,
It pains me to write this, for I do not wish to add to your great distress. But if I do not tell you, you will know soon enough through that special bond we share—we two who have been paired from the beginning. The physicians tell me I have but a short time now.

I rejoice at the news that you grow stronger by the day. A pox on Baptiste, who is known far and wide for his villainy!

In keeping with our scheme, I shall travel to the Low Countries and take up lodgings there under the name of another. It is a place of comfort and ease that I shall well and goodly enjoy. And it will make my last days most pleasant.

Despair not, for we have long known this day was approaching. You will make a most noble Duke—a credit to our fine house. We are alchemists in reverse, dear brother, transmuting your steady offerings of gold and silver and jewels into base brick and stone. Come what may, our home and family shall have the means to court good fortune. Through your work and mine, Marleigh—and the Blys—are secure.

Guard yourself well when you do set foot on our native soil, for allegiances here change as oft as the tides. Spies are everywhere, and your actions—once lauded—have not gone unno-

ticed. In keeping with our stratagem, I have tread always the middle ground lo these many years. Under my name, you will be safe. And who knows that I could not truly be George and you Henry— we who mirror each other?

I have arranged safe passage for your family to Tuscany. There, unknown to the world as George or Henry, you may recover more fully.

Rejoice that your fine, strapping lads shall soon be by your side. As will your sweetheart Jayne. Truly it will do her much good to finally have her dear husband near. And you much good in return.

Father is most well—hale and hearty as ever. He may bury us both!

I am proud to call you brother. Prouder still that you will carry my name. In you rests the hope and future of our honorable family. Be well, brother! Health and long life be yours!

*Your devoted brother always,
Henry*

Kate wiped a tear from her eye. She tapped Maxi on the shoulder, and silently handed her the paper, watching her friend's face intently as she read.

When Maxi finally placed the letter on the table, she reached up and brushed the moisture from her own eyes.

"He made it," Maxi said finally. "That old sea dog had one more trick up his sleeve."

"He did," Kate said, wiping her eyes. "And this was the best one of all."

Maxi raised her lemonade glass. "A toast to Sir George Bly, Duke of Marleigh. An officer, a gentleman, a pirate, and a scamp. Definitely one of us."

Acknowledgments

A very big shout-out to Dr. Kathryn O'Donnell Miyar, state osteologist for the Florida Department of State, Bureau of Archaeological Research. Not only did she take the time to explain what happens next when someone makes an accidental archaeological discovery—she made it fun! And any mistakes in this story are definitely mine alone.

And many thanks to Liz Chehayl, the Brian Holley curator of collections at the Naples Botanical Garden, for her expert help with Maxi's garden and the lush vegetation of Coral Cay! (Any errors are definitely mine!)

A heartfelt thank-you to the wonderful team at St. Martin's Press. Especially my editor, Alexandra Sehulster, who has made this book and the Cookie House series a dream come true. For you, a tall glass of cold lemonade, a batch of warm cookies, and a very grateful "thank you!" Also a big hug to editorial assistant Mara Delgado Sánchez, for her endless patience, time, and kindness. Two huge bouquets to Holly Rice and Kayla

Janas in the St. Martin's/Minotaur publicity department, who have worked miracles to spread the word about Kate McGuire, Oliver, the Cookie House, and Coral Cay. And a very big "thank you" to social media wizard Stephen Erickson, who's always generous with his time and expertise. Many kudos also to eagle-eyed copy editor, John Simko. And huge thanks to Mattew Carrera, who designed the cover, and Mary Ann Lasher, who did the terrific (and delicious-looking) cover illustration. Last—and definitely not least—thank you to the world's best agent, Erin Niumata of Folio Literary Agency: You've been my friend and sounding board every step of the way.

Read on for a sample of the next exciting
Cookie House mystery by **Eve Calder**

A TALE OF TWO COOKIES

Available in May 2021 from St. Martin's Paperbacks!

Kate McGuire felt the spray of the salt water against her face, as the boat plowed through the choppy water. Beside her, pup Oliver peered over the railing into the teal blue sea.

Instinctively, she reached down and stroked the soft, caramel-colored hair on the back of his neck, just above his orange life vest.

"So what do you think of your first boat ride?" she asked softly. "Or *is* it your first boat ride?"

The pup's past was still something of a mystery. From what she'd been able to learn, Oliver just appeared in Coral Cay one chilly March day. No one knew where he'd come from, but there had been no shortage of people who wanted to give the small, fuzzy puppy a good home.

Instead, the golden-doodle (or maybe labradoodle— no one was quite sure about that, either) played the field, spending a night or three at various homes before moving on. So now Oliver was the unofficial mayor of Coral Cay—welcomed and wanted just about everywhere in town.

But when Kate moved to the small Florida island— and into an upstairs room at the Cookie House bakery a few months ago—Oliver stopped wandering.

For the most part.

"So what do you think?" Desiree yelled excitedly to Kate over the roar of the engine and the waves slapping the sides of the boat.

"The island looks so different from the water," Kate shouted.

"That's what I love about traveling by boat," Desiree said. "Complete change in perspective. Jimmy Buffett was right."

As the boat slowed, Judson Cooper emerged on deck, a boyish smile on his broad, tan face. "Look!" he shouted over the din. "Someone's waving at us from shore!"

As they rounded the headland, Kate looked over and recognized the quaint cottage nestled in the cove. In its yard, two figures were each giving them a full-armed wave.

"That's Iris and Sunny," Kate said, waving back.

"Woof!" Oliver barked over the din. "Woof, woof."

"See? He knows them," Kate said with a grin.

"You weren't kidding," Desiree said. "You really do know everyone in town."

"Well, to be fair, it's a very small town."

"And everyone comes into that bakery," Judson added, patting his midsection. "As I can attest."

"Do I even want to ask who's driving the boat?" Kate asked, laughing.

"Just call him Captain Jack Scanlon," Judd said, winking. "And he's not half-bad for a veterinarian." He gave a mock salute and headed back up to the wheelhouse.

"I still can't believe you guys are having your wedding here," Kate said.

"Well, my first time around, I did it my mom's way. Poofy white dress, stiff satin high heels, and four bridesmaids. And the marriage lasted, what? Fifteen minutes? This time, we're doing it our way. Barefoot on the beach."

"It sounds wonderful," Kate said.

At that moment, Judd reappeared. "I forgot to mention," he called, as he approached. "Liam phoned this morning. He and Sarah are both flying in. They'll be here tonight."

"Judd, that's fantastic!" Desiree exclaimed. "What happened? How did you change their minds?"

"Search me," he said. "The boy called me. Of his own volition. No arm twisting whatsoever."

"Judd's kids aren't exactly my biggest fans," Desiree explained.

"It's not you, it's any woman in my life," Judson countered.

"Well, I'm grateful," Desiree said. "Whatever the reason. Especially if it means they hate me just a little bit less."

"Oh no," Kate said. "They can't possibly hate you. Maybe they just don't want to share their dad."

"It's not me they have a problem sharing, it's my bank account," he said, shaking his head. "Or, as they've taken to calling it, their inheritance."

"Judson, that is not true," Desiree said. "Although they were definitely not in favor of our summer wanderings. Three months away from the office—criss-crossing the globe. What was it Liam said when we told him? 'Over my dead body.'"

"I hate to correct you, honey, but what he actually said to me was 'over your dead body, Dad.' That kid of mine, he doesn't mince words." He shrugged, grinned amiably, and ambled back to the pilothouse.

Kate tried not to look shocked. She couldn't imagine anyone not taking an immediate liking to Desiree. Bubbly, funny, and down-to-earth, she made everyone feel at home instantly. Maybe that was why she was so good at her job—lead concierge for the Manhattan flagship of a major luxury hotel group.

Or at least, she had been.

A few weeks ago, Kate had gotten a call from her old

friend. Only in her mid-fifties, Desiree was retiring. And getting married.

The groom was, at least in certain circles, something of a celebrity: Judson Cooper. A globe-trotting marine biologist, the man made headlines with his efforts to protect the oceans and safeguard sea life around the world—from battling whaling off the coast of Japan to working to revitalize the Great Barrier Reef.

He'd also made a small fortune with a couple of inventions—one that harvested water-borne garbage and another that transformed liquid petrol-chemical spills into solids, which could then be easily sifted from the water.

Kate couldn't believe it when Desiree announced they were holding their intimate beach wedding on Coral Cay.

"I don't know why not," her friend had said, laughing. "You've told me so much about the place, I feel like I know it already. And Judson wants to kick back for a few weeks and spend some time at one of his pet projects just up the coast. A marine wildlife rehab sanctuary."

"Sounds like the perfect honeymoon for a city girl," Kate had teased.

"I know, right? But the whole thing feels just . . . magical. And perfect."

And now here they were. The wedding was tomorrow evening. Sunset on the beach. To be followed by a bonfire, beach cookout, and cake—a two-tier key lime number with coconut frosting that was currently under Sam Hepplewhite's watchful eye back at the Cookie House.

As Kate and Desiree lurched their way carefully to the back of the boat, Kate had to admit she'd never seen her friend happier. And it was contagious. As they settled into the cushioned bench seat, Kate stole a glance at Jack Scanlon in the elevated glass wheelhouse, deep in conversation with Judson Cooper at the helm. The vet brushed a lock of sandy brown hair off his forehead, caught her eye across the boat, and smiled.

Kate smiled, blushed, and quickly looked away.

"Hmmm, so I'm not the only one doing well in the romance department," Desiree said under her breath.

Kate shook her head. "Uh-uh. Nope. Not happening. Small island."

"Hey, I'm just relieved you ditched that other guy. Mr. Millionaire."

"You were always so nice to him," Kate said, amazed.

"Because *you* liked him. I always thought he was kind of hollow. Handsome, but he knew it."

Kate giggled. "Oh, did he ever know it."

"Well, you can do a lot better. And clearly, you are."

Kate risked a glance at the pilothouse: Judson at the wheel, Jack next to him looking out at the water—and Oliver happily wedged between them, all four paws planted wide for balance.

"Seriously, thanks for all the help with this," Desiree said, almost shyly.

"Are you kidding? After all the events you've arranged? You deserve this. Besides, I just happen to know the best florist in Coral Cay. Maxi may own the only flower shop on the island, but she could hold her own in Manhattan any day."

"I know. You should see the bouquet she designed. A strand of white orchids. Simple and beautiful. Which is pretty much our motto for the whole wedding."

"I love the idea of a beach party," Kate said. "Although, knowing this place, you may get a few uninvited guests. The folks around here love a good party."

"The more the merrier," Desiree said happily.

"On the bright side, they seldom show up empty-handed," Kate added.

Suddenly the engine cut out. Except for the slapping of the waves on the side of the boat, all was still. While the engine's sudden cessation didn't appear to bother Judson Cooper, something else clearly did. He scrambled down onto the deck, adjusted his binoculars, and peered toward the shore.

"What is it?" Jack asked, leaning out the door of the wheelhouse.

Kate looked to Desiree. But her friend was focused on her fiancé.

"That definitely shouldn't be there," Judson muttered.

"What?" Kate said. "What is it?"

"That cigarette boat," Judson said quietly. "I knew I recognized it. Dammit! Not again."

"Judson, what is it?" Desiree said as she rose from her seat and made her way haltingly toward the front of the boat. "You're scaring me."

"Nothing to worry about, sweetheart. Just business as usual, unfortunately. But we're going to have to cut this trip a little short. I need to reach out to a few people I know and have a little chat."

"Are we in some kind of danger?" Kate asked, alarmed.

"Nah, same old same old," Judson said casually. "Unfortunately, it all goes with the territory. But it's nothing. Really."

He rubbed Desiree's back. "And it's definitely not going to affect our plans."

And with that, he climbed back into the wheelhouse, carefully shifted the throttle forward, and steered the boat farther out toward open water.